# THE ARRIVALS

# THE ARRIVALS

## MELISSA MARR

HarperCollins*Publishers*

HarperCollins*Publishers*
77–85 Fulham Palace Road,
Hammersmith, London W6 8JB

www.harpercollins.co.uk

Published by HarperCollins*Publishers* 2013
1

A catalogue record for this book
is available from the British Library

ISBN: 978 0 00 734928 9

Designed by Jamie Lynn Kerner

Printed and bound in Great Britain by
Clays Ltd, St Ives plc

**MIX**
Paper from
responsible sources
**FSC** **FSC™ C007454**
www.fsc.org

*To Dad, for years of westerns, action movies, and guns.*
*(P.S. You don't have to read this book either. I just need you*
*to read these next two sentences: Thanks for being everything I*
*ever needed in a father. I love you.)*

# THE ARRIVALS

# CHAPTER 1

Kitty saw the bullets tear into Mary's belly, watched the red stain cover the flowered dress that she'd just stitched up for her closest friend, and her first thought was that there was no way she could repair that kind of damage. The dress was ruined. Close on the heels of that thought was: *someone needs to kill the bastard that shot Mary.*

They were supposed to be at a meeting, a peaceful, weapons-not-needed negotiation with representatives of a local monastic order. They were supposed to be collecting a payment. They were definitely not supposed to be dealing with trigger-happy monks, but reality had collided with expectations several minutes and a few corpses ago when the monks had pulled guns out from under their gray robes. Worse yet, as Kitty reached for her six-shooter, she heard the atonal mutterings as several of the monks started their prayers.

She slid the gun back into the holster. She'd much rather shoot than deal with the alternatives, but bullets and spells tended to mix poorly. Her partner, Edgar, tossed her a knife. Kitty caught it and kept moving, scanning the area as she walked. There were the two praying monks, two more that her brother, Jack, was dealing with, and the one she'd lost track of in the initial round of gunfire. She couldn't shoot the praying ones, and Jack was handling his. It was the missing monk—the one who'd shot Mary—who had to die *now*. She needed to flush the monk out or lure him out. She stopped and turned slowly in a circle, watching for her prey and waiting for him to do the obvious.

Edgar's expression was tense as he watched her. He never liked it when she was brash, and if she were honest, she'd be even worse if the roles were reversed. She averted her gaze from him and was about to move toward the shadowed interior of the nearest building when a bullet came from the building and grazed her shoulder.

"Found you," she whispered as the second bullet hit the ground next to her.

The monk stepped out of the building; simultaneously, she charged him. The monk closed his eyes and joined his voice to the other praying monks, summoning their demon's aid. He spoke faster, and Kitty felt the charge in the air around her as she reached him. It figured that he was the one who was accepting possession.

Kitty shoved the blade into the monk's throat and twisted. As she stabbed him, she pushed her will into the monk's body and concentrated on making her words manifest. The monk's blood burned her where it splashed her face and forearm.

He opened his eyes, and Kitty could see the shifting colors that revealed that his demon was already sliding into his bleeding body. He couldn't keep speaking his spell, but she hadn't been fast enough to completely stop it. The last thing she wanted was a demon walking around in a bloody, dead-monk suit.

"Magic it is," she said.

The monk took a step backward, trying to elude her. His lips still moved, although she couldn't hear any words. She wasn't sure if the whisper of the spell was enough, but she wasn't going to take any chances.

"Speak no more." She pulled the knife from his throat and jammed the blade into his left eye, before quickly repeating the action with his right eye. "See no more."

He started to fall to the sandy ground as she withdrew the knife, pulling her will back to her, and letting his life spill out the wounds.

Kitty followed his body to the ground as she jammed the blade into his chest with all the force she could muster. "Live no more."

As she pushed the knife into the monk's chest, Edgar came up behind her. His shadow fell over the corpse, and she was briefly tempted to ask for help. She didn't ask, and he didn't reach down to pull her to her feet—probably because she had snarled the last time he'd tried.

Carefully, Kitty came to her feet, swaying only a little as the backlash from blood magic hit her. "I'm fine," she lied before he could comment.

Edgar didn't touch her, but they both knew he was close enough that she'd be in his arms in a blink if she started to fall. She wasn't a waif of a woman, but Edgar was all muscle, more than capable of hefting her into his arms. That didn't mean that she *wanted* to be hoisted into the air. It was a point of pride to her that she could stand on her own two feet after working magic.

Slowly, she turned to face him. "You have blood on your trousers."

"True." He stared at her, read her silences and her movements with the sort of familiarity that comes from too many years to count. "You aren't ready to try to walk yet."

Kitty pursed her lips. She was the only one of the Arrivals who could work spells like some of the residents of the Wasteland, but doing so made her feel like her insides were being shredded. Whatever had yanked the Arrivals out of their rightful times and places had changed her when it brought them to this world. She was too much like the native Wastelanders for her liking, but not so much like them that she could work spells without consequences.

After a moment she leaned against him a little. "I hate spells."

"Is it getting easier, or are you hiding the pain better?"

"What pain?" she joked as the brief numbness of both the fight high and the spellwork receded. The agony of the bullet she'd ignored hit her, and the feel of the bloodburn on her face and arms added a chaser to the sharp sting on her shoulder. She could feel tears slipping down her cheeks, but she wasn't stupid enough to wipe her eyes with monastic blood on her hands. Instead, she bowed her head, and a few curls that had come undone fell forward, helping hide the tears. As steadily as she could, she reached down and withdrew the knife. With exaggerated care, she wiped it on the monk's gray tunic.

It didn't buy her enough time to hide the pain. Maybe it would've done so with one of the others, but Edgar was too observant for her to hide most anything from him. When she stood, he had one of his dandified handkerchiefs in hand.

"There's no shame in resting." Edgar pushed her curls back and then wiped the tears and blood from her face.

"I don't need to," she said, but she put a hand on his chest. The pain would end. The wounds would heal. She just needed to wait them out.

Edgar didn't comment on the fact that she was shaking. "Jack took care of the last two. You and I could wait here while I catch my breath."

Kitty shook her head. Edgar was many things, but worn out after a tussle with a few monks wasn't ever on that list. She wouldn't be either, except for the impact of the spell.

"There's no way Jack will agree to that." Kitty shivered slightly as her body worked through the consequences of the magic. "These were the monks we *saw,* but there are others. Jack will want to travel."

Edgar wrapped an arm around her, holding her steady as her shaking grew worse. "Fuck Jack."

Kitty leaned her head against Edgar. "I'm fine. I'll rest at the inn tonight and be fine by morning when we head to camp."

Even though he didn't argue, his glower left no doubts as to his opinion on the matter. If she truly couldn't travel, she'd tell them, but she could make it as far as Gallows. What she couldn't do was be responsible for conflict between the two men who looked after their group. She let herself lean on Edgar for another moment before stepping away.

When she turned, Jack and Francis were watching her. Francis' face was carefully expressionless, and he held himself still, giving the overall impression of a cautious, slightly battered scarecrow. His long scraggly ponytail was singed at the end, and he had missed a smear of blood on his temple.

Kitty smiled at Francis reassuringly, before letting her gaze drift to her brother. No matter how difficult a conflict was, and no matter how many of them were killed or injured, Jack was always implacable. He was their leader, and to him, that meant focusing on the *now*. He looked much the same as he had for most of Kitty's life: like a cross between a preacher and an outlaw. He had the lean frame that served him well in fights, and the baby blues that made him seem angelic enough to stand at a pulpit. Currently, his gaze was fastened on her studiously.

He cradled Mary in his arms, and Kitty forced herself to look at her brother's eyes instead of at Mary. It was a scant comfort, not looking at her friend, but Kitty still had the childhood hope that her brother could somehow make everything right. He couldn't, not usually and certainly not today.

She knew without having to hear the words, but Jack said them all the same: "She's dead, Katherine."

"I figured." It hurt to even say the words, to admit the truth, but pretending wasn't an option. Mary was dead. The only thing left to them now was waiting—and plotting revenge. Kitty walked up closer to Jack and brushed a hand over the dead woman's hair.

In a procession of sorts, they started the walk back to town. Edgar and Francis kept watch on the windows of the burned-out monastery and any cover where enemies could hide. The monks had said that they were the only ones who stayed at their quarters, but they'd also said they wanted to break bread in peace.

The shadows were starting to gather, and Kitty wondered if they would all be safer staying at the monastery rather than tangling with whatever might wait in the shadows. This world held more threats than she wanted to think about, and more and more their group seemed to end up on the wrong side of them.

"We could wait here for the night," she suggested. "Everyone's tired, and the monsters have too much of an edge in the dark."

"No," Jack said. "We need to get moving."

Edgar flashed a scowl at Jack that Kitty pretended not to see. Edgar knew better than anyone that she was weaker right now than she let on, but Jack had to think of all of them. She'd do whatever her brother decided.

Francis didn't get involved in the decision; he never did. Instead, he glanced at her, assessing her injuries. She knew that he'd bring her some tincture, salve, or vile tea by morning. He was forever trying whatever remedies every snake-oil salesman sold—or mixing his own experimental treatments. A good number of his homemade concoctions were mildly useful, even though far too many of them tasted bad enough to make a person consider staying injured.

"Hey, Francis? I could use one of those muscle soaks when we get back to Gallows." Kitty put a hand on his forearm briefly. When he stopped walking, she reached up to wipe away the blood on his temple. She reached up and patted his cheek fondly.

"We can't stay in the inn tonight, Katherine. It's not safe enough. We'll head back to the camp." Jack had stopped when she had. Her brother wasn't going to admit that he could see how tired she was, but he would adjust his stride so *she* didn't have to say it.

She smiled at him. She could make it as far as Gallows, but walking the extra miles to camp would be too much. "No," Kitty objected. "We can stay in Gallows."

"The inn isn't safe enough right now." Jack wouldn't do anything he thought would endanger the group unnecessarily, even for her. "We'll pack up when we reach Gallows and be on the road before full dark."

"Tomorrow," she said.

"The brethren are likely to have others here. We can make it to camp tonight. The inn's not—"

"I'll keep watch for Kit," Edgar interrupted. "You and Francis can take Mary back to camp tonight."

At the same time, both Kitty and Jack said, "But—"

"Kit needs to rest." Edgar's voice was even.

"We should stay together," Jack argued.

Edgar leveled a daunting look at him. "We're almost to Gallows, Jack. Either we all stay there, or we divide. Whether she's willing to admit it or not, Kit needs rest."

For a moment, Jack looked at Kitty with the sort of penetrating gaze that made her want to lie to him. She didn't often succeed at that, but she felt like a failure for putting him in this position. He didn't understand how much any sort of death magic drained her.

Before Kitty could lie and say that she was well enough to travel tonight; that she didn't want to abandon Mary; that she wasn't exhausted from being shot, bloodburned, and backlashed, Edgar added in that absurdly reasonable tone, "Mary's dead, Kit. You won't do anyone any good in this state, and Mary won't wake for six days."

"If at all," Jack added. She could tell his answer had changed as he'd studied the girl.

"If at all," Edgar concurred.

Jack nodded, and they fell into silence as they walked. There wasn't a whole lot to say. Either Mary would wake, or she wouldn't. No one knew why any of the Arrivals did or didn't wake after they'd been killed. Most everyone woke a few times, but there was no pattern to the hows or the whys of it. They got poisoned, shot, gutted, drained, or killed in any number of ways, but they often stood back up alive and perfectly healthy on the sixth day as if they'd only been sleeping—except when they didn't.

It wasn't until they reached the junction where they had to go separate ways that Jack suggested, "Francis maybe ought to go with y—"

"No," Kitty cut him off. "You're carrying Mary, and you have further to go. If you run into trouble, you'll need him."

"Be careful. Please?"

"Like Edgar would let me be anything else when I'm injured." She tried for a reassuring smile.

"And you'll come straight back to camp in the morning?" Jack prompted.

Kitty wanted to argue that he was being difficult, but she'd earned his suspicions—plus she was too tired to argue. She nodded. "Promise."

Neither Francis nor Edgar said a word, but she knew that they'd both obey Jack if it came down to a direct order. And while she wouldn't admit it aloud, she knew that they *should* obey him. There weren't a lot of things she believed after all these years in the Wasteland, but the one truth that she held on to like it was her religion was that her brother was worth obeying. She'd follow him to Hell without a moment's hesitation. For the first few years after they'd arrived here, she was pretty sure she *had* followed him to Hell. In the Wasteland, any number of impossible things lived and breathed. The one unified truth here was that the denizens of the Wasteland all thought the Arrivals were the most unnatural creatures in this world. Sometimes, Kitty thought they were right.

Tonight, though, they were simply a weary group of displaced humans. Kitty watched Jack carry Mary away, saw Francis scan the area for threats, and hoped that come morning no one else would be dead—and that in six days, Mary would be alive again.

# CHAPTER 2

By the time Edgar and Katherine returned to camp the next day, Jack had already finished an extra patrol and begun debating going back out. It wasn't that he was avoiding mourning; it was that he didn't know if he *should* mourn. Until the next six days passed, he wouldn't know if Mary would wake. If she didn't, there would be a void in his life. They weren't in love, but they'd been less and less likely to sleep in separate quarters over the past few months.

That was the only excuse Jack could give for putting Mary in his tent instead of her own. He'd given her the bed they'd often shared, and then he'd left the tent—and the camp—to patrol. Afterward, he'd slept on the floor for a few hours, and when day broke, he'd patrolled again. This wasn't the first time she'd died, but it was the first time since they'd become . . . whatever they were.

He'd covered Mary's body with a blanket as if she merely slept. He'd replaced her bloodied and torn dress with a nightdress, adding to the illusion of rest. Unfortunately, the glass of whiskey he held in his hand at this early hour unraveled the edges of the comforting lie that he'd tried to construct. She was dead.

There was no way to predict which deaths were permanent and which were temporary. Jack had spent many a week waiting by the bedsides of Arrivals who didn't wake—but he'd spent even more time alongside the beds of those who stood up six days later and continued their lives here in the Wasteland with nothing more than a few lingering bruises. After twenty-six years in this new world, he'd found no pattern to it, no way to make sense of it. The native Wastelanders didn't die and wake; that odd state was reserved for the Arrivals, those who had been born in another world.

Jack had just retrieved a second cup from his cupboard when he heard raised voices outside his tent. He'd known his sister wouldn't be pleased. Katherine would have expected to find Mary in the tent she and Mary had shared, and Jack wasn't the least bit surprised to see his baby sister scowl at him as she shoved open the tent flap.

"Are you feeling any better?" he asked.

"What were you thinking?" His sister stomped into the room, stopping beside the tiny table where he sat.

Jack gestured at the empty chair, but Katherine stood with her hands on her hips and her lips pressed into a tight line. When she didn't move, he said, "Mary slept here most nights lately. It seemed right for her to wait here now."

Katherine's temper visibly deflated, and she sank into the chair across from him. "Damn it, Jack. You can't ever let anyone help you, can you?"

He poured her drink and slid it to her. "So it would be easier on you?"

His sister let her breath out in a loud sigh. "No, but—"

"Let this one go, Katherine." Jack concentrated on his whiskey, taking a sip and letting it roll over his tongue. It wasn't precisely as bad as the swill they'd served up in saloons in California, but it wasn't the expensive stuff either. He didn't remember the last time he'd had truly good whiskey—or the money to buy it. The Arrivals worked mostly for the governor or for private citizens in the Wasteland. They weren't ever flush with cash. That said, Jack took pride in the fact that they worked for the good of the Wasteland. The jobs they took were ones that bettered their world, paid next to nothing—and irritated Ajani, the power-grabbing despot who was steadily destroying the Wasteland.

"The brethren didn't seem to take offense at anything before they opened fire," Katherine said, pulling Jack's attention away from whiskey, finances, and politics.

"I had the same thought when I was mulling things over," Jack allowed. Even though death wasn't always forever in the Wasteland, there *were* some things that were as predictable here as they'd been back in California. One unchanging truth was that meetings didn't suddenly change from peace to bullets unless there was a reason—or treachery.

"So . . . ?" Katherine's fingers tapped in an impatient rhythm on the table.

"I'm going to see Governor Soanes; he's still over in Covenant for a few days. The lindwurm job will wait till after . . ." Jack glanced at Mary. "I'll see the governor, be back here before the sixth day, and then we'll get back to work."

"You know I'm not going to let you go to Covenant without me." Katherine stared at him and sipped her drink as if she were calm.

But Jack had played poker with her, taught her the first of her tricks for handling the mood of a table, so he knew when she was digging in her heels. "Edgar won't be happy if you go out without him the day after you were injured," Jack said, "and I need him here."

Katherine shrugged. "So tell him to stay here."

"Spells leave you useless for a fight," he said evenly.

"And you're useless at spells. You need me on this one, Jackson. Just a shooter isn't enough, or you'd be arguing more."

Jack had tried to think of a better solution while he'd sat in the dark with his drink and his dead lover, but she was right. For most jobs, he had shooters aplenty. The Arrivals were all people who'd been on the wrong side of ethical at one point. Katherine had been a gambler and fancy woman, and Jack had been a gambler and shootist in his day. Early on, the first few people who'd come through to the Wasteland after Jack and Katherine were cut from the same cloth: willing to pull a trigger, but mostly as a consequence of the lifestyles they'd known or the skills they'd needed for survival. Most of those early Arrivals died—or joined Ajani. In more recent years, those who arrived were a mix of different sorts. Some were rough because of the things they'd had to do to survive, but more were folks whose moral compass was a bit unsteady. One of the few things they all had in common was that not a one of them since Katherine had been able to do spellwork.

Jack downed the rest of his drink. "Get your gear. I'll tell Edgar."

After a silent nod of acknowledgment, Katherine stood, walked over to the bed, kissed Mary's forehead, and left. Once his sister was gone, Jack sighed. He *did* need her help, and they both knew it. He'd needed her to make the decision, though. Even after all of the years he'd spent raising her and the years they'd spent in this world, he could still be surprised by the choices she made. He'd expected that neither one of them would cope well being trapped in camp while they waited to see if Mary woke, but he couldn't always be certain when it came to Katherine's opinions or reactions.

A short while later, Jack and Katherine were ready to set out across the Gallows Desert. It was a two-day journey to Covenant if all went well, so they'd packed water, bullets, and provisions. They only took one bedroll, which Jack currently carried, as they'd have to sleep in shifts.

As they'd approached the gate to exit camp, Edgar looked directly at Jack and announced, "If she's killed, I'll have to shoot you."

"I know." Jack nodded at him and stepped outside the gate to give Edgar and Katherine a moment.

Katherine, however, huffed at her on-again, off-again lover and walked past both him and Jack.

If Jack thought for a moment that he could trust anyone else to keep order in his absence, he'd have taken Edgar along on the journey, but no one was more competent than Edgar at handling the group in Jack's absence.

The trip across the desert and past the tiny town of Gallows was spent mostly in silence. That was one of the great joys of spending time with his sister: unlike some people—many of them women— Katherine had no patience for idle chatter. Aside from the essentials, the siblings remained quiet that day and much of the morning. As they traveled, they saw collapsed mines, starving Wastelanders, and scars on the ground from carelessly set-off explosives. Jack had already seen enough of Ajani's footprints on this world over the years, but the destruction left behind by Ajani's greed reaffirmed his deep-seated hatred of the man. The use of explosives in mining meant that able-bodied men were injured regularly in pursuit of riches that they'd never craved before falling under Ajani's influence.

As Jack understood it, until Ajani had taken over the mines, mining was largely handled by those born to it. The native miners used only natural methods, as if teasing the ground to give up treasures. They never took more than what was necessary for the production of weapons or tools. They didn't strip the grounds for the sake of stockpiling.

Then Ajani bought out, stole, or simply took over most of the mines. Now people not meant for work underground tunneled into dangerous areas, creating unstable ground on the surface, and were far too often killed in tunnel collapses. Boomtowns like Covenant had sprung up, growing too fast and resulting in dens of chaos and violence. Then, as soon as a vein was exhausted, the town died.

It was no wonder Garuda, the Wasteland's most important bloedzuiger, hated Ajani with a depth of passion that rivaled even Jack's.

There was nothing wrong with progress, with the evolution of a society, with developments in technology, but when avarice directed progress, the natural order of a community was destroyed. Lives were lost, and the Wasteland itself was being decimated.

When Jack and Katherine entered Covenant the next day, he wasn't sure if the uneventful journey was a blessing or not. He'd half hoped for some sort of fight to help relieve his mood, and he knew his sister wouldn't mind a bit of outlet either. At least the exertion of travel was better than waiting next to Mary's body.

"Not a monk in sight," Jack said as they walked toward the governor's quarters.

"No one else knew about the meeting, Jack. If it wasn't the brethren, that means the governor . . ." Katherine's words trailed off.

"I know, but that doesn't make a lick of sense." Jack gave voice to the thought that had plagued him for much of their hike across the desert. He'd weighed it out in his mind, trying to find a reason why Governor Soanes would send them into a trap. They'd worked for him from almost the time they'd arrived in the Wasteland, hunting down those who broke laws or those who were skirting close to breaking them. In some cases, they'd delivered warnings; in others, they'd executed more final orders.

"Maybe it's personal. The brethren haven't ever been very tolerant of the law," Jack mused.

"Could be, but why? We haven't taken them to task for anything." Katherine had obviously been pondering some of the very same thoughts he had. "If Soanes had word of a threat, he should've told us. If he didn't, the brethren are playing their cards awfully close to the vest."

"Just keep your eyes open," Jack murmured as they approached two of the governor's guards who stood on either side of the door to the squat, faded building.

The guards hadn't expected him, but they'd known Jack long enough that they simply nodded in greeting. One of them gave Katherine a far too friendly look, but instead of her usual harsh words or occasional physical demonstration of exactly how much she did *not* like being leered at, Katherine merely smiled.

Jack opened the door, and as she entered he asked in a low voice, "What was that?"

"Groundwork if we need another pair of eyes," she answered just as quietly.

The thought of needing spies in the governor's office wasn't one that set well with Jack, but he was, regrettably, already suspicious enough of the governor that he didn't object. Once they were inside, they waited while the next guard sent his partner in to inform Governor Soanes of their presence.

As they walked into the governor's office, Jack studied the Wastelander who had been his boss of sorts for years. He was a man who'd grown increasingly larger and slower from too much time behind a desk. Unlike a lot of the residents of the Wasteland, Soanes aged at the rate Jack associated with people back home. When they met, not long after Jack arrived, they'd been close in age, but after twenty-plus years, the governor looked like he was old enough to be Jack's father. The Arrivals did more work for him than anyone else, and Jack had believed they'd had a common goal: preserving order as much as they could, helping divert crises even as Ajani worked to amass wealth and influence. Now Jack had to wonder if the governor had changed his stance.

"Jack, Kitty," the governor greeted. "I wasn't expecting you."

The problem, however, was that the squat man didn't appear to be at all surprised by their presence. His words and his expression were at odds, and Jack couldn't tell whether it was simply because the governor was good at hiding his surprise—or if he was lying.

# CHAPTER 3

When Kitty had walked into Governor Soanes' office, she'd had to stamp down the impulse to start trouble as a test of his mettle. He wasn't in any shape to fight, a detail that irritated her even in her most generous moods. She had no love for Ajani, the man who caused most of their problems, or for Garuda, the bloedzuiger her brother called friend, but at least those Wastelanders were able to defend themselves in a conflict. Soanes, however, had the look of something bloated. His gut protruded like a woman at the end of pregnancy, and his face had the look of a dog she'd had as a girl: jowls flapping about like the skin had started to stretch. Yet, much like that dog, he seemed more lazy than dangerous. The idea of him exerting himself to send the brethren after the Arrivals seemed to go against his persona.

"The brethren attacked us," Kitty said as she dropped into one of the pair of chairs in front of the oversize desk where the governor sat. She twisted sideways, bending one leg and draping the other over the arm of the chair. Her dust and sand-coated boots would leave a mess behind, but it was in keeping with the demeanor of pure cussedness that she adopted around Governor Soanes. Since that day over two decades ago when she'd left home to follow after Jack, she'd learned to play a number of roles. When she was with Jack or Edgar, she felt like she could sometimes set all of that aside, but this was business. In dealing with Soanes, Jack would undoubtedly be polite, so Kitty would be brash.

The governor gestured to the empty chair beside Kitty, but Jack pointed to his holster and said, "Unless I'm disarmed, I'm more comfortable standing."

Soanes nodded, but a slight frown crossed his face before he turned his attention to Kitty. He asked, "Did you . . . *eliminate* the monks?"

"Eliminate? We were supposed to be negotiating with them in peace; that was the order, wasn't it?" Kitty flashed him a smile that was as falsely friendly as his always were.

And right on cue, with a warning tone in his voice and a hand on her shoulder, Jack said, "Katherine . . ."

"No, no. Kitty has a point," the governor placated. "The objective was a peaceful negotiation." He leaned back in his chair, which creaked but didn't spill him to the floor. "To clarify, I see you here, so I'd surmised that the monks are no longer a problem. I chose my words poorly."

"They killed one of ours." Jack didn't let any emotion into his voice, but if anyone knew him, they'd hear the emotion all the same.

"Dead dead or temporarily dead?"

Before Kitty could reply, Jack's grip on her shoulder tightened in a restraining way, and he said, "We won't know for a few more days."

He squeezed again, this time with a couple of quick pinches, and Kitty took that to mean she was to speak now. "The brethren's attack was unprovoked," she started. "That kind of thing doesn't usually happen without reason."

"What my sister means to say is that we were wondering where you got your information before you passed it on to me." Jack still sounded even-tempered, but the hand that was on her shoulder felt like a steel grip.

"Now, Jack, you know I can't answer that," Soanes said.

"Actually, that isn't what I meant, Jackson," Kitty said. "What I *meant to say* was that it seems suspicious that a peaceful meeting led to bullets and magic." She came to her feet and stood beside her brother, positioning herself beside him rather than in front of him in case there was violence. She didn't imagine that the governor was particularly adept with any weapons he might have concealed within his reach, but that only made him dangerous in a different way. An armed fool could be more dangerous than an experienced shooter.

"If you have some information that would make this clearer, I'd be mighty relieved to hear it." Jack stared directly at the governor. "I've fought for the good of the Wasteland for half my life."

"And we're grateful for that, for all of you, but that doesn't mean I can violate the responsibilities of my office by telling you things that are brought to me in private." The governor tilted his head back so as to stare up at them from across the expanse of his desk. "If all of these years together aren't reason enough for you to trust me, I'm not sure what else to say."

For a long moment no one spoke. Kitty waited for Jack to make the call. That was how it worked: he made the decisions, the rest of the Arrivals—herself included—obeyed his decrees. Someone had to be in charge. In their little group, that person was and had always been her brother. It wasn't a task she wanted for herself, and she certainly wouldn't give her allegiance to anyone else.

"You'll follow up," Jack half asked, half demanded.

"Of course!" Governor Soanes beamed at them. "You'll let me know if that death is a permanent one, I assume, and you'll take care of the monks?"

"We took the job," Jack said. "We've never left one unfinished before."

"I never could abide by demon summoning." The governor's expression was one of blatant disgust, and for the first time Kitty thought he was being completely honest. He might be hiding things, probably more than even she suspected, but his feelings about the brethren were crystal clear.

A few moments later, Kitty and Jack stood outside the governor's office.

"I'm not ready to travel," she admitted. The thought of trekking back out to camp today was daunting. "A cold drink and a long nap would go a long ways to making the trip back to camp easier."

"If we stay here tonight, we'll still be back the day before Mary's due to wake," Jack allowed.

The siblings walked toward the tavern. They'd discuss their thoughts on their visit to the governor, but not here where there were too many witnesses—all of whom were undoubtedly well aware that Jack and Kitty were the two Arrivals who'd been in the Wasteland the longest. Even if they did talk, however, there wasn't much to say. The governor knew they had doubts, and he'd answered in a way that was typical for this world: retreating behind the idea of tradition as if that were the only answer he could give. Admittedly, it was sometimes the answer, but politicians were politicians in every world. He'd not disclose everything he knew unless he had no other choice. A different man might have gathered evidence before presenting his doubts to the governor, but Jack was as direct as politicians were cagey.

They'd almost reached the tavern they usually frequented while they were in Covenant when Jack tensed. "Stay out of this, Katherine," he murmured low enough that only Kitty would hear him.

She followed his gaze to where a tall man who looked a lot like a better-dressed, longer-haired version of Jack was hitching up the Wasteland version of a horse to the rail outside one of the less savory taverns in Covenant. Not coincidentally, it was also the tavern Kitty preferred.

"Daniel," Kitty greeted in her friendliest voice. "Did you come to your senses or are you still an idiot?"

"I came to my senses years ago, Kitty." Daniel stepped away from his animal. "Ajani gave me the life I deserve. He'd give *you* everything."

"Except the things that matter," Kitty corrected.

Daniel shrugged.

"Are you alone?" she asked, looking around the quickly emptying street. None of Ajani's other lackeys appeared to be in sight, but that didn't mean that they—or Ajani himself—weren't nearby.

"The boss isn't here, but if you wanted him, I could send—"

"No," she interrupted. Before she could say more, Daniel lunged at Jack, and the two men were throwing punches.

Kitty sighed. Daniel had been one of their own, one she'd trusted and liked, but he'd left when Kitty had ended their ill-thought-out relationship. As far as she saw it, they'd been friends who sometimes went to bed together. Unfortunately, as it turned out, Daniel thought he felt something more for her, *and* he'd also been there to spy on the Arrivals.

As a result, Jack had the dual provocations of overprotectiveness toward her and intolerance for deceit. The result was that the two men couldn't seem to cross paths without fists flying. They'd killed each other repeatedly early on after Daniel had left, but these days Daniel never drew his weapon. Jack, of course, couldn't see his way clear to shoot him if he knew that Daniel was refusing to use bullets. Her brother was honor-bound to the point of foolishness. She wasn't.

"You have ten minutes, Jack, and then if he's still upright, I'm shooting him."

For his part, Daniel was a good fighter. Once upon a time, she'd enjoyed watching him in action. Since he'd become one of Ajani's top people, he'd shown himself capable of a type of creative violence that was disquieting to her. Currently, he was fighting fair—and well.

Kitty drew the revolver on her left hip and flicked open the chamber. She tapped out two bullets and replaced them with a pair of Francis' toxin-filled rounds.

"Thought you said ten *minutes,* Kitty." Daniel glanced at her and grinned. "If Edgar is telling you minutes are that brief, maybe I ought to remind—"

"Watch yourself, Danny." She pulled back the hammer and grinned at her former bedmate.

"At least Edgar is worthy of my sister," Jack snarled as he hit Daniel with even more force than before.

Daniel staggered back as Jack landed another blow. He locked eyes with Kitty as he wiped the blood from his mouth. "I don't think you'll do it."

Jack shook his head and muttered something, but Kitty didn't hear it over the crack of her gun.

The bullet hit Daniel in the upper thigh. Kitty wouldn't shoot a Wastelander so casually, but Daniel was—like all of Ajani's group—impervious to death. Even if he did die from the wound, he'd wake back up. Unlike the Arrivals who stayed with Jack, Ajani's people didn't ever stay dead.

She pulled back the hammer as she debated where to shoot him the second time, but before she fired again, Jack said, "Katherine! Enough."

She rolled her eyes. "Just because you don't shoot him anymore doesn't mean *I* can't."

"And that's the other reason Ajani wants you. You're bloodthirsty." Daniel ripped off his shirt to wrap around his wound. He still looked damn good with less clothes, and he knew it. She barely resisted smiling at the familiar warmth in his voice as he asked, "A little help?"

"Go to hell."

"Didn't we already do that?" Daniel asked quietly.

When neither Kitty nor Jack replied, Daniel looked down and

wrapped the shirt as best he could around his bleeding leg. He tied the arms of the shirt into a knot, using them like straps to fasten the makeshift bandage. When he looked up, he had a far too friendly expression on his face, but all he said was, "Burns like fire, Kit. Something Francis cooked up?"

Jack shook his head at the two of them, touched his lip gingerly, and looked at the blood now on his fingers. "Come on, Katherine. There's no need to stand around with a go'damned lickfinger."

The look Daniel was giving her was the same one he'd used years ago when he wanted to talk privately. Kitty glanced at her brother and said, "I'll be right in."

Jack gave her a pointed look. "Don't kill him . . . or do anything else stupid."

Daniel laughed and waved Jack away. "Give the others my best."

But Jack was already heading into the inn. Once he was gone, Kitty squatted down beside Daniel. She sighed. "Jack would let you come home. It doesn't have to be like this."

"Are you over Edgar?"

She forced herself not to flinch away from Daniel's attentive gaze, to keep her expression mild, but it didn't change anything. "What's between you and me has nothing to do with Edgar. You were my friend."

"Are you offering the same sort of friendship we used to have?" he asked baldly. "I hear that he's still banned from your bed. Tell me we can pick up where we were, and we can call it whatever you want."

"I can't."

"Then I'll stay with Ajani." Daniel sighed. "Living like you and Jack isn't something I'm going to do just for the hell of it, Kit. I like comfort, and I like money. The only thing I want that I don't have in Ajani's employ is your *friendship*." He paused, but she couldn't say anything he would want to hear. "Ajani wants you because of what you are, but he has no idea *who* you really are. Honestly, Kit, I think it would kill me to see you with him. Worse than seeing you with Edgar."

"I'm not *with* Edgar," Kitty insisted. "We're friends, but not . . ."

"You're with him enough to refuse me." Daniel gave her a rueful smile. "None of the others Ajani has gathered can work spells. It's still only you, and he is going crazy over it lately. He rants like a child denied a favorite toy. Be careful."

Over the years Kitty had gotten very good at hiding her feelings, but she failed in that moment: her surprise was as obvious as her doubt. "So you're *my* spy now?"

He shrugged. "If that's all you'll let me be . . . I'm not working for the Arrivals, but there's not much I wouldn't do to protect you. Lately, I'm not so sure the boss is firing on all cylinders. Something's up. I just thought you should know." Then he held a hand out to her. "Help me up?"

"I'm the reason you're down," she objected, but she took his hand all the same and stood. Bracing her feet, she tugged, and he pushed off the ground with his uninjured leg and other arm.

When he was on his feet, he used her hand to jerk her toward him.

Before he could kiss her, she'd raised her gun and pressed the barrel against his stomach. "Don't make me shoot you again."

His answering laughter was so familiar that she smiled in spite of herself.

"I could stay here tonight, Kitty," he said. "Edgar wouldn't have to know. Hell, no one has to know. It doesn't even have to mean anything."

For a moment, she considered it. She wasn't sharing Edgar's bed, and she didn't owe anyone any explanations. It wasn't like she was able to catch a disease or get pregnant, not here in the Wasteland, but no amount of rationalization would change the fact that Daniel worked for Ajani. Weakly, she said, "I just shot you."

"True," Daniel murmured. "There *would* be positions we couldn't—"

"No," she interrupted. She stepped away from him and glanced toward the tavern, as much to look for Jack as not to look at Daniel. "Edgar would forgive me for a meaningless fuck, but you're not meaningless."

"Thank you for that." Daniel squeezed her hand. "Be careful, and— as much as I hate saying this—try to stay with Edgar or Jack. I'm not sure the boss would follow the rules anymore if he saw an opportunity to take you."

After Daniel released her hand and limped away, Kitty stood watching him. They'd once been friends, but that didn't mean she understood him . . . or truly trusted him. In his life before waking up in the Wasteland, Daniel had been a drug dealer. He lied as easily as he breathed.

In this, though, she believed him. For the first time in a lot of years, he'd sounded like the man she'd once cared for. Whatever flaws he had, he'd just put himself at risk, and taken a bullet to the thigh to warn her. She could only hope that Ajani didn't find out.

# CHAPTER 4

Jack was trying not to notice that their return trip across the desert was slower than the trip to Covenant had been. Maybe it was simply a result of not wanting to return to camp and wait. They'd know within the next two days if Mary would return to them, and until they knew, it was hard to focus on much else—or hurry back to camp.

Unfortunately, the world didn't pause for death. The monks were still out there; the job remained unfinished. Jack had an uneasy feeling after their conversation with Governor Soanes—and seeing Daniel hadn't helped matters.

"How did Daniel know we were in Covenant?" Jack prompted.

"Damned if I know." Katherine's expression became closed, and he knew she was hiding something. If she'd been anyone else, he'd be mistrustful, assuming that she was passing information to Daniel, but although his sister was guilty of a lot of things over the years, none of them was treachery.

He waited.

They were over halfway to camp when she said, "I think he was there to talk to me, but I don't know *how* he knew we'd be in Covenant."

Jack nodded.

A few more minutes passed before she added, "He says Ajani is coming off the rails lately. He wanted to warn us."

"Warn *you*," Jack corrected. "Should I ask if he left after you spoke?"

"You shouldn't have to ask, Jack," she snapped. Then she sighed. "Do *you* know how Danny knew where to find us?"

"I don't." Jack trusted the rest of the Arrivals. *Mostly.* Melody had spent some time with Ajani last year, and Jack suspected she still had some contact with his people. She was the most likely source of any information leak; on the other hand, it wasn't too hard to guess that Jack would be going to see the governor after Mary's death. Anyone in Gallows could've seen them and sent word to Ajani. Hell, Daniel might've been in Gallows and heard it himself, for all they knew.

"Was the governor expecting us?" Jack mused.

Beside him, Katherine sighed again. "It sure seemed like it, but I can't say for certain. If I had any real answers, I'd share them. All I know right now is that the monks were supposed to be looking for peace, but they weren't; that Soanes wants them dead; that Daniel thinks Ajani is unstable; and that if Mary doesn't wake up, we'll have a new Arrival to deal with on top of the rest of the bullshit."

"What happened to women being the gentler sex?" Jack shot her a pretend grumpy look; he couldn't stand seeing her look so defeated. "Shouldn't you be offering some sort of comforting reply?"

Katherine rolled her eyes, but her lips curved in a small smile. It wasn't much, but it was enough to make him relax a little. She was able to hold her own against most of what the Wasteland threw at them, and she was the only one from their world who could do spellwork, but the emotional stuff threw her into maudlin moods, and Jack wasn't an idiot: he knew his sister still had feelings for Daniel. She shot him often enough to prove to everyone she didn't, but it wasn't particularly convincing.

"I'll figure it all out, Katherine," Jack promised her quietly. "And whether or not Mary wakes, we'll get through this too."

He wished yet again that he'd had the sense to tuck her away in some school back east instead of letting her stay in California with him. If he'd put her where she'd have been safe, she wouldn't have been brought to the Wasteland; if he'd thought about her safety instead of giving in to his own arrogant belief that he could keep her safe, she'd be in a better world where she could have a proper life. Instead, she was trapped here in the Wasteland, dealing with monsters and death, scuffling in the dirt and blood, and knowing as well as he did that there was no end in sight. He looked over at her and repeated, "I'll figure it out."

Unfortunately, the following day, when they were back at camp, Jack had no clearer idea of what to do. They'd know by the next day whether Mary's death was permanent or not. In some reserve of hope that he still clung to after all these years, he hoped that death in this world would mean waking up back in a better one. He didn't much care whether that better world was the one they'd once known or some sort of afterlife where the Arrivals would find peace. He told himself Heaven was a child's hope, but if so many impossible things were real, believing in Heaven, in a forgiving God, seemed a little more possible.

His beliefs had dwindled over the years, but as he sat near Mary he whispered a prayer. Then he decided to do something he'd never done before. While Katherine slept in her tent that night, Jack went to the only other person he'd ever met who was capable of standing up to her.

Edgar looked up as Jack entered the tent. Not surprisingly, Edgar was sitting at his table cleaning his weapons. Before coming to the Wasteland, he had been a hired gun for a thriving crime syndicate, so he was as fastidious about weapons maintenance as Jack was. Edgar wasn't quite the dapper killer he'd been when he arrived in the Wasteland, but he was still an unusual man. His word was binding; his kills were calculated. The job was business, nothing more, nothing less. His willingness to shoot was only tempered by a sense of loyalty, and Edgar Cordova's loyalty was very narrowly assigned: Katherine was his beloved; Jack was his boss. As to which of the Reed siblings outranked the other when they were at odds, it varied, depending on what Edgar thought most sensible at the time.

"I need your help," Jack started.

Edgar resumed cleaning the pistol in front of him and asked, "With what?"

"I hate asking you to stand between Katherine and me," Jack started.

"But you're going to."

Jack stepped farther into the tent. It was as practically laid out as the man who slept in it, utilitarian but with a few unexpected exceptions. In his room in every one of their personal quarters, Edgar had a device that allowed his trousers to hang so they wouldn't wrinkle and a clothes rack for his shirts and jackets. Beyond his clothing contraptions, Edgar's tent was very basic. A plain dark wood partition concealed the toilet; a weapons chest stood to the side; and in the middle of the room was a bed. Jack stopped at the small table where Edgar sat.

"She's having a hard time with Mary's death," Jack said.

"She always does when one of us dies." Edgar wiped down the barrel of the pistol and set it aside. "So do you."

"True." Jack didn't want to talk about his own reaction. Of all the people in this world or the last, Edgar was one of the few he didn't keep at a distance.

"I want to wait alone with Mary," he admitted. "I need you to keep my sister out of my tent."

Edgar shook his head. "Kit won't be happy."

"I'll tell her I ordered you to do it," Jack offered.

The look Edgar gave him would make more than a few people piss themselves in fear, but Jack knew him better than that. If Edgar were genuinely angry, he wouldn't waste Jack's time or his own with scowling.

Once they returned to Jack's tent, Edgar took one of Jack's chairs and positioned it outside. As Jack went back inside to wait, Edgar said, "If Mary stays dead, I'm letting Kit past me eventually. You can have until midday."

Jack nodded and resumed his vigil by Mary's body. Now that Edgar stood outside to stop Katherine from coming into the tent, Jack would have privacy. None of the other Arrivals were particularly close to Mary; it wouldn't require any special measures to keep them out. Edgar cared only for Katherine; Francis likewise had a brotherly fondness for Katherine. Melody was too self-centered to be close to much of anyone, and if Hector had emotions, no one knew about it. Part of Jack's reason was simply a need for privacy if he needed to mourn. The rest was a desire for space in order to think about what might come next for the group. Over the years, the group had fluctuated slightly in number, but right now they were at their lowest. Aside from the emotional toll it would take on Jack and Katherine, losing Mary could cause problems if the next Arrival chose to work for Ajani instead of staying with them.

He sat beside Mary, thinking about what came next, but not finding any answers—or signs of returning life. It wasn't unheard of for the Arrivals to wake a few hours shy of midday or even at dawn, but it wasn't typical. Jack knew that, but he hoped all the same. Hours passed in silence, and more than a few prayers passed his lips. He hadn't realized he'd even remembered them that well until now.

When morning came, Katherine's cussing and Edgar's calm words broke the silence, and Jack felt a moment of guilt for keeping Katherine out. His sister wanted to be there for him, and he knew she'd been close with Mary, but the cold truth was that he didn't want his sister there watching him. He didn't love Mary, had never known the sort of love Katherine and Edgar shared, and he wasn't entirely sure he was capable of it. What he did know was that Mary had loved *him,* and right now he wanted to be worthy of that love.

"If you come back, I'll try to love you," he promised.

Mary didn't stir.

For several more hours, Jack alternated between praying and making promises to the dead woman in his bed, but by midday, she was still motionless.

"I'm sorry," he told her, and then he left his tent.

Edgar looked up at him when he walked out. Beside him was Katherine. They both opened their mouths to speak, but Jack shook his head and said, "I'm going on patrol."

His sister reached out to him, wrapping her arms around him, but all he could say was "I'm sorry," even though the words weren't any more use to her than they had been to Mary. Yet another of the Arrivals was dead, and in the next few days, someone else would appear in the Wasteland to replace her, and Jack would once again try his best not to fail that person. And all the while he would try to convince him or her not to join Ajani—even though that was the only surefire way Jack knew of to keep the newest Arrival from permanent death. That was the ugly truth of it: if they worked for Ajani, they'd be truly free of death. Unfortunately, they'd also be indebted to the one person in the Wasteland whom Jack would willingly die or kill to destroy.

# CHAPTER 5

When Chloe opened her eyes, she was stretched flat on her back, staring up at an odd-looking sky. She wasn't sure where she was, but she *was* sure that it was not Washington, D.C. Although she hadn't seen the whole of the city in the few months she'd lived there, she could pretty much guarantee that there were no sand dunes or fields of what looked like cotton in the heart of the nation's capital.

All she could move was her head. From her neck down, her body was tingling. She tried to move her legs, to sit, but all that happened was a weird jerking, as if her body was trying but couldn't complete the movements. She could feel the trickle of sweat rolling off her skin like small insects crawling all over her, but she couldn't move to wipe it away.

She tried to stave off panic by studying what she could see around her. To her right was a barren stretch of desert surrounded by a sturdy but peculiar-looking metal fence. A rutted road of dirt and sand cut between the desert and the field. The cotton plants had tufts of white on them, but they didn't look nearly as prickly as real cotton plants.

Above her, the sky looked . . . *wrong*. It was mostly blue like skies were supposed to be, but the sun was high above her as if it were midday even though sunset streaks of reds and purples were painted across the blue. She frowned as she looked to her left: there were two moons visible in the sky.

The more she looked, the more she suspected that she had to be hallucinating—except it had been a long time since she'd even smoked a joint much less taken anything that would result in full-color hallucinations. She'd broken her sobriety last night, but that seemed unlikely to have led to something this severe. It wasn't like she'd been sipping some sort of potentially toxic moonshine. She'd been in a bar where even the well liquors were high end.

The ability to move seemed to be slowly creeping downward. Chloe wiggled her fingers and stretched her arms. The pins-and-needles feeling was a welcome sensation. She fingered the pendant she wore on a chain around her neck. Her aunt had given it to her for five years' sobriety—which she had ended last night.

The last thing she remembered was having an obscenely overpriced drink in a suit-filled bar. It wasn't her usual sort of digs, but it was the first place she'd seen after she'd found her fiancé, Andrew, and her boss humping like feral bunnies. She'd walked out of her apartment, the apartment *he* had moved into only a month ago. She hadn't even slammed the door. She'd left them there fucking in her home and wandered for a few hours until the warm light of a bar beckoned. It had been a long time since she'd even come close to breaking her sobriety, but it was either that or go home to a bed she couldn't sleep in now. The images of walking into the bar, of ordering several drinks, of ignoring Andrew's calls: those were all clear. After that, it was all a blank until she woke up wherever she was now.

"I told you she was bound to be out here," a man's voice said.

Chloe turned her head to see a man who looked like he'd stepped out of a western TV show, dressed in patched brown trousers and a plain button-up shirt.

"Don't be smug, Jack." The woman who came to stand beside him was wearing a strange skirt that was hitched up above her knees in the front but hung to her ankles in the back. The strange cut of it exposed a pair of what looked like battered red leather boots that laced up to the knee. The peculiar skirt was topped with a snug, low-cut blouse that exposed far more bosom than even the most daring swimsuit Chloe owned.

The woman held out a hand to Chloe. "Name's Kitty."

"This is a very vivid hallucination," Chloe told her.

"And that's Jack . . . short for jackass," Kitty continued as if Chloe hadn't spoken. She kept her hand outstretched. "Come on now. Standing's going to hurt no matter when you do it."

When Chloe didn't respond, the woman reached down, gripped Chloe's hand, and hauled her to her feet.

Chloe's legs weren't quite as reliable as her arms were. She wobbled and had to close her eyes against a wave of dizziness that was followed instantly by the pressing need to vomit. Kitty held her steady as she did just that.

"Hush," Kitty murmured. "It passes soon enough. What are you called?"

"Chloe." She kept her eyes closed as she marshaled the strength to stay upright. After a few moments she opened one eye tentatively to see the two strangers watching her.

The man held out a neatly folded square of cloth.

"It's clean," Kitty said.

After Chloe took it and wiped her mouth and chin, Jack bowed his head slightly. "I'm Jackson, but everyone calls me Jack."

The woman holding her upright interjected, "Except when we're calling you—"

"This is my sister, Katherine," Jack continued. "She's not nearly as vulgar as she appears."

"*Kitty*, not Katherine," the woman corrected. She smiled and cajoled, "Come on, Chloe. You'll get your bearings soon enough, or you'll succumb to madness. Either way, it'll be easier after you get past the travel sickness and rest awhile."

"Travel sickness . . ." Chloe echoed. "I'm just hungover, and you're a hallucination . . . or a coma dream." She glanced toward the pasture, where she saw what looked like an elephant-size iguana. "This is all a coma dream."

"Of course it is, sweetie." Kitty's arm tightened around Chloe's waist. "Why don't we head back to the camp? You can catch some sleep, and then we'll talk about everything."

After a moment's pause, Chloe decided that there weren't a whole lot of options before her. She could go along with the people in her dream/hallucination, or she could stand around staring at the giant *lizard* while she waited for reality to right itself.

"I'm not dead, right?" Chloe asked.

Jack flashed her a grin before saying, "Well, no one's ever accused Katherine of being an angel."

"And jackass here isn't as much a devil as he'd like everyone to think," Kitty added in a soft, consoling voice. "It'll all be all right, Chloe. We'll go back to camp and rest a bit, and soon enough you'll feel right as rain."

# CHAPTER 6

They were only a mile outside camp when Jack noticed the unfamiliar tracks and decided that it was in everyone's best interest to carry the disoriented woman. She'd been chattier than most, rambling about concussions and brain tumors affecting her perceptions and then explaining that she must be in a hospital filled with drugs that were creating elaborate hallucinations. She finally fell quiet when Jack lifted her into his arms and walked faster.

Katherine picked up her pace without question.

Jack did his best to think about getting them to camp safely—without thinking about the last woman he'd carried into camp. Mary was truly dead. Thinking about her didn't change anything. The new one—*Chloe,* he reminded himself—was lighter than Mary. It was harder each time to remind himself that they were all individuals, people, not simply replacements for the Arrivals who'd died.

He knew that this one—*Chloe*—was from a later year than most of them, possibly around Mary's time period. Her clothes were different. She wore the tightest pair of denim trousers, of jeans, that he'd ever seen. A blouse of some sort of delicate material was covered by a soft leather jacket that narrowed at the waist like a woman's dress would. With such revealing clothes, any man would've noticed her. Jack was neither a saint nor a preacher; he definitely noticed her charms—and immediately felt guilty for it.

As Jack, Katherine, and Chloe reached the perimeter of the camp, Jack saw Edgar leaning against the barrel that served as a stool at the guard point. He looked at them with his usual methodical assessment.

"Kit," Edgar said with no obvious inflection. Then the taciturn man glanced at Chloe, who rested half asleep in Jack's arms. "Jack . . . and . . . ?"

"Chloe." The girl lifted her head from Jack's shoulder and looked at Edgar. "I'm not sure of anything else today, but I'm definitely Chloe."

Jack lowered Chloe's feet to the ground, but he kept an arm around her waist. She wavered a little as she stood, but despite the exhaustion, shock, and lingering travel sickness, she was upright. In truth, she was doing remarkably well. "Go with Katherine, Chloe. You're safe here."

Without any of her usual sass, Katherine stepped up to Chloe's other side and wrapped an arm around her middle just under Jack's arm. "Lean on me," she offered.

Once Chloe shifted her weight onto Katherine, Jack lowered his arm and released the woman into his sister's care.

Edgar lit a cigarillo. He was studying Katherine as intently as he always did when she returned to camp after a patrol. Katherine continued pretending not to notice, but neither of them persuaded anyone—including themselves. If anything ever happened to Edgar, Jack would have no idea how to look after his sister. He was tempted to lock the two of them in a room to sort themselves out, but he'd tried that once before with less than grand results.

The two women slowly tottered toward Katherine's tent. Once they were inside and Katherine closed the tent flap, Jack turned to Edgar. "She's the new Arrival."

"I figured, but you don't usually cart them in like that," Edgar said, holding out a second neatly wrapped cigarillo.

Jack shook his head. "Can't. I need to do another patrol, and the stink of that makes it harder to scent what's around me."

Mutely, Edgar pocketed the cigarillo.

"You'll stay at the gate?" Jack prompted.

Edgar took a drag and exhaled a plume of smoke before he answered. "I don't shirk my duties, Jack. I'll talk to her after my shift." His tone was mild enough, but he was undoubtedly already tense after Katherine had insisted on going out with Jack. Typically, Edgar patrolled with Katherine; he stood night watch when she was in camp. Right now Katherine was struggling. She never coped well when one of the Arrivals died, worse when it was someone like Mary, whom she'd called a friend.

Jack nodded. It was the best he could hope for, all things considered.

"What's she like?" Edgar asked.

"The new Arrival? Hard to say." Jack pulled his attention away from the tent. "She kept calling us hallucinations."

Edgar snorted. "Another Francis. Did she tell you her 'real name' was Dewdrop or Star?"

Jack grinned. "No. Near as I can tell, she isn't from the same years as him. She feels . . . newer than anyone else has been."

Each new Arrival wasn't from a later time than his or her predecessors, but they were from a general window of time. Jack and Katherine had lived in the late 1800s; Mary had been from almost a century later. No one had come from a time earlier than Jack's, and everyone else was from the 1900s. The areas weren't the same either. Edgar was from Chicago; Melody wouldn't give the same answer twice on where she was from. Francis thought he'd been in somewhere called Seattle when he'd been brought over to the Wasteland.

Jack and Katherine had been the first, and Jack had spent more than a few nights wondering if they were all here as a result of something he'd done forever ago. He had no idea what that something could've been, and he'd thought on it often enough the past twenty-six years. He'd also spent years trying to figure out a pattern to the times and places, but he'd had very little luck. All he knew for sure was that those who arrived in this world needed someone to help guide them, and he'd taken that task as his own. The transition to this world was hard. If he could have spared everyone from having to make it, he would.

For a moment, the only sound was the crackling of the tobacco in Edgar's lit cigarillo. Neither he nor Jack mentioned the fact that they'd been expecting Chloe—or someone like her. Nor did they mention the worry that she'd attract Ajani's attention too soon.

Jack had been waiting for that peculiar itch under his skin that always heralded a new Arrival; he'd wondered more than a few times if Ajani felt the same thing, but there was nothing to indicate that Ajani was anything more than a Wastelander who'd found the Arrivals particularly useful as employees. For Jack, though, there was a pull to a particular location, generally near to where the last of their group had died. Even without a sense of it, Jack would know to watch for the Arrival. Mary had only been dead a little over a week, but the replacement almost always arrived within a month. That was how it went: when one of them finally died, someone else arrived in the Wasteland. The only oddity was that Chloe had arrived much sooner than they usually did.

Edgar interrupted Jack's musing when he asked, "Do you need me to do anything?" His tone said what his words didn't: he had no special thing in mind, but if Jack did, he'd be obliging. That was one of the joys of dealing with Edgar: there wasn't a lot of guesswork where he was concerned.

Jack pondered the question. Sometimes he had a better sense than others about what to do about the new ones. With Edgar, Jack had known almost instantly that he needed to keep the man away from any weapons until Edgar had determined that the Arrivals weren't a threat to him. With some of the others—people long dead now—they'd had to keep weapons out of reach to keep them from harming themselves. Chloe didn't fit into either of those categories.

"Not right now," Jack said. "Maybe take Katherine out tomorrow so I can talk to Chloe without her hovering and badgering."

Edgar nodded.

"I don't know if she mentioned it, but Daniel was in Covenant." Jack kept his voice pitched low.

"She hadn't mentioned it yet." Edgar's characteristic calm failed a little; his nostrils flared and his lips pressed together tightly. In a blink, though, the expression vanished, and he asked in a deceptively calm voice, "Anything interesting happen?"

"Katherine shot him," Jack started, and then he summarized what he knew of the meeting. He paused a moment before adding, "He warned her that Ajani is crazier than usual of late. I trust my sister, but she's far too forgiving where Daniel is concerned."

"I'm not."

"Likewise." Out of habit, Jack flicked open the chambers of his revolvers. Neither the silver bullets in the right gun nor the cold iron ones in the left were much use against demons, but there were plenty of other monsters in the dark.

Silently, Edgar held out one of the shotguns that they kept at the perimeter for patrols—or for any attempts at infiltration. Jack took it, cracked the barrel to check that it was loaded, and ignored Edgar's small snort when he did so. They both knew it was loaded, and they both knew that neither one of them would be able to walk into the darkness without checking for himself. Trust didn't outweigh habit.

"I'll be back within two hours," Jack said, and he left camp. When he could, he patrolled on his own. The rest of the team usually worked in pairs, but Jack needed his space, especially in the wake of a death. They all dealt with defeat in their own way. Some of them didn't seem to react to the losses at all, but Jack suspected that he and Kitty felt each death more powerfully because they had been here the longest. So many people had arrived, become part of their family of sorts, and then died.

Jack couldn't make sense of it, wasn't sure what came after this life—or if anything they did made a difference. The others all looked to him for answers that he no longer even thought he might have. All he knew was that whether it was in the world he'd once known or here in the Wasteland, the only time he thought there might be some great divine deity out there was when he was alone with nature. So he patrolled in the Gallows Desert, watching for demons or monks as he trekked across sand and rock under constellations that were nothing like those he'd seen in the California desert.

# CHAPTER 7

In a house far from the stifling heat and pervasive sand, Ajani rested in a darkened chamber. It wasn't his most comfortable home, but it was opulent enough to be tolerable as he recovered from his latest endeavor. Somewhere nearby, an indoor waterfall splashed and murmured in soothing tones. He kept his eyes shut and tried to concentrate on the relaxing sounds, on the steady inhalations of breath, on anything but the raging headache that made him feel as if dying would be preferable to this pain.

The headache had lessened some in the hours since the new Arrival had come through to the Wasteland. Ajani no longer felt like his body was being reorganized inside, and the vomiting had stopped. As long as he didn't move, the nosebleed would stay away too. Better, however, didn't mean well. Opening a gate to the other world was somewhere between magic and science. It *felt* like magic, like turning a body inside out and squashing it into space that didn't quite want to hold body-shaped things. Regardless of whether it was magic, science, or something in between, it hurt like the devil.

Sometimes it seemed that the headaches had grown worse over the years. Other times, Ajani suspected that he'd simply become less tolerant of pain. It didn't matter, though: great men had always suffered for their causes. He would suffer for his, and in time, the natives would thank him for his sacrifices and those back home would know that he was a true visionary. He might not have discovered the path to a new world in the same fashion as most explorers had, but like the rest of those good men who'd expanded the queen's empire, he'd made sacrifices. He was shaping an entire *world* for her empire instead of a mere island or continent. Numerous mines employed teams of natives extracting precious metals and gems from the ground to be delivered to the queen.

There were no interesting artifacts here, as there had been in Egypt, and he had no desire to gather too many exotic species of animals. He'd collected a few in a private zoo, but jewels and metals were far more useful than lindwurms or cynanthropes. He wasn't sure how well he could transport creatures either. Moving living beings through time and space was difficult as it was. It was a remarkable victory that he'd accomplished this much.

The distance between worlds seemed so vast when seen from the ground. Wide swaths of darkness, sprinkled with stars, the distance between them so unfathomable—until a man realized that the dark distance was like fabric. With the right tools, the fabric could be bent, fashioned into waves, and then pierced like a needle through folded cloth. A tiny hole—a doorway to another world—could be opened, and vast spaces could be crossed in a moment.

The consequence, unfortunately, was that it left him exhausted and sick. When he'd been in England, a place as removed from the Wasteland as possible, he'd learned that he could open a doorway rather by accident. Egyptology was the fashionable thing. The queen had been expanding her empire, and everyone had grasped whatever heathen artifacts they could. Ajani was no different.

Only a third son, grateful not to be his father's heir but not interested in pursuing a life of service either, Ajani had been at a loss—until he'd bought a mummified body. With the body came canopic jars, shabti, and a coffin text. The text was scrawled in the margins of a torn page from a book that had been tucked under the jar. While holding the canopic jar, he'd read that text aloud.

> I am lord of eternity in the crossing of the sky.
> I am not afraid in my limbs,
> I shall open the light-land, I shall enter and dwell in it . . .
> Make way for me . . . I am he who passes by the guards . . .
> I am equipped and effective in opening his portal!
> With the speaking of this spell, I am like Re in the eastern sky,
> like Osiris in the netherworld. I will go through the circle of
> darkness, without the breath stilling within me ever!

And a doorway had opened. The universe folded as the words created a tunnel leading from his rather comfortable sitting room to somewhere he couldn't see.

If Ajani had known what waited, he might have hesitated, but he'd been well in his cups by then, and despite plenty of practice in the art of drunkenness, he'd failed to observe any of the logical principles he'd typically have employed. Fortunately, it was not the netherworld he found when he stepped through the portal. He'd ended up in the Wasteland, a godforsaken world filled with heathens and monsters, deviants and demons, and no aristocracy at all.

So Ajani had done what any of the queen's best men would've done: he began to work to correct the shortcomings of the Wasteland, to bring its inhabitants the benefit of the superiority of the British Empire, to guide and rule the natives of this primitive world.

Reminding himself that what he did was for the betterment of the world was at least some small consolation today. Yesterday, he'd brought another useful soldier to this world. Today, he would wait for his body to repair the cost of yesterday's success.

# CHAPTER 8

That night, Kitty looked after Chloe as the new woman worked through the fevers that accompanied arrival in the Wasteland. The unexpected benefit of this was that it gave her an excuse to avoid Edgar. He'd stopped outside her tent when he'd finished his shift, but he wouldn't come inside without invitation, especially when she was tending a new Arrival.

Kitty had done this so often for so many people that it was almost routine. Unfortunately, being used to a thing didn't make it any less wearying. She sat at the same bedside where Mary had once thrashed in the throes of her arrival fever; she dipped her cloth into the same white basin and watched over another woman who would wake in an unfamiliar world.

The first few days were hard on the body. By midday the next day, Chloe's worst bout with the fever had passed, but she was still resting. She'd woken only briefly, which was fairly normal. The transition between the world the Arrivals had known and the Wasteland left every one of them exhausted. Now that the worst was past, Melody could watch Chloe for a couple hours. Francis would take over when he finished his shift. Usually Kitty would take the opportunity to catch up on the sleep she'd missed the first day—and the sleep she would miss again tomorrow. By the end of the third day, Kitty would be stuck in her tent waiting for Chloe to wake. It wasn't a *rule* per se, but she preferred that the new Arrivals awoke to the sight of either her or Jack. Everyone else went along with her plan, even if they didn't always understand. The others had never woken up alone, utterly lost and unsure of absolutely everything; they didn't understand the shock of it all. Jack did.

When he and Kitty had arrived in the Wasteland, they knew nothing about the world around them, nothing about the people or creatures in it, and even less about how they ended up in this place. After twenty-six years, they knew plenty about the world, the people, and the creatures. They shared the knowledge with new Arrivals and helped their transition. It was the *right* thing to do.

Today, though, Kitty wanted to be somewhere else—not resting, not dealing with Mary's death or Chloe's arrival. The group had been living at this campsite for more than a week since the situation with the brethren. What Kitty needed was a break: time away from everyone's watchful gaze, space away from the horrible anticipation that followed every death.

She changed into something less suited for work, and then after verifying that Edgar was nowhere in sight, she made her way to the gate, where she found Francis twisted into one of his contorted positions that seemed like they should be impossible. He was trying another of his plant-based creams, so his entire visage was tinted blue. Unlike most of them, Francis burned a bright red even with the sun protection the rest of them used. He'd developed it, and it worked well enough for everyone else. He just burned more easily. Kitty couldn't help but smile at his blue face.

"I need to head into Gallows," she said.

"Alone?" His gaze flickered over to her only briefly before returning to dutifully watching the expanse of desert.

Kitty sorted through a few of the weapons that were kept at the gate, buying herself time, trying to decide how much she had to admit. There was no way to pretend she wasn't going to a tavern dressed as she now was. Her skirt was of a lightweight fabric and tied up in the front with a series of ribbons, giving her freedom of movement and exposing a lot of leg from the front. The back of it had no ties, so it brushed almost to the ground, and the degree of detail made abundantly clear that, despite the fabric, this wasn't a dress for walking in the desert. Sand would collect at the hem, and unless she was careful, plants would snag it until it looked like a rag.

She dropped a few throwing knives into her bag and settled on, "Jack's already out there, so we'll catch up before I head into town."

She wasn't completely lying. She suspected that her brother would catch up with her; whether or not that would be before or after she reached town, she couldn't say. It depended on when he found out she'd left.

"If Edgar asks, you know I have to tell him." Francis didn't look at her this time. "If Jack comes back without you—"

"You sound like you doubt me."

"I smoked an awful lot of weed when I was back home, tripped a lot too, but that doesn't mean I'm stupid." Francis continued to scan the desert.

She sighed.

"Didn't say I wouldn't play along," he said quietly. "You take the dying harder than the rest of us. Go out, and have fun. Don't get killed, or Edgar and Jack will . . . honestly, I'm not sure what they'd do. They don't like you going out alone."

"*They* go alone." Kitty tried not to sound angry, but her brother was out in the desert alone right now. Edgar undoubtedly had been earlier. They acted like she wasn't capable of protecting herself, yet she was the only one of the group able to work Wastelander magic. She had been here just as long as Jack, longer than Edgar. Long before any of the others had arrived, she and Jack had fought and killed creatures that didn't even exist in the world they'd once called home. "There's no reason I shouldn't be able to go alone."

Even as she said it, she thought about Daniel's warning, but he was no better than Jack or Edgar. Everyone acted like she was some sort of frail creature that needed sheltering—at least they did until they needed spellwork or bullets. They were fine with her fighting skills, but only when they were fighting along with her. It was maddening.

Francis held out a gun, which she accepted and slipped into a holster that she'd already fastened under her skirt, high on her leg where it was easy to access but hidden from view.

"They go out alone because they've been here the longest," he said.

"I've been here as long as Jack and *longer* than Edgar," she corrected.

"True point." Francis' voice was bland as he asked, "What years were they born?"

"Shut up, Francis." She wasn't going to *say* he was right, but she used his own phrase—"shut up"—which Mary had been fond of as well. She'd picked up the words and habits of later-born Arrivals over time, even though some of the things they said and did were still perplexing to her. She would admit, though, that Francis had a good point: Jack was a lot less willing to evolve; he clung to his old notions as if there was a chance they'd all be going back someday. Kitty had tried to move forward over the years, but both Jack *and* Edgar retained some of their more irritating attitudes from home when it came to her safety.

"Just be careful." Francis uncoiled his lanky body from the barrel that he used as a chair of sorts and gave her a one-armed hug. "Seriously, Kitty: don't get killed."

"I'll be fine," she promised. "I just need a little fun."

Several hours later, Kitty was trying to tell herself she was having fun, but reasoning with drunks with guns wasn't the sort of evidence that was helpful in convincing herself to believe that lie. The tiny outpost town of Gallows was the best she could do this far into the desert, and all things considered, it wasn't a bad little town. She'd had more than a few fun nights in Gallows. *Mostly with Edgar, or . . .* She stopped herself before she could think of the Arrivals she'd called friends over the years.

After pushing that thought away, she looked at the scrawny drunk beside her and started, "Be sensible, Lira. You don't want to—"

A face full of wine interrupted her attempt at calming words.

Kitty swiped an arm across her face; the sickly-sweet scent of cheap wine was almost as irritating as the wet hair that now clung to her skin. She started counting in her head, willing herself not to lose her temper.

The bartender dropped behind the bar, and the drunk to her left started to raise her gun.

Kitty punched her.

"Thanks." Lira grinned, as if she hadn't just doused Kitty with wine.

For a moment, Kitty considered resuming her counting, but the moment was brief. She'd planned to spend one night pretending life was normal, and she was stinking of wine she hadn't drunk, knuckles stinging, while the woman who'd started the argument smiled at her like they were friends. Admittedly, she'd known Lira for years—the quarrelsome woman was one of the shift managers—but a few conversations and arguments didn't make them friends. More to the point, friends didn't throw wine in a person's face.

"Lord, save me from fools," Kitty said, and then she punched Lira too.

Years ago, she'd have stepped out of their way and let the two drunk fools shoot each other to their hearts' content, but Jack's oft-quoted admonishment echoed even in his absence: *It's our calling.*

"Calling, my ass," Kitty muttered as she took in the sight of several skirmishes in the bar. Now that the manager was out and the bartender wasn't trying to keep order, the patrons were behaving like naughty children. She could step in, but Jack wasn't there to nag her, and she was feeling contrary. So she lifted her own drink in a toast and put her back to the bar to watch the show. Sometimes, being in a bar brawl made her almost feel like she was back home—if she could ignore the fact that this world was filled with magic and creatures that could step right into storybooks. People were people, even if they weren't always human. Trouble was trouble, even if it was started by monsters. That was the truth of it.

She made a game of silently predicting the winners of various fights until the smell of smoke made her look around the room. The fire wasn't coming from any of the empty barrels that stood as tables. The wall tapestries were all fine. The wafting smoke was drifting in from outside.

"Down!" she yelled.

Both of the front windows blasted inward, and red-tinted glass rained over all of them.

The chaos inside the pub stilled. Patrons who'd been ready enough to cosh each other over the head two minutes ago suddenly helped the folks they'd been fighting.

The bartender crouched behind the bar, so only his eyes and the top of his head were visible. "Aren't you going to do something?"

One of the cooks crawled along the floor, shoving a bucket of unidentified bits of uncooked meat toward Kitty. "Here."

She shot a frown over the crowd: they were watching her like she was all that stood between them and disaster. She wasn't. Any one of them could step up, but they didn't, and they wouldn't.

For all Jack's preaching at her, and despite all the straight-up weird shit she'd seen in the twenty-six years or so since she'd left the normal world and California far behind, she could count on humanity's basic predictability in a situation. The moment *real* trouble started, most people hid. Now that they needed help, she was everyone's best friend. If she were a softer soul, it would bother her. Okay, maybe it still did, but not so as she'd be mentioning it anytime soon.

Kitty sighed, but she twisted her damp hair into a knot and snatched up the bucket. "Stay inside."

Without waiting to see if they listened, she clomped across the floor and pushed open the half doors that hung in front of her. She suspected that the lindwurm that had vanished from Cozy's Ranch had found its way into Gallows.

Luckily, the beast that sprawled out in the street was a juvenile, more smoke than fire. It rested on its scaled belly with its legs splayed, but that didn't mean it couldn't move quickly if it was so inclined. Kitty hiked up the edge of her skirt and tied it off so it wouldn't tangle around her legs when she had to run.

"Lookie here." She eased to the side. The lindwurm's head snaked to the left, keeping her in sight.

She tossed a slimy piece of meat onto the ground in front of it. In a whip-quick movement, it snatched the snack with a long thin tongue and then slithered toward her.

"That's right. You just follow Miss Kitty," she coaxed.

One big opal eye tracked her as she backed away from the building. It didn't rush her or exhale fire in her direction—although a little plume of smoke drifted from its oversize nostrils.

She kept backing away, tossing handfuls of meat toward the lindwurm. After a few tense moments, it slithered forward a little more.

She wouldn't want to try this with a full-grown lindwurm, but the young weren't as agile or as surly. It was likely hungry, and once it'd had enough to eat, it'd nap. All she needed to do was lure it out away from buildings without getting herself cooked in the process. The sands that stretched around Gallows were the reason this was lindwurm-farming territory: farmlands like back home would've been reduced to nothing but prairie fires here.

A few more pieces lured the lindwurm farther from the buildings, but it wasn't moving far or fast. She couldn't tell it to wait while she fetched more meat, and a quick glance around made it obvious that no one was coming to bring her a backup bucket. Lindwurm herding was the sort of task that required help, and while she'd done it solo before, more often than not it had resulted in waking up after a few days dead.

"Any decent folks care to offer a little help?" Kitty called.

Not surprisingly, doors and shutters stayed closed.

The lindwurm was getting bored, and she was low on meat. It exhaled a small puff of flame, and she darted to the side.

"Seriously?" she grumbled. "Getting toasted was not my plan for the night!"

"Then maybe you shouldn't have gone out alone, Katherine." Jack's voice was uncommonly welcome just then. She didn't need to look at him to know that his mouth was already pressed into a stern line that ruined what was an otherwise handsome face and that his pretty baby blues were ruined by a you-disappoint-me look.

Kitty hid her sigh of relief at seeing him by picking a fight with him. "I didn't feel like dealing with you *or* Edgar, jackass. I wanted to relax."

"Clearly," Jack drawled, angling to the right of the increasingly restless lindwurm. "Upsetting lizards seems like a fine way to spend an evening."

"Not my fault."

"It never is," Jack said. He paused only a moment before adding, "Reins and collar look intact. You could've—"

"I'm not a wrangler."

"Yet another good reason not to go out alone." He glanced her way, and once she met his gaze, he prompted, "Ready?"

"Go." She tossed one of the remaining scraps of meat to the left.

As the lindwurm twisted its neck to snatch the treat, Jack hoisted himself atop the scaled beast. He wore the same grin he wore in a fight or anything remotely likely to get him injured. He was too dour most of the time, spewing rules the way she spit out cusses. In an adventure, though, he was all smiles.

"Hitch up your skirt and run," he yelled.

The lindwurm's tail lashed around at him, drawing blood, but it didn't roast him. An older beast would've. All that this one did was buck and slash. So far, Jack was only getting the edge of its temper.

Kitty ran toward the butcher's shop, shoved open the door, and tore down a fair-size bit of mutton. Slimy meat in hand, she raced back to the lindwurm.

It stilled again as it spotted her.

She held the mutton aloft—and away from her body—as she walked closer to the lindwurm. "I hate this part."

"Be ready to bolt," Jack reminded her.

As the lindwurm tasted the air, scenting at the meat she held in front of her, she said in as flat a voice as she could muster, "He decides to cook his dinner, and I'm going to be crispy."

"You'd get a few days off."

Kitty tossed the mutton before the lindwurm got any closer to her, and it pounced on the meat as soon as it landed in the sand.

While it gnawed on the mutton, Jack took hold of the reins that were fastened around the creature's back and steered it into the sand fields. Kitty followed on foot until they were far enough away that any belches or coughs or intentional flames would all be too short to ignite the pub or anything else. If she was able to get on its back, she could've done the same, but no one with half a brain would try to mount a lind-wurm without having a partner to distract it first—or without being too bold for one's britches.

Jack slid to the ground now that the lindwurm was out of range of the shops. Once he came to stand beside Kitty, she ripped the ruffle off her skirt and started to wrap it around the gash in his left bicep.

"You should've told me you were going out," he chastised. He put his right hand on her shoulder as she bandaged his other arm. "Or told Edgar. You know better."

She yanked on the two ends of the ruffle. "You're welcome, Kit. Always glad to help, especially after I've been a jackass and pushed you away to let myself drown in guilt. Sorry I can't let you be there for me. Really." She knotted the bright red ruffle on his arm and lifted her gaze to meet his eyes. "Sorry your dress got trashed too, Kit. I'll buy you a new one to replace it. I'm really glad you're not hurt, and oh . . . thanks for finding the missing lizard."

"Are you done?"

Kitty sighed. "You'll feel better if you argue with me, Jack."

"What's to argue? You're right, even if I'm not going to say any of that womanish stuff." He plucked a dirt-and-wine-coated curl off her cheek and tucked it behind her ear. "I know you're a grown woman, but you're still my little sister."

She leaned her forehead against his shoulder, counting silently to herself before she said something else she shouldn't.

After a few moments, she stepped away. The riffraff in the pub had started to wander outside, and she wasn't going to fight with Jack *or* get all sappy with him in front of strangers.

"That beast's not going to get home by itself," Betsy said from behind her. "And you can't leave it here."

Kitty rolled her eyes and started counting again. Dealing with the absentee proprietress wasn't going to help her mood. The woman hired half-incompetent staff, and then treated the tavern like her own personal prowling grounds. It didn't do a lot to inspire respect in Kitty.

In a blink, Jack stepped past her and smiled at Betsy.

*You can take a gambler out of the saloon, but you can't take the charm out of a gambler,* Kitty thought. Once upon a time, she'd had to rely on her charm too, but since they'd ended up here, she'd grown to prefer bullets to smiles. Still, old habits were more useful than new ones sometimes. Kitty affixed the falsely guileless smile she resented wearing and turned so she was by Jack's side. Family stood together. That truth had been a guiding force in her life since she was a child.

"Surely we can leave it here while we go on out to Cozy's Ranch to see if this is one of his." Jack gestured at the resting lindwurm and smiled.

Betsy laughed. "And hope that Cozy's going to be quick about it? You're pretty, Jackson, but I'm not young enough to be swayed by pretty." She gave him a hungry look and added, "At least not *just* pretty."

Jack ignored her invitation and flashed his grin. "Worth a try."

"Not really." Betsy shook her head, but she winked at Jack before she called out, "Lindwurm special until the beast is gone. Half-price pints." Then she went back into the pub, calling for brooms and a glassmaker as she went.

In moments, most of the patrons had gone back inside—all but a small group of miners who had been an eager part of the fracas earlier. Like all of the native miners here, they were stocky, squat people with no whites around their pupils and large, batlike ears. The popular theory was that they'd developed their diminutive stature, overlarge ears, and solid black eyes as a result of countless generations working in the earth—a theory that made just enough sense to lessen the sense of unease Kitty felt when she looked at them.

"I don't suppose you have any lindwurm-strength chain nearby?" Jack asked.

Two of the men stepped past their brethren. The first glared up at Jack and said, "Maybe."

The second got to the heart of the matter: "Are you accusing us of something?"

Kitty walked toward him, using the fact that he was eye level with her hips to her advantage. With the way that her skirt was hitched up in the front, the miners were seeing a lot of leg. When she was close enough that the miner had to look up at her or admit that he was distracted by her bare skin, she stopped.

When he lifted his eyes to hers, she said, "We're simply asking for chain. Do *I* look like I have a lindwurm chain hidden on me?"

The miners stared at her intently with their unsettling eyes, and after a few moments, they conceded that she was in need of some chain. Neither Kitty nor Jack commented on the chain they'd retrieved, which matched the links still fastened around the lindwurm's neck. Kitty and Jack had agreed a few years ago that those who had been so adversely affected by Ajani's enterprises merited a bit of selective blindness. The miners topped that list.

"I don't suppose you could handle taking it out of here?" Kitty asked, directing her offer to all of them rather than any one specific miner. "If it took a day or so to reach Cozy, I'm sure he'd overlook the delay in exchange for not having to fetch it home."

The answering rumble of assents was all she needed. Cozy was a surly bastard, and he was all too willing to ignore centuries of traditions to line his pockets with Ajani's money. Like a lot of the lindwurm farmers, he'd raised his prices so high that miners couldn't afford to rent, much less buy, lindwurms. Ajani levied steep taxes on the farmers if they did business with anyone other than those he authorized—and that didn't include miners. Years ago, the miners had refused to sell their family mines to Ajani, but he'd retaliated by systematically denying them the tools to ply their trade. The resulting conditions meant that the people who'd made their living in the mines for generations, who'd been the only ones to do so and had physically evolved for that work, were now starving. It also meant that they occasionally liberated a few lindwurms that they couldn't legally rent.

Kitty smiled at the miners, happy to have found a solution that benefited them. Wrestling with the beast hadn't been fun, but she couldn't blame them for not stepping in. What mattered now was that no one was hurt, Ajani would lose a little profit, and the miners would remember that she had lent them the lindwurm—even though it was one they'd already stolen.

Situation resolved, Kitty linked her arm through Jack's as they strolled toward camp. The dirt and dust that were inevitable in the Wasteland seemed thicker than usual—or maybe it was just that they clung to her more because of the wine.

They were a little over a mile away before Jack spoke. "I'm sorry about Mary . . . and about keeping you out while she . . . while I waited."

"Her death wasn't your fault, but next time, *tell* me that you're kicking me out instead of making Edgar do your dirty work." Kitty knew that Mary had been important to her brother too, but he wasn't weeping. He'd taught her years ago that tears were for the weak. *Maybe that was why he didn't want her in the tent.* She knew Mary had been in love with him, but she had been pretty sure he hadn't reciprocated those feelings. If he had, he hadn't told Mary—and he still wasn't telling Kitty.

Jack didn't reply to her, so Kitty tried to lighten her tone and added,

"Now, if you're looking to apologize, we can talk about you ruining my evening. *That* was your fault."

"After wine bathing and lindwurm dancing, I can see how you'd be disappointed to leave," Jack drawled. "Out of curiosity, what number did you make it to before you decided not to hit me?"

She didn't bother telling him that she was glad that he'd shown up to help. She didn't even admit that if she could've invited him to go out rabble-rousing, she would've because she knew he needed to let off steam more than any of the rest of them. Instead, she rolled her eyes and answered, "I'll let you know when I get to it."

Jack laughed, and they headed back toward camp in a more comfortable silence.

When they were almost at the gate, Jack suggested, "I could be there when the woman wakes."

Kitty smiled. "Because you're so good at dealing with weeping women?"

"Don't know that this one's a crier," Jack mused.

"Chloe. Not 'this one,' Jackson. Her name is *Chloe*." Kitty didn't admit that she'd done the same thing in her mind, tried to not-name the new arrival. Names made people real. Sometimes, that was the part Kitty wanted to avoid: them being real. If they weren't real, maybe their eventual deaths would hurt less.

"Right." Jack nodded. "I don't think *Chloe* will be a crier."

"Let's just hope she's not the sort to side with Ajani."

Jack grimaced, but he didn't comment. They both knew that the possibility of Ajani wooing Chloe away was a very real one. Sooner or later, he'd come around. Until he did, they'd just do what they could to help Chloe get settled. It was all they could do—well, that, and worry.

They'd been in this exact same situation well over a dozen times since they'd arrived in the Wasteland. If Kitty were truly honest with herself, she'd admit that *this* was what she needed—not losing herself in drink or in the company of a Wastelander. What she needed was this togetherness with the only person who could possibly feel the same worries, think of the same deaths, remember the same long-gone faces. She needed her only remaining family.

# CHAPTER 9

After leaving Katherine at camp, Jack fled. He felt foolish for offering to be there for Chloe, especially when there was work to do. The monks and the demon they'd summoned still needed finding. Morning would be soon enough for following up on Edgar's temper and Francis' gullibility. Jack had brought Katherine home safely, but he knew—and he suspected that Edgar did too—that she'd simply needed a break. Chloe's arrival was hard; Mary's death was still fresh. His baby sister tried to hold her emotions in, but she'd reached her limit. She'd confronted the governor, shot Daniel, patrolled with Jack, and then she'd nursed Chloe through that first horrible day of transition sickness. Unless someone forced her to rest, she'd spend the next few days helping Chloe, who would feel like she had some combination of poisoning and madness. For all the things Katherine did that made him crazy, he couldn't ever fault her for the way she cared for the new Arrivals.

*We all cope in our own ways.*

Katherine had gone looking for trouble, and Jack was walking alone in the dark. For him, peace was best found in open spaces. The desert breathed around him as he walked away from camp. Sometimes he felt like he could get lost here, like he could let the sand and sky swallow him whole. It was like being back in the world where they'd all been born, back where things made sense. Despite what some of the others thought, he was certain that they weren't going to be swept back en masse to the world they'd once known. Aside from the obvious problem of not knowing what year they'd be dropped into—*our own year? the current year?*—there hadn't been more than one person to arrive in the Wasteland at a time, except for Katherine and him. Whatever brought them through did it slowly and did it solo.

The shadows shifted around him as he walked, and he was struck by the strange futility of the way they made their living here. Governor Soanes had recruited them when it was just him and Katherine, and they'd grown into a motley unit of sorts when the others arrived. After all these years, he felt like killing the things that went bump in the night was no different from his brief stint as a U.S. Marshal in the West: a lot of fuss for very little progress.

Ajani actively recruited the new Arrivals when possible, offering them positions in his private militia. Instead of using their ability to awaken after dying for some measure of good in their new world, Ajani harnessed it for personal gain. Jack did his best to keep his people out of Ajani's sight, but they all had to deal with him eventually. The man had been steadily causing problems in the Wasteland, ignoring more and more of the traditions, pack rules, and bloedzuiger etiquette. What he couldn't buy, he stole. Those he couldn't convince, he killed. Frustratingly—for reasons Jack couldn't figure out—Ajani's people didn't ever stay dead. Once they joined Ajani, they lived forever. *So far.* It gave him an almost godlike status with some of the Wastelanders— and made him seem impossible to kill.

But Ajani wasn't likely to be leaving trails in the desert. Hell, he wasn't likely to dirty his custom-made shoes by *walking* in the desert, and following the trail before him was what Jack needed to deal with tonight. When he had returned to camp with Katherine earlier, he'd found more of the tracks he'd sighted yesterday when they found Chloe. These were even closer to camp. If they'd been genuine tracks, the wind would've swept them away. The drifting sand wasn't like mud; it didn't hold prints. The fact that these were repeatedly near camp and anchored in the sand meant that someone was inviting his attention.

Jack squatted down to look at the prints. They'd been made by boots with a sturdy heel and deep tread. If not for the slightly deeper indentation on the inward curve and the smaller size, he could think they were his own prints. Aside from troublesome humans, the only desert-dwelling monsters likely to wear shoes were bloedzuigers. Any two-natured thing would be traveling on paws in this landscape, and neither demons nor spirits left prints.

Warily, Jack followed the trail until he found the creature who'd laid out the invitation in the sand. Gaunt, sallow-skinned, with lips too red and eyes too pronounced, Garuda was the first bloedzuiger who had sought Jack without malice years ago when he was new to the Wasteland.

Garuda looked him over the way discerning diners examined their meals. "I see that you are staying healthy."

Jack made a noncommittal noise and studied the area around them. The bloedzuigers had to observe traditions, Wasteland etiquette, as it were, and until those traditions were respected, he and Garuda couldn't get to whatever business prompted the invitation. Jack didn't see anything, but he watched the darkness and waited.

Garuda folded himself into an improbable position on a rock, legs and arms bent at inhuman angles, looking rather like a praying mantis. He tilted his head and stared into the shadows at Jack's left. Jack followed his gaze as a second bloedzuiger launched itself at him. Reflexively, Jack drew and fired on the slavering creature before it reached him.

Jack turned to Garuda. "Really? A newborn?"

Garuda shrugged.

A third bloedzuiger came at Jack from behind him, moving quickly enough that he didn't notice until its teeth had already closed on the heavy leather of his jacket. Venom slid over the material.

Jack stabbed his knife into the soft flesh under the creature's chin.

It let out a shriek and clawed at the hilt of the knife with one hand while swinging at Jack with the other. In time, it would become a proper predator—if it survived that long. For now, though, it was nothing more than a mass of spindly limbs and dripping fangs bound to obey its master.

It looked at Garuda for instructions.

Garuda motioned it forward with a careless wave of stick-thin fingers. The gesture was elegant for their sort, but it still resembled the waving of insect legs.

The bloedzuiger went to its master and stood motionless as Garuda withdrew the knife and tossed it toward Jack.

He moved so it fell to the ground at his feet. "Thank you."

The bloedzuiger grinned and pointed out, "You missed."

"True." After Jack rolled the knife in the sand with the toe of his boot, he lifted it with his left hand, being careful not to get the blood on him. Blood wasn't as dangerous as venom, but blood from mouth wounds was liable to have venom in it. *That* was a problem. It wouldn't do permanent damage unless it got into his veins, but it still blistered the skin something awful.

Just to be safe, Jack stabbed the knife into the sand so any toxins could be wiped clean. "Are we done here, then? Just those two?"

Garuda looked at the two hapless bloedzuigers he'd brought, smiled, and said, "I didn't want to waste valuable time with our pleasantries."

There was no point arguing that defending himself against bloedzuigers wasn't pleasant. Traditions were what they were, and expecting them to change was like thinking the second moon would disappear. Of course, Garuda wasn't above adding a surprise attack after he'd suggested they were done, so Jack looked around before he approached the rock where the bloedzuiger perched.

"You wanted to talk?"

"I hear things, Jackson." Garuda's emaciated fingers tapped against the rock with a clicking, rasping sound. "The brethren has a benefactor who's interested in your little pack."

Jack didn't correct Garuda's terminology. The old bloedzuiger made sense of the Arrivals by imposing his own species' dynamics on them. It had made him decide that Jack was his equal, and that particular decision was useful more often than not. The label of a thing mattered less than the results—not that Jack could convince his baby sister of that. She had issues with Garuda that Jack didn't understand.

"Ajani?" Jack asked. "He was over in the Divide last I'd heard. Are you sure?"

Garuda lifted his shoulder slightly in a small shrug. He wouldn't accuse any Wastelander without evidence, but he obviously thought that Ajani was involved. If he believed that it was someone insignificant, he wouldn't trouble himself to seek Jack. Such squabbles were, in bloedzuiger society, unavoidable and unimportant. There were rules, etiquette that had to be observed. *Everything* with bloedzuigers involved etiquette.

"I'll look into it," Jack said. He'd learned years ago to take Garuda's warnings seriously. Among the creatures that roamed the Wasteland, none had held power and influence as long as Garuda. Ajani and the governor were powerful now, but Garuda had walked the Wasteland before either of those men drew their first breaths. Of course, that also meant that the bloedzuiger had more reasons than most to mistrust both Ajani and the governor.

Garuda stared into the distance, pointedly not looking at Jack. "Have you spoken to the governor lately?"

"I have. I need to find the rest of the brethren and deal with the demon troubles." Jack watched the bloedzuiger with the sort of attention that came from years of conversations between them. What was unsaid was often as useful as what was said.

"Yet you cannot travel while your new packmate recovers," Garuda mused. "If someone were looking for you, now would be a good time. You've been in one place for a while already because of the brethren. If the governor were no longer to be trusted or if the brethren were to be employed by someone who means you ill, you would be quite vulnerable right now."

Jack knew the bloedzuiger was suspicious of everyone, but he couldn't see why the governor would tie himself to Ajani. The two were at odds over politics and territories too often for that to make sense. The brotherhood working with Ajani made a certain sense, but not the governor. "I can handle the brethren."

"And the demon?"

"Hopefully we'll find it soon. If not, we'll come back."

Garuda raised both brows. "So you would ask me to believe you can 'handle' the brethren, a demon, and any treachery?"

"We always do," Jack said. He did what he could to maintain order in the Wasteland, but he wasn't going to ignore any insights Garuda was willing to offer. That was the path that led to injury sooner or later. Maybe this time the bloedzuiger was wrong, but even if he *was* wrong now, he'd been right often enough that Jack had learned years ago to take his warnings seriously.

At a gesture from Garuda, one of the newborns toddled over and extended his wrist. "If you'd like refreshment, it would be our privilege as your host," Garuda said.

Jack didn't point out that Garuda had no obligation to offer a host gift since they were in the middle of the desert. "I don't want to insult you, but—"

With the striking speed of a viper, Garuda took Jack's knife from the hilt on his thigh and slashed open the newborn bloedzuiger's wrist just below the pack brand on its forearm. "You would throw my gift away?"

There were few things in the Wasteland more disgusting or more appealing than Verrot. Jack swallowed and stepped away, trying to put the vile temptation out of reach.

"Don't be infantile," Garuda chided.

"I don't need—"

Garuda drew Jack's knife across his own wrist then and held it up, not to Jack but to the other bloedzuiger. The creature latched on to Garuda's arm like a rabid animal. After a minute, Garuda stopped it. The whole time he watched Jack watch them.

"Come now, Jack. I've filtered it for you." He cut the creature's wrist again and lifted it to Jack. "Don't court injury by refusing my hospitality."

Drinking from a newborn wasn't a new experience, but the side effects of Verrot were always unsettling. With painful slowness, Jack came forward and lowered his mouth. The scents of rot and disease made his eyes water as he swallowed.

He sealed his lips over the wound on the young bloedzuiger's wrist as best he could. He could feel the blood smearing on the sides of his face; the cut was too wide. *Wasteful.* Then he sucked, and thinking became more difficult. He had no idea how much time had passed or how much of the foul stuff he swallowed, but when Garuda pulled the creature's arm away from his mouth, Jack growled at him.

Garuda smiled, and Jack backed away, struggling for self-control. He knew he'd crave Verrot like he was starving without it for the next few weeks. He also knew that it would give him the extra strength, stamina, and a not insubstantial connection to Garuda for much longer. Once a person drank Verrot, the bloedzuiger whose blood it was and that creature's master could locate the drinker.

As Jack fought not to snatch the bloody wrist back, Garuda motioned the other bloedzuiger over and drained its blood into a thick brown glass bottle. "My gift for your pack."

"You don't need to do this," Jack finally managed to say. "Your gift was already far too generous without . . . this."

Garuda grinned briefly, and then motioned over the bloedzuiger Jack had drunk from. Its remaining blood filled not quite a third of a second bottle.

The two young bloedzuigers looked completed desiccated. It was odd that so little blood animated them, but something in their physiology made their bodies consume any blood they produced or ingested. If they survived, they'd learn to function despite their ravenous hunger. These two wouldn't survive.

"If you wouldn't mind?" Garuda prompted.

Silently, Jack beheaded them. He felt a twinge of guilt he did his best to subdue. If these two weren't Garuda's, they would've tried to kill him when he'd crossed their line of sight, and even though they were Garuda's, they wouldn't have paused if he died as a result of their greetings. They were barely conscious beasts.

*But they're still dead because of me.*

Maybe it was because of the blood Jack had taken or maybe just because he knew Jack, but Garuda obviously knew what Jack was thinking.

"I brought two I no longer needed, Jackson," he said. He stood, straightening his praying-mantis-thin limbs, and held out the two bottles. "They served me more by this act than they would've if they'd lived."

Jack accepted the bottles without commenting.

"I have few friends." Garuda paused and gave Jack a tentative smile. "That is the word you offered me, is it not?"

"It is," Jack agreed.

"Ajani grows less reasonable as he gains power. I find the governor's actions troubling, and the brethren's strike illogical. Perhaps it is only my paranoia, but if not, your pack will need strength and my aid. I call you friend as well, Jackson. Garuda stepped over the corpses of the bloedzuigers. If anyone could find a way to make Ajani not rise again, I would offer every treasure I have amassed."

"If I could make him stay dead, I would do it for my own peace of mind," Jack admitted. "I don't know how."

"I look for that answer as well," Garuda murmured. Then, in nothing more than a few blinks, he vanished into the black desert.

Jack resumed his patrol. His only other options were standing around staring into the dark or returning to the camp, where he'd feel like a caged animal. Neither of those sounded particularly appealing. He felt his heartbeat roaring in his ears, the sound so loud that he felt like his heart was in his mouth instead of his chest. Sometimes drinking Verrot was akin to dying. The one time he'd drunk from Garuda himself, only one mouthful, he'd actually died. His heart had stopped. He'd also woken to life within hours rather than the usual six days. That secret he guarded like few others.

Keeping the rest of the Arrivals safe meant convincing them to drink Verrot. The Arrivals carried very few of their superstitions from the lives they'd known before coming to the Wasteland, but the fear of bloedzuigers was a primal thing that seemed to linger. The bloedzuigers weren't as dissimilar from the vampires of foolish legends as he'd like to argue, but Jack still trusted Garuda as he trusted no other Waste-lander. The bloedzuiger wouldn't send more than a bottle of Verrot to the camp unless he was more than a little certain that Ajani was getting close. That meant Ajani would come for Chloe sooner than Jack would like.

# CHAPTER 10

When Kitty returned to her tent, she found Francis waiting. Much to her relief, he'd replaced Melody as nursemaid to the still-resting new Arrival. Chloe was safe enough with Melody; tending the injured was something she took to quite well. Conversations with her, on the other hand, were sometimes trying, and Kitty wasn't up to dealing with her craziness tonight.

"She's due to wake soon." Francis stood and stretched, seeming oddly equine in his movements as he extended his spindly legs and arms. "The fever's gone, though."

"Vomiting?"

"None tonight. I think the worst of the transition is past." He hugged Kitty. "I'm glad you're not dead or hurt."

With a small smile, Kitty shooed him toward the tent flap. "You knew I'd be fine."

Francis followed her to the exit. "I also knew to tell Jack to go after you when I saw him."

"You're a good friend." Kitty opened the flap of the tent. "Now, go make yourself scarce before Edgar gets off shift. I haven't talked to him about my little adventure yet, but he's bound to know by now."

"You owe me." Francis ducked out of the tent, but paused. "If he's furious . . ."

"You know I'll talk to him, *and* yes, I do owe you." She gave him an affectionate smile. If she were able to have children, she'd want one a lot like Francis. He was curious, but he was kind and constant, trustworthy in a way few people were, and brought out a protective streak in her.

A noise from inside drew her attention. Kitty told Francis, "Go on. I need to look after Chloe."

The transition process was exhausting enough that Chloe wasn't truly awake. Odds were that she'd remember very little of her first couple days, but the body still had needs even when the mind was too feverish to remember. Kitty gave a woozy Chloe a cup of water with some of Francis' vitamin mix stirred into it. Then she helped her to the facilities, washed the sweat from her face, and tucked her back into the cot that had last belonged to Mary. It wasn't as if the process was rote, but after a couple dozen people, it was predictable.

Kitty wasn't a hypocrite, so she wouldn't be holding Chloe's murderous past against her. Every one of the Arrivals was a killer; it was the one thing they all shared. Whether or not they knew *why* or *who* Chloe had slain, they knew she had. She wouldn't have arrived in the Wasteland if she hadn't taken a life. Back in California, Kitty herself had needed to put down a customer who'd gotten a bit too rough and, in another instance, a man who'd drawn on her over a card dispute. Sometimes, a man simply needed killing.

Once the new girl was again sleeping soundly on the dead girl's bed, Kitty had to make the unhappy choice between talking to Edgar and taking the coward's way out a little longer. Neither option was particularly appealing. She didn't think herself weak, but telling Edgar things he wouldn't like was never fun. Hurting him was one of the few things that made her feel guilt.

She stalled on the inevitable, busying herself with sorting through the clothes she had on hand to find a few things for Chloe to choose from the next day. She examined the skirt she'd ruined earlier. She spent a bit of time with as much of a wash as she could manage with the basin and cloth inside her tent. Finally, she fastened one of her modified bone-lined corsets and pulled on a blouse and a pair of trousers. She couldn't imagine wearing ones as revealing as Chloe's had been, but she did admit that trousers weren't completely abhorrent to her. She was a lot more comfortable in them than she'd been when she'd first arrived here, but they still made her feel half naked even after years wearing them. She didn't have any short enough for Chloe, but she could hem a pair of Mary's easier than if she'd had to lengthen them. Kitty closed her eyes against a sudden memory of doing just that for Mary when she'd arrived, of sitting at bedside after bedside preparing to help each new Arrival in the years before Mary.

With effort, Kitty stared at Chloe. Those women were all dead. Chloe wasn't.

"Maudlin thoughts never help," Kitty chastised herself. She went to one of her trunks and withdrew a sheet of thick native paper and a series of pencils. Then she distracted herself by drawing a portrait of Chloe. At some point early on, she'd taken to doing portraits of all of the Arrivals. She never knew how long they'd be around. A few didn't wake up after their first death, and others were with the team for years. She hadn't been able to find a pattern to it. More important, neither had Jack, and he'd always spent a lot of time studying every possible aspect of their situation.

When Kitty finished the portrait, she added it to the stack of images she'd kept in a polished wooden box. Sometimes she lingered over the images, but the loss of Mary was too raw still. She closed and locked the box, returned it to its hidden place, and returned her precious pencils to the trunk where she stored them. After that, she couldn't devise any other activities that would enable her to stay in her tent without disturbing the sleeping woman on the cot, so she gave in to the inescapable: she slipped out of the tent, letting the flap drop closed behind her with a soft *wump*.

The desert was still warm, but the harsh heat of the day had dulled. The moons offered enough light that she could see almost bluish shadows. Briefly, she was tempted to go back inside and fuss with her hair, to paint her face, to find a proper skirt to wear. It was foolishness. Edgar had seen her when she'd been gutted by a rabid boar. He'd seen her when she was blood-soaked and barely upright after a fight with a bloedzuiger. He'd seen her die a few times. There was no reason to try to pretty herself up for him, but she still did so far too often.

After a scan of the area to assure herself that none of the others were around, she walked over to the guard station. Edgar undoubtedly expected her to come to see him, had expected her for some time, but he didn't take his eyes off the vast expanse of shadowed desert. She studied him as she approached the guard station. It wasn't a difficult thing to look at Edgar. Sometimes when they were at a camp, he wore simple black trousers, simple black shirts, and well-worn boots. In town or for negotiations, he often donned a jacket too. Rare flashes of color came in a necktie or a carefully folded pocket square. Despite his lingering adherence to the attire of the world he knew when he lived in Chicago, he claimed he had no desire to go back there. His big concession to life in the Wasteland was that he now openly draped himself in weapons, much as some women did with baubles.

Kitty knew that she could stand in the dark and watch him all night and he'd never glance her way. He wouldn't shirk his duties to look for her. He'd simply wait, and if she didn't come to him during his shift, he'd come to her tent tomorrow. There was no way to avoid the conversation.

Whoever was on guard duty was all that stood between the Arrivals and the creatures that roamed in the dark. All of their campsites were surrounded by blessed, mixed-metal fences, as well as spells. That meant there was only one way in or out, and that access point was guarded at all times. In a few towns, they'd take rooms in one of the inns, but when what they hunted was more troublesome than usual, Jack insisted they stay outside town. Many a monster needed putting down, but that didn't mean that the monsters were animals. They were as wise as men—more so, too often—and smart enough to use the townsfolk as pawns or spies.

Aside from the monsters and the man in front of her, being in the desert reminded her of the boomtown where she'd lived in the 1870s, not that it was home, but it was a simpler life than the one she had been living since coming to the Wasteland. There, she'd danced and relieved fools of their money in exchange for a few minutes of sloppy groping or a little bit of creative card playing. Here, the illusory peace of the desert was broken too often by the growls, shrieks, and inhuman cries of the things that lived out there.

"Edgar," she started.

"You exhaust me sometimes, Kit." He didn't mince words; he never had. "What were you thinking going into town alone so late in the day? You know what sort of things are out there at night."

"I was hoping to stay till morning," she said quietly.

That earned her a look that made her want to flinch. Instead, she lifted her chin. Edgar wasn't her husband; he had no right to look at her like she'd stepped out on him. She didn't say that, though, not to Edgar or to anyone else.

He looked back out at the desert. "With someone in particular? Daniel?"

She sighed. "No. I just wanted to . . . get away from here, from all of this. Don't you ever want to just escape?"

Edgar shrugged. "I get to kill things, and sometimes I get you.

Why would I want anything different? The dying always hurts, and the waking back up does too, but it's not so bad."

"So what does it matter if I'm out there alone?" She wanted to step in front of him, make him look at her, but neither of them would allow their conflicts to endanger the camp. "I'd heal. Whatever they do to me, I heal."

"Tell that to Mary or Patrick or Des—"

"*They* weren't first," she interrupted. Her temper stirred. "Me and Jack? Nothing kills us. Everyone else comes and then one day you all die on me. Me? I'm left alive in this hell."

"I haven't died, Kit. You may be just as mortal as I am, or maybe I'm just as immortal as you. Until either of us dies for real, there's no way to know." Edgar reached out and caught her hand. "You should tell Jack next time you want to go out on your own, if you're not going to tell me."

"I know." She paused, wanting to pull her hand from his almost as much as she hoped he'd pull her closer. "Please don't be mad at Francis. He told Jack as soon as he returned from patrol."

"He could've told me," Edgar said.

She shook her head. "You intimidate him."

"Good." Edgar released her hand and held out a holster. "If you're standing guard with me, might as well gear up."

"About Daniel—"

"No." Edgar glanced her way for only a heartbeat. "If he comes back here, I won't stay. I won't work for Ajani like he did, but I won't stay here and watch you be with him."

"I know," she whispered.

"I'm patient, Kit, more than I want to be, but you and I both know where you belong."

"I can't."

He laughed without any actual humor. "Yes, you can. You didn't stop loving me because we're sleeping apart."

Kitty couldn't lie to him, so she said nothing.

"Stay away from Daniel, Kit," Edgar said. "I'll forgive a lot, but there are limits."

Shakily, she admitted, "That's why I said no." She hesitated and then added, "I don't want you to leave."

"That's a start," Edgar murmured.

And at that, they both lapsed into silence. They did fine when they didn't talk. Conversation led to arguments. When they fought whatever monster they hunted, when they patrolled, when they did most anything but talk, they were fine.

Edgar had been on the shady side of the law before he came to the Wasteland, a truth she would've known even if he hadn't told her about his life. He'd been employed by an organization that made its money from gambling, clubs, and alcohol. When he'd told her that the U.S. government had outlawed alcohol in his time, she wondered if he and she were really from the same world, but other Arrivals verified that there was a brief, odd period when the transportation and distribution of alcohol was illegal.

With Edgar, there were no illusions. He had no qualms about who he was or what he'd done—in Chicago or in the Wasteland. He had been a hired gun there, and he'd transferred his loyalty to Jack when he'd woken up here. The only times he ever ran into trouble were because of her.

A few hours later, when Jack relieved them, they were together in their usual comfortable silence—a detail Jack acknowledged with a relieved smile. "I can finish guard."

Edgar nodded and divested himself of a few of the weapons that stayed with the guard post. "Post's all yours."

Kitty offered, "I'll stay here with—"

"No," they both said.

Jack softened the refusal by adding, "I'd like a little quiet. I need to think."

Edgar, on the other hand, simply looked at her in that way of his that made her feel like she wasn't wearing anything at all. The ease they'd shared when he was on duty evaporated when he zeroed in on her.

She turned away, but she'd only made it a few steps before he was at her side.

"Kit." He stopped her with both hands on her waist, holding her steady but not forcing her to turn to him or pulling her against him.

She could move away if she wanted to, but she really didn't want to.

"It wasn't your fault Mary died." Edgar didn't force her to turn around. "Sometimes people just die. We're alive; she's not, and it's horrible, and it hurts, and you want to do something reckless because of it."

She turned around then. "I don't want her to be dead."

"Being careless isn't going to change that. Pushing me further away isn't either." Edgar had kept his hands on her waist, and even though it seemed foolish that such a small touch could comfort her, it did. It did other things too; it sparked needs that she wasn't going to admit to having.

"You're alive, Kit." Edgar stayed motionless, waiting for her. "The rest of us are too. I'm sorry that Mary's gone. I'm sorry you're hurting, but we are still alive. Don't forget that."

What he didn't say—or force Kitty to say—was that they were more alive together than either of them was alone. She was standing in the shadows with the man she loved. It didn't undo the hurt she felt at Mary's passing, but for a moment the pure joy she also felt with Edgar was enough to chase all the bad away. She wasn't going to let herself slip into the depression that threatened to engulf her every time one of the Arrivals died for good. Edgar gave her the strength to handle that. The nagging reminder that she counted on him, that he was the only one who could keep that depression at bay, was followed by the chilling memory of when he had died. He was vulnerable too.

She stared into his eyes and admitted, "You always know what to say."

"I try." He brushed her hair back on both sides so he was cupping her face.

Before he could do the next logical thing—the very thing she wanted too damn much—Kitty pulled away from him. He frowned as she moved away, but she'd seen that frown on his face so often the past year that it didn't hurt her quite as much as it once had.

She folded her arms across her chest to keep from reaching out to him. "Chloe will die too. How do I help her learn how to live in this world? How do I keep doing this?"

"You just do." He wasn't being cruel. It was simply the way Edgar's mind worked: he dealt with what *was,* played the hand he had, and didn't see any other way to live.

Kitty felt tears trickle from her eyes.

"They come, they stay, and sometimes they don't survive," Edgar told her. "I don't know why some of us do, but I do know it's not your fault—or Jack's."

Kitty closed her eyes. She didn't know if she agreed, but she didn't know if she could argue either. As much as she wanted him to comfort her, to tell her whatever lies he could, she'd watched people die before and after Edgar arrived. She couldn't let herself count on him to help her through her grief now because all she could think every time one of the Arrivals died permanently was *please don't let it be Jack or Edgar next time.*

She opened her eyes and stepped farther away. "I'm going to check on Chloe."

"Melody can watch her, so we can go to my—"

"No."

"So you were going to spend the night with someone else, considered fucking *Daniel,* but you'll reject me?" His voice had an angry edge to it, and Kitty couldn't even deny that she deserved his anger.

"I'm sorry."

"My patience will run out too," Edgar added.

A foolish part of her wanted to ask him how much longer that would take, but he'd hear the words as the invitation they were. If she wasn't going to warm Daniel's sheets out of awareness that it would hurt *him*, she certainly wasn't going to use the man she actually loved. If she did, they'd be right back where they'd started when she'd realized she needed to step away.

Finally, he said only, "Sleep well, Kit."

"You too," she said. She wasn't about to admit that she never slept well when he wasn't beside her. Everything felt wrong without him, but she hadn't slept next to him since the last time he recovered from dying. When he died a little over a year ago, she'd spent six terrifying days praying to every god, monster, and devil she could think of. When he woke up, they'd locked themselves away for six more days. On the seventh day, she'd returned to her own bed alone and tried her damnedest to exorcise him from her heart.

Like every other night when she'd left him, she felt him watching her as she walked back to her tent. She told herself it was better this way, but that didn't make it any easier—or true.

# CHAPTER 11

Chloe wasn't quite as confused when she woke this time. She remembered stretching out on the cot in an oversize tent filled with boxes and bins. Before that, she remembered a walk through the desert after waking up half paralyzed under a strange sky with an extra moon. She remembered being carried by a cowboy, and she had a hazy memory of being cared for by a woman who acted like a nurse but looked like a burlesque dancer. What Chloe couldn't recall was anything between being at the bar and that first moment waking up on the ground. More important, she had begun to suspect that this wasn't a hallucination. She had no logical explanation for the weird sky, the large lizard that looked suspiciously like a dragon, or the Wild West characters who'd brought her to this strange campsite. If they weren't a hallucination and this wasn't a coma dream of some sort, she was in a new world—which was scientifically improbable and, quite bluntly, scary as hell.

She took a deep breath. *Breathing means not dead.* Just to be sure, she checked her pulse.

"It's real. You're awake." Kitty stood in the doorway of the tent. She still looked like a dancer, and the soft voice was still more soothing than any nurse's Chloe had ever met.

"Thank you," Chloe said. "You were here. I remember . . . some."

"Good." Kitty let the heavy material fall shut behind her. In her hand, she clutched a long swath of fabric. "You'll adjust, but it'll take a few more days to get your strength back."

"How long did I sleep? Strength back from what?" Chloe swung her feet to the ground. When she didn't feel dizzy or queasy, she stood.

Kitty watched her. "Almost forty hours, but you sort of woke to drink and use the necessary. The fever makes it a little hazy for most folks." Her voice grew even more comforting. "You're adjusting from the trip here, but the worst is passed."

"Right. The trip . . . here," Chloe echoed.

She walked over to a curtained area that she vaguely remembered Kitty showing her at some point. It was a small victory to not have to ask for the strange woman's support to go to the toilet and washing area.

When she returned, Kitty gave her an approving look. "You're not dreaming. Not dead. Not in a coma." She ticked each item off on her fingers. The cloth in her hand fluttered with each motion. "You're in the Wasteland. Why? No one seems to know. I've been here twenty-six years. Same as Jack."

"But . . . you don't look"—Chloe did quick math—"like someone from the 1980s . . . or like you're old enough to have been anywhere that long."

"We don't age once we get here. This is it." Kitty held her arms out in a look-at-that gesture. "I'll never get any older on the outside—or have kids, as far as we can tell."

Chloe stared at her, trying to digest the idea of not aging. That part didn't sound awful. The idea of never having kids, on the other hand, sounded less appealing. It wasn't that she'd planned to have them anytime soon, but the idea of not having the choice to ever have them was sobering.

Kitty walked past her and picked up a torn skirt. "And it wasn't the 1980s when I came to the Wasteland. Time's off between here and home. It was 1870 at home when I came here. Sometimes there are big gaps in the times people are from. No one's come through who's later than 1989 or earlier than me and Jack."

"I'm later." Chloe tried to concentrate on the details, the words Kitty was saying. If not, if she thought about the big picture, the sheer impossibility of it all, she might fall apart. "It's 2013 at home. I walked into a bar. Then I was here."

Kitty looked at her for a moment, shrugged, and said, "It was bound to happen."

When Chloe didn't reply, Kitty carried the skirt and her needle and thread to a spot on the ground. She sat on the floor with the skirt and ruffle in her lap. Somehow, that seemed more absurd than anything else so far, or maybe Chloe had simply reached her threshold for absurdity. She began laughing, but after a few moments the laughs began to sound suspiciously like sobs.

"You're doing fine, all things considered," Kitty said, not unkindly. Then she looked down at her sewing as if she couldn't tell that Chloe was crying.

Chloe stared at the 1800s woman who was calmly sewing in the middle of a tent in the desert, and Kitty very obviously pretended not to be waiting for her to pull it together—or maybe she didn't care if Chloe pulled it together. There was no way to know short of asking, and Chloe didn't feel much like doing that. They stayed that way for a few minutes until Chloe broke the silence by asking, "Why me?"

Kitty lifted her gaze from the skirt, met Chloe's eyes. "No one knows."

"How? How can you say you've been here that long and don't know?" Her voice grew a bit shrill as panic edged back closer to the surface.

The smile Kitty offered veered closer to sardonic than anything else. She pulled the thread through another stitch and then another before saying, "Depends on who you ask. My brother thinks we're here as a punishment for some sort of sins, and we need to atone for our failings."

"I had a *drink*," Chloe objected. "Lots of people drink. I was an ass for years when I was a lush, but I've been sober the past five years. What in the hell am I being punished for?" She swiped at her cheeks. "One drink shouldn't mean I wake up in wherever this is."

"There's a washbasin with cool water." Kitty pointed at a stoneware basin with tiny little flowers painted all over it.

Chloe was splashing water on her face when she heard Kitty say, "She's fine, Jack. Get to bed. You patrolled and then stood guard. When did you sleep last?"

"Hector offered to finish out the last hour of my shift," Jack said.

Chloe didn't want to turn around and face the cowboy who had carried her out of the desert last night. As she patted her face dry, she forced herself to picture her fiancé screwing her boss instead of thinking about how kind Jack had been. She might not be in the world she knew, but there were constants she suspected were the same no matter what world she lived in. *And he can't look as good as I thought he did. I was half out of it.*

Appropriately fortified, she turned to see baby blues, perfect cheekbones, and lean muscles. She'd never been a cowboy fan, but one look at him had her revising that stance. Realizing she was staring, she tried to speak but only managed to say, "Damn . . . I mean . . . Hi. I . . . Thank you. For carrying me, I mean."

Kitty laughed. Whether at the look of wide-eyed confusion on her brother's face or at Chloe's mortified stuttering, Chloe couldn't say.

Jack clearly didn't know what to say either. He looked at his sister and then at Chloe. "No need to thank me." He cleared his throat. "I just stopped here because . . . you're new. It takes time to adjust and . . ." His words trailed off, and he bounced a little as if he was having trouble standing still.

"He's trying not to say that he's our fearless leader or that he has a crippling need to meddle," Kitty interjected.

"Katherine," Jack warned in a voice that held no real threat. Chloe could see that he was clenching his jaw. In his hand was a mostly empty bottle of some sort of wine.

Chloe stared at it. Until she'd seen it, she'd been wondering if maybe through some act of god or magic or science, she'd come to their world without the alcoholism that had hovered at the edge of her life for so many years. Clearly, she hadn't. She fisted her hands and backed away as he lifted the bottle.

"Before I hit the bunk, I wanted to bring this by." He walked farther into the tent, and Chloe had the stray thought that he was moving slowly and deliberately like a hunter expecting his prey to bolt.

Kitty was staring at the bottle suspiciously. "Where did that come from?"

"I don't drink," Chloe forced herself to say. "Please take it away."

"It'll help." Jack pulled the stopper out of the bottle. "It's medicinal."

Kitty stepped between them. "What is that?"

Chloe started shaking. *One drink wouldn't hurt.* Things were already a mess. She held out her hand.

Jack pushed past his sister, grabbed a cup that had been left beside the bed where Chloe had been sleeping, and poured the port-colored liquid into it. He didn't look at Kitty as he said, "You know what it is, Katherine. Verrot. Ajani's coming around soon, and we don't have time for a slow recovery."

"Jackson!" Kitty grabbed his arm. "I don't care. You can't give her—"

"Drink it," he interrupted as he handed Chloe the cup.

Shakily, Chloe lifted it to her lips. She wasn't sure what Verrot was, but the moment the liquid hit her tongue she knew it wasn't wine or any other type of booze she'd tried over the years. She'd consumed some truly horrible rotgut during the worst of her drunken spells, but this made everything she'd ever had seem delicious in comparison— and yet, she swallowed it greedily. She couldn't bring herself to lower the cup from her mouth.

"It'll help," he murmured.

Kitty was yelling at him, but Chloe couldn't concentrate on a word she said. Fortunately, Jack stood between her and his sister, and Chloe had a strange burst of relief that he did so, because even though the Verrot was vile, she wasn't sure she could willingly let Kitty take the cup.

Chloe was licking the last drops from the cup like a child with a bowl of ice cream when she realized what Kitty was saying: "You gave her fucking *vampire* blood on her first day?" She shoved Jack toward the door of the tent. "Get out. Now."

It was all Chloe could do to lower the now empty cup. Very carefully, she said, "Excuse me? Is that a brand or—"

"No." Kitty came back over to her, took the cup, and led her to a chair. "It's exactly what it sounds like." Gently, she stroked a hand over Chloe's hair. "It's not always so weird here, and as much as it pains me to say it, I'm certain he thinks he had a good reason to give it to you."

"To give me *vampire blood*?" Chloe clarified. A part of her was oddly relieved that it was vampire blood because if alcohol was that good here, she'd be so far into the bottle that she'd never crawl out again. "Like *blood* from a . . ."

"They're called bloedzuigers. They're not like in the stories at home; they're not dead or anything. They just live a long time, and their blood is restorative." Kitty paused as if she was determining what to say. "You'll be fine, though. It's a shitty way to start your first day here, but you can handle it."

"Okay," Chloe said. She repeated the word, more firmly this time. "It's *okay*." She leaned back, trying not to push past Kitty and run. She felt like her entire body was on fast-forward, like she could do anything—and she would do anything to get another taste of the Verrot. "I feel very good right now. Thank you. Is there more?"

# CHAPTER 12

Before Jack could land himself in more trouble, he walked away from his sister's tent. He was awake enough to patrol, but as Katherine had pointed out, he'd been awake well over a day and a half. He wasn't even sure if he *could* sleep. Verrot didn't result in a collapse after days awake; it simply alleviated the need for as much rest.

He knew Katherine had an objection to Verrot. After her first encounter with it, she'd avoided it every chance she could, and if he tried to argue, she raised hell the likes of which he hadn't ever seen from her over anything else. Even Edgar couldn't reason with her on the subject. If she *did* drink it, she was as likely to barricade herself in a room as to take off on her own.

There were a lot of things in the world Jack didn't understand, but his sister's issue with Verrot—with bloedzuigers as a species—was pretty damn high on his list. Garuda was the closest thing they had to a friend among the Wastelanders. He had offered his support more times than Jack could count for almost twenty years. Maybe it was the agelessness that they all had, which Garuda's kind shared; maybe it was some shared ideal that the old bloedzuiger valued; maybe it was simply because Garuda liked the way Jack opposed Ajani. What mattered, though, was that Garuda had offered his aid to Jack in times of need, and every time he'd done so without requesting payment. Despite all of that, Katherine always overreacted to anything concerning bloedzuigers.

Still, Jack could allow that his walking in and offering Verrot to Chloe without any conversation with Katherine on the subject hadn't been the most graceful way to handle things. The truth was that Chloe was a liability—and that Jack wasn't thinking anywhere near as clearly as he should. If he'd had time to ride out the initial rush of the Verrot, he'd have handled things better, but for reasons he wasn't grasping just yet, this particular high was clouding his mind a little more than usual.

He took a calming breath. His mind was speeding. The challenge now was to harness the speed. *Maybe another patrol.* Killing something sounded very relaxing.

First, though, he needed to drop off the Verrot in his tent, but he couldn't stay there. He had to check in on Hector—or maybe that was just the excuse he clung to in order to keep from facing the reality that sleep wouldn't be coming soon or fast. *Or at all.* If Mary were still alive, it would have been less of an issue.

Since she'd died, he'd felt like he should mourn her more than he was because they'd had an understanding, but that would be a lie of the sort that he and Mary had agreed not to indulge in at the beginning of their arrangement. Neither one of them had any illusions about what they were. He wished they had sometimes. He hadn't felt anything more than physical needs for anyone in far too long. He cared for his baby sister, and he respected Edgar to the degree that he'd call it affection of a sort. Lately, it didn't seem enough. He wanted to feel, to care about something beyond the job, and if he were honest with himself, he'd admit that he sometimes suspected that he only cared about the job out of habit.

The cause, the ideal that had once driven him, was the slight thread of belief that they could improve their situation by doing the right thing. Unfortunately, he hadn't believed that in years. Nothing that he did or said mattered. He was pretty sure that this was where they were until they died; he just couldn't confess to the others. Even if he had no faith, he pretended to because it gave the others something to cling to. The only thing Jack truly believed anymore was that he would do his level best to look after the small band of people who'd ended up in the Wasteland.

Some days Jack wasn't sure if he wanted to know why they'd all ended up in the Wasteland; on other days he wanted that answer the way a drunkard wanted one more drink. The bits of truth that he'd parsed together weren't comforting, but he couldn't stop trying to make the Arrivals' peculiar lot in life make sense. Back in California, he hadn't been a particularly God-fearing man. If he were a confessing man, he might even admit that he'd broken most of the command-ments. *Repeatedly.*

He wasn't exactly a good example either. It was his fault that Katherine had taken up gambling and ended up working in a saloon. Such habits wouldn't have been her way if not for his own failings. He hadn't protected her, hadn't made sure she was tucked away in a good position or wed like a lady should be. Instead, when his parents passed on, he'd brought Katherine with him like baggage. Worse yet, he'd brought her here to the Wasteland. She'd been holding on to his arm when he last stood in a sodden alleyway in California, and the next thing they knew, they were in a strange new world. More than a few times he'd wondered if his failings had caught the attention of some god or devil who'd cast them out of their home into this world where monstrosities roamed. And, after more than two decades in the place, he still had no idea how to improve their future.

When Jack returned to the guard post, Hector barely hid his look of surprise. He was one of the least subtle of their group, quick to anger and quick to laughter. Hector attracted a different sort of attention in the Wasteland than the rest of the team, mostly because his wiry muscles were liberally decorated with tattoos. The art of body decoration wasn't something Jack had seen back home, but in the Wasteland it was common. Here, every bloedzuiger had a pack brand, and many members of the monastic order had their own inked symbols. Other Wastelanders had tribe affiliations or achievement decorations on their flesh. Among the Arrivals, though, it was rare—but Hector was happy to use his art as a way to ease the discomfort the native Wastelanders felt with the Arrivals.

He leaned back on his stool and glanced over at Jack. "Did you forget something?"

"No." With effort, Jack kept himself from speaking too quickly or too much. "I'll finish shift."

"Sure." Hector grabbed his personal knives and headed out. He was a decent enough man, never asking questions that Jack didn't know how to answer—or if he had such questions, he didn't belabor the point by pressing them when Jack ignored them. All told, Hector was an asset that Jack would miss when he eventually didn't wake up.

It was nice to have at least one or two relatively uncomplicated people in his life. *Like Mary.* Francis often bordered on uncomplicated, but right now he was second only to Katherine on Jack's needing-a-smack-in-the-head list. Admittedly, though, that list changed often. Depending on how Edgar was handling Katherine's behavior and how Chloe handled the Verrot, any of them could easily knock Francis back to the bottom of Jack's list of problem children.

Jack spent the next few hours scanning the desert, wishing he was out in it rather than trying to stand in one place. Forcing himself to do so, testing his own discipline, was a better theory than reality. He paced while he watched animals run, fly, and scuttle. He loaded, unloaded, and reloaded guns. He sharpened blades. By the time Francis arrived to take the midnight shift, Jack was ready to forgive him for letting Katherine leave camp simply because he showed up on time. Standing guard while he was humming with this much energy was far more trying than it had ever been.

"She's not helpless, and she was upset, and she wasn't going in the dark, and I told you not too long after." Francis's words were one long rambling stream, followed by a gulp of breath.

"I know." Jack stood and stretched as if he were as tired as he should be.

"Edgar's going to kill me, isn't he?" Francis pushed his floppy hair back.

"I suspect that all depends on Katherine. Just don't be stupid again."

Francis rocked back on his heels, pushed his thin brown ponytail over his shoulder, and stared at Jack like a dog that had lived on the edge of town too long.

Jack shifted the rifle from his lap to the table beside him. It was still in reach, but now that the darkness had receded, he didn't need to be as alert. "Starting tomorrow, you're on early daylight guard. I'll give Edgar the early night shifts the next few days. That should buy you time for him to calm down before you have to cross paths." He concentrated on speaking at a normal pace as he detailed the plan he'd used far too many times already. "Don't do anything else stupid, Francis."

Francis nodded and turned his attention to the desert, and Jack walked toward the tents.

Katherine stood outside her tent with her arms folded over her chest, her boot-clad foot tapping in the sand and a look on her face that reminded him almost painfully of their mother.

"You simple fucking idjit." Katherine stomped toward him. If there'd been boards under their feet, her footsteps would've resounded like warning alarms. As it was, her stomping toward him merely set dust to swirl around her, creating the illusion of steam radiating from her. Jack couldn't stop grinning even as she reached up and poked a finger into his chest.

"Where did you get it? Never mind. It was that bony bastard, wasn't it? You know better. Seriously!" She was now shaking her finger at him. "I know you drank it too. Are you a . . . never mind, we both know you are." She finished her diatribe with a little half-muffled scream and then added, "Say something!"

"You look like Mam right now."

All of the steam left her in a whoosh of a sigh. "That's not fair."

Jack knew he should take advantage of her moment of softness, so he said, "Ajani is involved in the monk situation. I need you to drink it too."

"Jack—"

"Don't make me resort to something barbaric to make you drink it," he half begged. "We're down one fighter, and if Ajani is coming around again, you and Edgar are the biggest targets."

"And you. And Hector, and Francis, and Melody because he'll see them as expendable. And Chloe because she's new." Katherine ticked off their names on her fingers. "Oh God, he's going to know about Chloe before she has a chance to adjust, isn't he?"

"That's why I gave her the Verrot," Jack pointed out as mildly as he could.

Katherine shivered a little. "There's no way he could've known Mary wouldn't wake, right? I mean, that's imposs—"

"He probably just heard that she *did* stay dead, so he'd be watching for the new arrival. We got to her first, though. With Garuda's gift, she'll recover from the transition faster. We all need to be ready if Ajani is coming around again." Jack pulled Katherine in for a hug even as he threatened, "I have another full bottle of it, plus what's left in that one. You're not leaving camp unless you drink it. If you try to leave without it, I'll leave you chained in the tent. I'll hate it as much as you will, but I'll do it if I have to, Katherine."

"Jackass," she muttered, but she hugged him back quickly before stepping away and folding her arms again.

"Everything will be fine," he promised her.

"So, there's no reason—"

"You're still drinking the Verrot," he interrupted. "Drink or stay in camp. I can't risk losing you, or risk Edgar being so worried he's useless. There are too many changes right now, Katherine."

*"Jackass,"* she repeated, but this time there was no hug to soften the temper.

# CHAPTER 13

Chloe was feeling a mix of trepidation and frustration as she waited for Kitty to walk back into the tent. She felt more alive than she'd felt ever in her life. Earlier that day, she'd explored the camp a bit with Kitty, but it was now the middle of the night and she still felt unable to stay still.

She'd sweated through her jeans and blouse, and they needed laundering, so she was now wearing a skirt that was slit up both sides—"so a girl can reach her thigh holster," Kitty had explained—and a shirt made out of a lightweight but coarse material. Chloe wasn't given a thigh holster or any other sort of weapons, but she was given a pair of very tall, battered, brown leather boots that Kitty had found in what appeared to be a steamer trunk. They were almost the right size, and a bit of wadded-up cloth shoved into the toe of each boot corrected the disparity. The high-slit skirt felt a little awkward, but in this terrain, boots were a vast improvement over even the low-heeled pumps she'd been wearing when she'd arrived. According to Kitty, they'd protect her leg from any desert-dwelling serpents or lizards that might decide to take a bite. Her pumps certainly didn't offer that benefit.

By the time Kitty entered the tent, Chloe was trying to stay still long enough to lace the boots. That was the only downside to them, staying still and fastening them when she felt like her body was vibrating with energy. She took another deep breath, hoping it would help her sound calmer, and asked, "Am I a prisoner or anything or can I go look around on my own?"

Kitty closed her eyes and rubbed her temples for a moment before she answered. "You're not a prisoner, Chloe. You need to realize, though, that you're new here and not thinking clearly either. It's the Verrot making you feel like this. It's a drug of a sort, but more dangerous because no one can get it out of a bloedzuiger without permission or murder. You need to ride out the initial high, and then you'll be fine. I thought the exercise earlier would've helped."

"Right. It did. Definitely." Chloe nodded so quickly that she felt like her teeth were rattling together. "Back at home, in my real world, I was a recovering alcoholic. I've done this part before. I might not understand your world, but being smashed I get."

She shuddered forcefully as the attempt to stand still became too trying. Her body was going to move, with or without her cooperation, and she wanted—*needed*—to be in control of that much at least. As levelly as possible, she asked, "Just tell me where I can't go."

Kitty batted Chloe's shaking hands out of the way and finished fastening the boots. "Later, when you calm down, I'll apologize for my brother. Right now I'll shelve it so you can go." She stood, forced Chloe to look at her, and enunciated very carefully, "Remember what I said about the fences? Don't touch them."

Then Kitty walked over and pushed open the tent flap. Chloe followed her to the doorway, and Kitty added, "You need to stay *inside* the camp. Everyone in camp is one of us. Outside camp"—she pointed into the darkened desert—"there are more monsters than I can explain when you're unable to even stand still. There are cities, forests, rivers, and oceans. There are people—Wastelanders they're called. *You* stay in camp. Got it?"

Impulsively, Chloe threw herself at Kitty in a tackling hug and then released her just as quickly. "Promise!"

Whatever reply Kitty offered was uttered so quietly that Chloe wouldn't have heard it even if she waited around, which she didn't. In a blink, she was outside, standing under two very bright moons and staring at a small tent city that seemed to be nearly empty. This was a far cry from D.C., and while she didn't know how she'd gotten here or how to figure *that* out, she had every intention of figuring out the world where she now found herself.

Carefully, she looked around, trying to decide where to go. She hadn't taken in too many details earlier. She started to explore, walking as slowly as she could with the Verrot singing in her veins. There were about a dozen tents scattered around, all of them far enough apart to make sure no resident violated another's privacy. A few fire pits were set in the ground, a strange thing to see in the desert. As Chloe went to investigate one, she saw that the sand was held back by metal rims, and ashy piles of wood and a few small bones mingled with sand in the bottom of the pit. She paced past the pit, avoiding eye contact with the very large man dressed all in black who stepped out of a tent as she passed. She was pretty sure she'd greeted him when she'd been brought to camp, but she couldn't remember for sure. She ducked her eyes and walked faster in the hopes that he might think she hadn't seen him. Standing still to talk seemed akin to torture just then—mild torture, but still . . .

As Chloe walked, she realized that the camp seemed to have a very clear perimeter. A line that had been worn into the ground hummed quietly. It appeared to be made of various metals and some sort of crystal. A metal fence extended just outside the line.

She had just stepped closer to the fence when she heard a voice say, "It'll kill you if you touch it. The fence, I mean."

"I know," she said, not exactly admitting that she had forgotten that particular detail. The Verrot made her feel like her body was capable of anything. Later, when the high passed, she would need to . . . do something about her access to it. If it didn't have a crash like drugs or liquor, maybe she could enjoy feeling like this. *Maybe it really isn't addictive.* She thought someone had said that earlier. For now, she shoved all her questions away and turned to see the man who'd brought the Verrot to her.

Jack looked as wired as she felt, eyes wide and lips parted. He also looked like he'd be a hell of a good time: muscles and attitude, knowing gaze and inviting lips, and just enough danger to make all of her warning systems go on alert.

"I'd rather you don't die when you've just arrived."

"Are there things here that *won't* kill me?" She backed away from the fence, putting herself closer to him, and wasn't sure if doing this made her more safe or less. "I'm pretty sure I saw a dragon last night. Your sister gave me a skirt cut so I can reach weapons—which she wisely didn't offer me considering how jittery I am because you drugged me with *vampire blood.*"

"They're not vampires; they're bloedzuigers. Katherine just dislikes them, so she calls them that." He shifted side to side a little, as if standing still was difficult for him too. "I might have been a little hasty about giving Verrot to you without explaining, but it makes you stronger. Drinking it meant you'd shake off the travel sickness faster. You're already well."

She licked her lips, thinking of the Verrot, and his gaze focused on her mouth. Somehow, that shift in attention made Chloe feel cornered. She inhaled and exhaled as slowly as she could, trying to force herself to relax. The fence was deadly, so she couldn't back away, and moving forward now meant moving closer still to a man who, in the short time she'd been here, had carried her across several miles of desert and given her a dangerous drug without warning.

"Being part of the team means trusting my judgment." Jack's gaze shifted to the desert behind her.

"Is there something behind me?"

"No. If there was, it couldn't cross the fence." He stared directly at her as he added, "I'm just used to looking for trouble."

He didn't look away from her, and she wondered if he was suggesting that she was trouble. They stood at an impasse of sorts for long enough that she was considering asking why, but then he turned abruptly and walked away from her.

For reasons that could've been either curiosity or stupidity, she ran after him. "What are you doing?"

"Walking."

"You drank it too." She caught up to him, feeling self-conscious about the way the borrowed skirt exposed so much skin, but still hoping he'd steal a look at her legs.

He stopped abruptly, forcing her to put a hand on him to steady herself or smash into him. The solid muscle under her hand was as defined as the body of the amateur boxer she'd dated briefly, so much so that she was hit by a guilty temptation to slide her hand down his back. Instead she yanked her hand away from Jack as quickly as she'd reached out.

Jack turned to face her. "Yes, I drank the same Verrot. I need to keep everyone safe; that's what I do. I patrol. I hunt. Most of us do." He put a hand to the gun at his hip. "We do what jobs we can here, try to be a force for good and help keep order. It's how we make our money, and how we atone for the sins that led to our being here."

"The what?" She stepped backward.

"Someone picked us. Each of the Arrivals has killed someone or done something else horrible before we got sucked into the Wasteland. That's the only thing we all have in common, Chloe." Jack swept his arm out in a gesture that made her look around the shadowy, moonlit camp again. "These people are all killers . . . Odds are that you are too."

Not too much he could've said would've been as effective at dousing any ember of lust she might have been nursing. *A killer?* Chloe stared at him, but didn't answer the question he was putting before her. That's what it was, really: he was asking her to admit to being a killer. *Fuck that.* What she'd done in the past was no one's business. She knew well enough that there were secrets that were not meant to be shared freely—and certainly not with a man she'd just met. She'd done what she'd done, and that wasn't something she had ever discussed. Rule number one in taking a life: never talk about it. Some secrets were too dangerous to share. Maybe the crimes of her old life weren't punishable here, but that didn't mean there was any reason to discuss them.

She started to walk away from him, but she'd only gone a few steps before he asked, "Can you shoot?"

"What?" She turned back to face him.

"Shoot, Chloe. Are you a decent shot? If you're going to be with us, you need to have the ability to defend yourself. Guns are easier to handle than knives or any of the native weapons."

"I've been known to hit a few targets," she hedged.

"I'm going out. I need to do a quick patrol anyhow." He motioned out at the barren landscape beyond the camp. "If you want to tag along, you can show me what you've got."

It wasn't an apology; it probably wasn't even meant as a hint of an apology. What it was, however, was a way of showing his willingness not to pursue the subject of her *sins,* as he called them. That was enough of a concession for her—especially as it came with an invitation to investigate the area outside of camp.

# CHAPTER 14

Jack didn't stop to speak to Francis as he reached the guard point. He grabbed a couple of guns and one of the prepacked bags as Francis introduced himself to Chloe. If Jack stopped, he might think about what he was doing, but thinking wasn't what either he or Chloe needed to do. He'd given her Verrot without even asking. He'd eased new Arrivals into this world for more than two decades. He wasn't usually this careless.

Jack handed a shotgun to Chloe. Even someone with lousy aim could do some worthy damage with a shotgun. "Here."

She accepted it, cracked the barrel with surprising familiarity, and snapped it shut. She didn't speak—and Jack was glad. Mary was dead; Ajani was involved; and he was feeling as jittery as a cat in a house full of rockers. He'd thought that Garuda's blood wouldn't be too potent since it was filtered through the newborn bloedzuiger, but he was obviously wrong.

"Tell Katherine we went out when she comes around asking questions," Jack told Francis. He grabbed a few more supplies and shoved them in the weapons bag he'd picked up. "Tell Edgar I said Katherine isn't allowed to leave camp. No one is till I get back. If Hector and Melody return before me, tell them too."

The need to move was growing, not abating, and Jack realized that he'd made a mistake. Not only had he given a new arrival Verrot, but he'd given her Verrot that was too pure. The newborn must also have drunk from Garuda before Jack arrived.

"Come on." He tossed the bag over his shoulder and headed into the desert.

Chloe followed him. That she was able to keep pace with him so easily was only possible because he'd given her some of Garuda's gift. Typically, the travel sickness took a few days to work itself out. In a few rare cases, he'd seen it take a week or more. Chloe, however, was far from sick. She sped up a little more, so she was in front of him rather than trailing him.

Mutely, Jack increased his pace.

She did the same.

In a few minutes, they were both running, racing across the not-yet-light desert with the sort of abandon that Jack rarely let himself enjoy. He steered their course, turning at the edge of a saguaro forest so they were racing down paths that wound among towering cactus. As far as the Gallows Desert went, it was safe enough.

Nowhere out here was truly safe, but there were a few creatures who hated the cactus forest. The biggest threats in this forest were the bloedzuigers and the two-natured, but for at least the next month, anyone with the blood of Garuda's pack in them could count themselves as packmates to the bloedzuigers. Jack had no doubt that Garuda had left some of his young ones in the area should Jack need their aid. When he was bound this way to Garuda, the old bloedzuiger could track him. That meant he'd leave resources behind for Jack's use, as well as potentially making an appearance if the threat was severe.

When they reached their destination, Jack grabbed Chloe's hand

and forced her to stop. The momentum spun her and propelled her into him. He instinctively dropped the weapons bag and put his hands on her hips to steady her.

For a moment, he thought she would step away, but she stared up at him, lips parted as if she'd speak. Instead, she kissed him, and he couldn't think of any reason to stop her. His hands brushed the slits on her skirt, and it only made sense to slide his hands under the fabric. When he discovered that there were no undergarments between her skin and his hands, he cupped her ass in his hands and pulled her tighter to him.

They'd gone from running to touching, and somewhere in his mind, he realized that this wasn't the best idea he'd ever had. They were in the desert at night. She was a stranger to this world. They'd both had near-pure Verrot.

Then she twined her arms around him and hitched a leg around him, and suddenly he couldn't think of anything else.

They hadn't stopping kissing yet, and in the distant, still-functioning part of his mind, it occurred to him again that it was a very bad idea to kiss her like this. Threads of reason tried to weave into his thoughts, but he was racing on the blood he'd ingested.

Chloe pushed harder against him, leaning her body into his so forcefully that he pulled his hands away and put them behind him to keep himself from crashing to the ground. He used his hands to steady their descent to the ground, but even so, he was grateful that he was fit and strengthened by Verrot.

As soon as they were on the ground, she was straddling him, and it seemed wrong to have so much clothing between them—especially when she ground down against him.

He tugged at the front panel of her skirt, and she lifted herself up, balancing on her knees and staring down at him with wide eyes as he pulled the material from between them. His thumb grazed her, and she stilled. In that moment clarity assailed him.

"No." He jerked away from her.

In a bloedzuiger-quick move, she stood looking down at him. She was breathing as heavily as he was, and her lips were swollen from their harsh kisses.

"No," she repeated in a whisper of a voice. She swallowed and tried again, slightly louder. "You're right. No. That . . . I didn't come out here for that. Maybe you did, but . . ."

"No. That wasn't my plan either," he agreed. "It's a bad idea right now."

Not trusting either one of them, Jack stayed prone on the ground. He watched her smooth down her skirt and then run her hands over her hair, as if straightening her appearance would change anything.

"Right. Bad idea." Her words agreed, but they sounded like a question. "I'm not like that," she added. "Maybe people around here are . . . like that, but I'm not."

"People are the same here as at home." Jack pushed himself up so he was on his knees, and he was suddenly very aware that he was eye level with Chloe's thighs. He forced himself to look upward and meet her eyes. "Your lack of undergarments is mighty distracting, Chloe."

She smoothed her skirt again. "I have a skirt on."

He grinned. "One that's cut up both sides high enough that if you were to walk over here, I could—"

"Bad idea," she repeated shakily. "You said so yourself."

"That I did." He stood, but didn't step any closer to her. "As a matter of accuracy, though, what I said was that it was a bad idea *now*. Once you get acclimated to the Wasteland, though, we maybe ought to discuss it again."

Rather than reply, Chloe picked up the bag of weapons and opened it. "Guns. Guns are good. I haven't practiced in a while. Gun laws in D.C. are crazy strict, but it's like riding a—"

"Man?" he interjected, feeling more lighthearted than normal thanks to both the Verrot and Chloe's kisses.

"Bicycle," she said firmly, but her lips curved in a brief smile before she continued: "Or a horse, in your case, I'd suppose. You don't forget how to shoot; it's like riding a *bicycle*."

The foul mood he'd been fighting earlier had vanished somewhere between running across the desert and thinking about burying his face between Chloe's thighs. Jack grinned at her before saying, "Right. Well, there aren't any gun laws in the Wasteland. Let's see what you can do with a revolver."

# CHAPTER 15

Even though he was crossing the desert in the least unpleasant mode of transportation available, Ajani wished someone else could handle the task. It seemed a bit of a perversity that the Wasteland had such an overabundance of dismal locales: barren deserts, hovel-filled frontier towns, thick forests crawling with wretched beasts, and oceans that were populated by still more monstrosities. Still, it was the desert he liked the least. For weeks after he'd visited it, sand seemed to appear everywhere. He could taste it now, an unpleasant, silty brine on his lips and tongue.

"Water," he ordered.

The sedan chair didn't alter its forward trudge through the desert as one of the locals he employed handed him a canteen of warm water through the window. The water wasn't at all refreshing, but given his lingering exhaustion and the desert heat, Ajani knew that drinking wine or brandy would be unwise. The perspiration on his skin had already caused a fine layer of sand to stick to him. He grimaced and blotted his face with a cloth.

Outside the sedan chair, Ashley, one of his most trusted fighters, gave him a look of disdain that would've resulted in a reprimand if she'd been anyone else. She was valuable enough that she got away with things no one else did. At first glance, she seemed like a delicate doll, a human replica of the sort of porcelain creation that his sisters would once have cherished. She was a petite woman with honey-blond hair, pale blue eyes fringed with exceptionally long eyelashes, and a smile that made her look angelic. In the world they'd both once called home, she'd had something she had called cystic fibrosis that had affected her lungs, but here—like the rest of his militia—she was functionally im-mortal. Having known limitations in that world had turned Ashley into the sort of warrior who seemed impervious to pain or discomfort. Even if he invited her to ride in the chair with him, he knew she'd refuse.

In his time, Ashley would've been just old enough to marry, but in her era, she had apparently been a student. He still found the idea of educating women a bit abhorrent, but after almost thirty years in the Wasteland, he was no longer shocked by anything.

"Would you like some?" He offered her the canteen.

"No." She stared straight ahead, steadfast in her duties even as she struggled to keep the distaste from her voice. "Perhaps the others would."

Ajani didn't look at Daniel, her counterpart in rank, or any of the other servants or guards. They wouldn't accept a drink after he'd said they didn't need one. Even if they were suffering from dehydration, it wouldn't kill most of his guards. Those he'd imported were unkillable. Those who weren't from home were natives: their sort had long since adapted to the harsh environment.

"They'll be fine," Ajani said.

"So will I." Ashley's lips pursed in irritation, but she didn't allow him to draw her into an argument.

"True," Ajani admitted. He wasn't sure if it was a result of the Coffin Text he used to open the portal to their world or some sort of transformation that resulted from crossing through to the Wasteland, but whatever ailments or diseases they'd had at home were gone here. They lived without physically aging. It made for the sort of incentive that created loyalty that couldn't be bought.

As the crude little frontier town came into better focus, Ajani felt a thrill of excitement. It wasn't the town itself that lifted his mood, but the possibilities of what he'd find there. One of the people who'd traveled to the Wasteland had expired, and with that, a new Arrival—a person full of potential—had come to this world.

*And Katherine will be there waiting.*

"Pick up the pace," he ordered. In a few short hours, he'd reach his lodgings in Gallows, wash away the travel grime, and greet the latest resident of the Wasteland. Each time, he hoped that the new Arrival would be like him—like Katherine. Even if this woman wasn't their equal, he'd welcome another good fighter. An emperor needed only one worthy wife, but many dutiful soldiers.

# CHAPTER 16

Chloe wasn't sure what she thought about the Wasteland or Jack or much of anything, but she knew what she thought of guns. There was something energizing about the weight of a pistol in her hand, and it didn't hurt that the power they allowed her was actually a good thing here. She wasn't going to blindly trust the people she was with, but she was happy to accept the use of the guns they had lying around their camp the way most campsites had firewood.

"I have a guy who makes a few things for us," Jack explained as he handed her what, upon inspection, appeared to be a nine-shot revolver with a long barrel. It wasn't completely dissimilar to the guns she'd shot years ago at home, but it was different enough that she turned it over in her hands and examined it. She flipped open the barrel and saw that the nine chambers were extra long. No bullet that she knew would require the length of these chambers. She held out her hand for bullets.

Silently, Jack dropped three narrow, pointed projectiles into her hand. He'd gone from ready to screw on the desert floor to adopting the demeanor of a distant gun-range instructor. If she were honest with herself, she wasn't sure what she thought of it . . . beyond the obvious: her taste in men wasn't particularly good. At home, she'd gone from loser to ex-con to the seemingly good guy she'd last seen screwing her boss. Here, she'd met all of three guys and was already rolling around with the one who'd given her the Wasteland equivalent of drugs.

*Some things never change.*

Chloe slid the odd bullets into the chambers and closed the barrel. "Target?"

He pointed at a distant rock outcropping that he probably assumed she couldn't hit, especially as the sky was still dim. It wasn't quite morning, but her vision was crisp enough since she'd had the Verrot that she could see more than well enough.

She aimed, inhaled, and pulled the trigger. The bullet made a whistling noise as it was propelled through the air and hit the outcropping almost square center. From this distance, it looked like the bullet shattered into tiny fragments on impact.

"Modified wood," Jack explained. "Francis usually has them all blessed too. I haven't seen any difference in the bullets after he treats them, but our Francis is a few steps past superstitious."

"He's the one at the gate?" She walked toward the rock she'd shot so she could see the damage.

Jack walked alongside her. "He is."

They practiced with various other handguns, rifles, and a shotgun until Jack was all smiles. "You've spent more than a little time with guns. What was it you did at home?"

Chloe shook her head. "Nothing important."

"Edgar was a hired gun; I was a gambler and a few other things. Francis sold drugs; Hector . . . no one's quite sure what he did. He just calls it 'carny work,' but he seems to have spent some time in prison for it." Jack held out a pair of throwing knives. "These are what he likes to use. Any knife skills?"

For a moment Chloe stared out at the desert behind Jack. She'd ended up in the midst of a group of criminals and cutthroats. *Mom always swore I'd end up in bad straits.* Chloe watched some sort of dog-like animal running across the sand and tried not to think about Jason cutting her. *Jason's dead now,* she reminded herself. *I made sure of it.* She looked back at Jack and said, "I'm not a knife fan."

"Fair enough." Jack picked up the bag and pulled out two other knives. "These are dummy knives. I'll show you the basics for close quarters."

"Jack? That animal is coming awfully close . . ." She pointed. If she were at home, she'd say it was definitely a canine of some sort. She wasn't sure what sort, though: it had the larger, pointed ears of a coyote, but the downward slope toward the back haunches was reminiscent of a hyena.

When Jack turned and saw it, he immediately shoved her toward the weapons bag and grabbed the knife he'd left on the rock. "Gun. Now."

Chloe withdrew a revolver, checked the chambers, and searched the bag for more rounds. "What is it?"

"Cynanthrope." He came to stand at her side.

She lifted the gun and sighted down on the thing. "I can take it out."

"Not it. *Them.*" He was scanning the area. "They're pack hunters. If there's one, there are others nearby. If you shoot one cyn and they weren't intending to attack, they will."

Chloe followed Jack's lead, searching the landscape for the rest of the cynanthrope pack. She hoped he was wrong or that the solitary canine was just passing by, but her hopes were quickly dashed as she saw several more of the creatures come into view. "Jack?"

"I see them." He sheathed the knife and withdrew his gun. "Hold steady."

There were at least seven of the creatures, and now that they were closer, Chloe could see that they were decidedly larger than coyotes. They were even bigger than the German Rottweilers that one of her exes had owned. Like those dogs, though, these creatures were all muscle and intimidating teeth. Her ex's dogs had been big sweeties, despite appearances, but she was pretty sure that the cynanthropes weren't cuddly. They prowled closer in a sort of hive-mind behavior, and Chloe wasn't so sure she agreed with Jack's order to wait. With that many of them, the odds of avoiding injury weren't looking good if they attacked.

One of the doglike creatures growled, and the others took up the sound, so it was like a growing roll of thunder that sounded far too much like an immense swarm of angry bees.

"Can I shoot yet?" she half begged. "I don't want to be kibble here."

"No." Jack put his back to hers, both allaying the temptation to back up and intensifying her desire to do so. If she moved away from the cynanthropes, she could knock Jack off balance and interfere with his ability to defend himself—or she could enjoy that brief comfort of knowing that he truly was behind her without taking her eyes off of the monsters.

The cynanthropes continued to growl, but the ones she could see in front of her and to the sides were motionless. She wasn't sure what they were waiting for or what to watch for, but before she could ask Jack, he yelled, "Dive left. Shoot."

She did so, but all she caught was an arm of a cactus as the cynanthrope she'd targeted dodged to the side. She aimed and fired again, this time hitting the tip of one of the creature's ears. "Damn it."

The cynanthropes weren't attacking. They'd moved to avoid her shots, but they weren't all leaping at her. Chloe fired at them, and they backed away. All things considered, the situation was going much better than she'd expected. Then, behind her, she heard growling.

She tore her gaze off the three of the creatures she could still see in front of her and saw that Jack was rolling in the sand with one of them trying to bite his throat. His gun was nearby in the sand, but both of his hands were busy trying to keep the creature off of him.

There was no way she could shoot it without risking shooting him. After another look to ascertain that the rest of the pack wasn't attacking, she walked over and grabbed the bag of weapons. With another glance at the unmoving cyns, she wished she understood the rules here better already. It would be handy if waking up in a strange world included a guide. Since it didn't, she had to trust what she hoped were semireliable instincts. She looked in the bag and withdrew a weapon that looked like something between a hunting knife and a short sword, and another pistol.

Taking time to reload wasn't something she was eager to do until she had to. Instead, she shot at the cyn that was closest. This time she hit it square in chest. It hissed in a very undoglike way, and another cyn raced closer. This was the one with the now-injured ear, and again it evaded her shot. It and the injured cyn both retreated, leaving only one of the cyns in front of her.

She turned toward Jack then, but before she could get close enough to help dislodge the cynanthrope that had him pinned to the ground, a loud whining of unmistakable fear came from all of the creatures at once. All of the creatures she could see, except for the one trying to eat Jack, fled in a rush.

As she looked up to see what had frightened the monsters away, she saw something even more horrific than the animals that had attacked them. One of the cyns, the one she'd shot, was being lifted into the air by a wrinkled, person-shaped thing. It ripped the throat out of the cynanthrope. Blood and flesh were clinging to its emaciated face as it turned to face her.

"Here, puppy, puppy," she muttered as she swung open the barrel and shook out the casings. After wishing the doglike creatures would vanish, she suddenly wanted a surge of them to appear. Maybe that would buy her time to figure out what to do about the new threat.

"Any tips?" she called as she finished chambering several rounds, snapped the barrel shut, and raised the revolver. Her thumb was already on the hammer, pulling it back, and her finger was ready to squeeze the trigger.

"It's on our side. Don't shoot!" Jack yelled.

Chloe looked at him like he was a madman. When things that look like slavering nightmares arrive and run toward a person, shooting is a perfectly sound response. In fact, shooting such things repeatedly was an even more rational plan. *I'm signed on to work with a lunatic.* She forced herself to ease off the hammer and glanced at Jack, who was still pinned under the growling cynanthrope. "What is it?"

"Bloedzuiger." He punched the cynanthrope in the snout.

With renewed horror, Chloe turned her attention to the thing. Red-tinged spittle bubbled on its lips. "*That's* a bloedzuiger?"

The sight of it evoked the nausea she hadn't felt when she'd learned she'd consumed blood. It was a disgusting, barely sentient-looking beast. Even the animals that had attacked them seemed more aware. This thing looked like it was frothing at the mouth.

"It'll obey you within reason," Jack yelled as he tried to keep the cynanthrope's teeth away from his throat. The creature was stronger than its size would seem to indicate, but Jack was holding it off so far. "Help, please."

She still wasn't sure she could shoot the creature attacking Jack without hitting him too. They were moving too quickly for her to get a clean shot, and she wasn't sure she wanted to turn away from the thing in front of her either. "I can't—"

Her words died midsentence as the bloedzuiger responded to Jack's request. It disposed of the remaining cynanthrope with a speed that was too quick to follow. Jack came to his feet as the monster that had rescued them stood with drool and blood dripping down its chest.

Despite the bloedzuiger's actions, Chloe couldn't force herself to lower the gun the whole way. She relaxed her arms slightly and lowered the barrel, but she still held it in both hands, ready to raise and fire. Jack came to her side, put a hand atop the barrel, and gently pushed it and her hands down until the gun was aiming into the sand.

"It won't hurt you," he assured her.

She wasn't entirely convinced that he was trustworthy—really, that *any* of the people she'd met were trustworthy—but the drooling creature that stood watching them as Jack inspected their injuries was at the top of her increasingly long list of things to mistrust. It was more like the old black-and-white movie vampires than the romantic versions of later movies. It also wasn't moving, so she turned her attention to the man who'd been fighting at her side.

Jack was cut in several places, but his wounds appeared to be healing as she stared at him. Her own cuts were likewise vanishing. She could feel the pain lessening by the moment, and she wondered why. Maybe it had to do with the Wasteland or the Verrot. If bloedzuigers were akin to vampires, did Verrot heal? Then a horrible thought followed that one: *if I die, will I turn into that?*

She glanced at the slavering bloedzuiger. This time, however, the eyes staring at her seemed to hold an eerie alertness. Its body was still and somehow contemplative, like a predator going still before attacking.

"Jack!" She lifted the gun she still held. "It's doing something."

He pushed the gun down again. "No. It's not doing anything. Its master is checking in on us."

"She a wise woman," the creature said. "A fair replacement for your dead packmate, I would say."

*Dead packmate?* Chloe looked quickly at Jack, but didn't pursue that line of questioning yet. She had no clear idea who or what to trust, but she had a primal mistrust of the bloedzuiger. Later, she would ask about the odd remark. For now, she simply watched it. *First crisis first.*

"Why is it . . ." Her gaze snapped back to the bloedzuiger as she realized that the "master" who was speaking was using this bloedzuiger's body but was not actually present. "Can it do that to us? Possess us?"

The bloedzuiger smiled, a truly horrific sight with the blood covering its cadaverous face. "My name is Garuda, and no, I cannot possess you or Jackson even though you've had Verrot."

Jack stepped between her and the possessed bloedzuiger. "Your aid is appreciated," he said.

"Monks are in Gallows." Garuda's gaze stayed fixed on Chloe as the bloedzuiger spoke to Jack. "I sent the newborn to tell you. I'm glad it served another purpose as well. It's almost light, though, so I need to call him home."

Jack nodded, and the younger bloedzuiger resumed the mien of a drooling beast. Garuda had departed as quickly as he'd arrived, and they were left with an apparently younger version of a bloedzuiger.

The bloedzuiger stared at Jack for a moment, and then turned and ran. It wasn't graceful, more like a charging bull than a gazelle, but the speed at which it moved was remarkable.

Chloe stared after it; in mere moments, she could see no sign of the bloedzuiger. All that she saw was the seemingly empty desert. She now knew that it wasn't truly empty: monsters on two feet and on four roamed out there. She wasn't sure what other secrets the desert held, but the world she was now apparently to call home was growing odder by the hour.

"I'm sure you have questions, and I'll answer what I can *after* we gather the rest of the team to head into Gallows," Jack promised.

"Gallows is a town? With monks?"

Jack nodded.

"So we're going there now?"

"We are," Jack said. The look in his eyes was steely enough that she had no doubt that he was a man she'd rather not cross, and she strongly suspected that he wasn't on friendly terms with the monks—although he was on such terms with the bloedzuigers.

"Right," she said quietly. "Let's go to Gallows."

She had no desire to remain in the desert, although, admittedly, she wasn't entirely sure that going to Gallows was any more appealing. The world she'd found herself in wasn't feeling like a very hospitable place. Only half jokingly, she asked, "I don't suppose you have a guide-book about desert dwellers or Wasteland monsters back at camp?"

Jack paused in his packing. "No, but you'll learn fast enough, Chloe. I give you my word. If you're one of us, you're my responsibility, and I do my level best to protect all of those in my care. Unless you mean me or mine harm, I'll do whatever I can to keep you safe."

"I don't mean you harm," she said. That much she knew; however, she didn't know Jack well enough to determine if she *was* one of them. She wasn't sure that a life in a crude desert outpost was what she wanted or if there was a way to go back home. All she could say for sure was that as Jack stared at her, she knew that she didn't want to be *against* him because although he hadn't articulated it, she was pretty sure that he'd do that same level best to strike down those who weren't a part of his small group of killers.

# CHAPTER 17

When Jack returned to camp that morning and announced that Chloe was a helluva shot, Kitty wasn't sure whether she was relieved or alarmed. No one knew how the Arrivals were picked, but on occasion, people with no fighting skills whatsoever did arrive. No one was quite sure what to do with them, but the group worked together to train them up right. On the other hand, those who arrived with skills in violence were either trouble or the sort of assets Ajani would try even harder to lure away. Any fighting aptitude Chloe had would be useful, but it alarmed Kitty a little that she was adept enough with firearms to impress Jack.

"There are monks in Gallows. Gear up if you're coming," Jack announced. Before Kitty could answer, he added, "Drink first, Katherine. You and Edgar both, or stay here. I left some with him already."

Then Jack walked away, calling for Francis, Hector, and Melody as he went. Chloe followed after him like everyone else in camp did, sheep following their shepherd blindly. Admittedly, the newest sheep looked a bit more bedraggled than she had earlier, but she was still trotting along behind Jack.

Kitty stared after them, briefly envisioning slapping her brother up alongside the head. She was perfectly capable of dealing with monks—or even Ajani—without drinking Verrot. She'd fought at

Jack's side for twenty-six goddamn years, and she'd done so with competence and determination. Sure, she'd died here and there, but she did so far less frequently these days.

Strong hands came down on her shoulders. "He's serious, Kit."

"I hate Verrot," she told Edgar as she turned to face him. He stood in his shirtsleeves and trousers, a concession to the desert heat that she always appreciated. There was nothing wrong with his suit jackets, but she enjoyed the sight of his slightly more relaxed attire too.

"If it helps, I won't drink it until you're feeling clearheaded," Edgar offered. "I can keep you from doing anything reckless, Kit, and Jack wouldn't ask me to stay behind if you go. He knows better."

Mutely, she turned away from him and walked to Edgar's tent. She pushed the door flap aside and went into the dark enclosure. The scent of the slightly bitter soap he favored greeted her, and without thinking, she took a deep breath. It was foolishness, but being here, among his things and surrounded by the scent she associated with him, eased her nerves like few things could. Her glance darted over the wooden contraption that held his trousers so they wouldn't wrinkle and the bed with the covers neatly straightened. Familiar longing filled her at the sight of that bed, and she turned her head away abruptly. It was dangerous being here.

She walked to the small table and two chairs near the door. On the table sat two clay mugs full of Verrot. "You drink it. I'm safe enough at camp." Kitty picked up a mug of the Verrot. "Here."

"Kit . . ." Edgar accepted the mug and promptly set it down untouched. "You can't expect me to believe you're going to stay behind instead of going after the monks who killed Mary."

Kitty walked away from Edgar. Jack would insist that Edgar stay if she didn't drink. That would leave the rest of the Arrivals vulnerable. Refusing to drink the Verrot meant depriving the team of two of the three best fighters, and both Jack and Edgar knew it.

"I won't stay dead even if I get killed," she grumbled. "You're at far more risk than I am."

For a moment Edgar stared at her with a small smile on his lips, and then he said what they both knew: "If you don't drink, I'm not going into Gallows either. Jack won't leave you here alone because you'd follow him."

"My brother's an ass."

"Maybe." Edgar carried the mug to her. "And he's worse than the most vicious shooters I knew at home every time you get dead." He held out the mug. "Come on, Kit."

She took it, looked at the Verrot, and made a decision that she probably should have made years ago. She stared at the noxious stuff and said, "I trust you more than I've trusted anyone in my life. More than Jack." She looked up to find Edgar staring at her. "It's different for me. When I drink it, I don't have the same . . . reactions."

Edgar waited. His expression gave nothing away, but she knew him well enough to tell that he was caught between hurt and angry.

"Every time I drink I can hear Garuda in my head, talking to me like we're in the same room," she continued. "He can see through me like he sees through the members of his pack. That's why I stay away from everyone when I've had to drink it . . . or when I pretend I've drunk it." She held the mug, neither drinking it nor setting it down. "Jack doesn't know."

"How long?"

Kitty didn't pretend to misunderstand. She wished she could; she hadn't told Edgar at first because she was embarrassed by her reaction to Verrot, hated the idea that she was *wrong* somehow. Later, she didn't tell him because she had hidden it already. She forced herself to hold Edgar's gaze as she admitted, "Always."

"You lied to me."

"Not really. I just didn't t—"

"You *lied,* Kit." Edgar pressed his lips together as if he were trying to keep from speaking.

When she said nothing, Edgar asked, "How long have I loved you?"

The rush of pleasure she felt at hearing the words from him again made her voice softer than she liked, but all she said was, "A while."

"Half of your life," he corrected. "If you can't trust me—"

"I *do* trust you." She paced away from him, not wanting to see his injured expression. She never wanted to hurt him, even though she often had. She sat on the edge of his bed. It was foolish, but being there made her relax a little. She lifted her gaze to look up at him. "I don't want to be different from everyone else. The magic thing is already enough. Melody is scared of me; Francis acts like I'm a saint because of it."

"Melody's an imbecile. So's Francis, for that matter." Edgar pulled out one of the chairs at the table on which the other mug of Verrot was sitting, pointedly not coming to her. "Do I treat you special because of it?"

When she shook her head, he asked, "Then why would I this time?"

He stretched his legs out in front of him, folded his hands together, and watched her. "I killed back home, kill here. I die and wake back up. I'm going to drink this"—he tilted his head toward the Verrot—"because it'll make me a better killer. At home, I'm not sure my bosses knew I could speak. They ordered; I did." He fixed his attention on her. "Everyone who gets pulled into the Wasteland is just like me. Maybe they killed for money or a cause or something else, but at the core, they're no different than you and me. You use magic. Hector throws his little knives. A monster or Wastelander is the same amount of dead either way."

Outside of the tent, Kitty could hear voices and knew that the others were getting ready to go into Gallows. She glanced at the closed tent flap. "I do trust you. I know I should've told you, but then I didn't, and then I couldn't." She kept her gaze away from him as she admitted, "I still love you. Just because we're not . . . what we were, that part hasn't changed."

"I know." He waited until she looked at him before continuing. "But you're still not going into Gallows unless you drink the Verrot."

"We could let Jack think I had," she suggested. "There's no way he'd know."

Edgar didn't even acknowledge that idea with words. He simply frowned and waited.

Resigned, Kitty sighed. "I don't want to tell Jack what it does to me." It was embarrassing, but there it was: she still hated that she was aberrant. "Please?"

Edgar gave her an assessing look before saying, "I'll keep your secret unless it endangers you or Jack." He retrieved the second mug and carried it to her. "Does it make you stronger like it does us?"

She nodded.

"Then drink with me, Kit. Jack and I will fight better knowing you're stronger." He stood in front of her, lifted his mug to his lips, and waited.

Mutely, she matched his movement, and together they drank.

# CHAPTER 18

Jack saw the calculated slowness in Edgar's steps as he and Katherine approached, and he knew that Edgar had drunk the Verrot—which also meant he'd convinced Katherine to drink it. Jack was glad that he'd figured out that the first bottle was more potent before he gave it to them. Katherine hated the Verrot enough that her temper would've been even worse if she'd had the extra-strong dose that Jack and Chloe had consumed.

"All's good?" Jack asked.

Edgar nodded.

Now that Edgar and Katherine had joined the rest of the group, everyone stepped outside the threshold of the camp, and Katherine said whatever words she needed to speak to lock their camp. Jack watched the impact of the spell hit her, and he hated that she had to do it. Eventually, they'd build a gate, as he'd had done with a couple of their sites. Until they had the funds to do that, Katherine worked her spells. Most creatures knew better than to try to cross that threshold, but there were scavengers aplenty in the Gallows Desert, so locking up was necessary.

The rest of the Arrivals waited while she spoke the spell. The tension in several of them made clear how difficult stillness was with Verrot in their systems.

Once Katherine was done, she simply began walking into the desert toward Gallows. The rest of the Arrivals fell into step. Edgar was at her side. Francis, Melody, and Hector walked behind them. That left Chloe beside Jack. They'd all accepted her into their ranks at his word, and much as they had done every other time the team added a replacement, they settled in to the new dynamic because they had to do so. When Mary was alive, she walked with Katherine or with Francis. Edgar and Jack would've still been either first or last, but sometimes Mary was the soothing presence that Katherine needed to keep her from feeling like she had to be frontmost. No one but his sister typically walked at Jack's side. Strangely, though, he found that he liked having Chloe beside him.

"Guns at the ready," Jack reminded them as they moved farther away from the camp. "Cyns jumped us earlier."

"This close to camp?" Francis asked.

Despite Melody's absurd attention to what she considered "ladylike" attire—knee-length skirt and a long-sleeved blouse—she made an unladylike sound and said, "Jack had Verrot before us, *Starshine*. He wasn't too close to camp."

"Told you 'Francis' is just fine," Francis muttered. He'd been increasingly prickly over the use of the bizarre name he'd used when he'd arrived in the Wasteland—not that Jack blamed him. Starshine *was* an odd name. Sometimes he wondered how the world he'd once known evolved into both Francis' "hippies" and Edgar's Prohibition. Maybe once they weren't in Ajani's sights, he'd ask Chloe about the world as she knew it.

The Wasteland didn't seem to change as rapidly as the world they'd all known as their home. Jack wasn't entirely sure why change came so slowly here, but in conversation with Garuda, he had come to believe that it was tied to the average life span of a Wastelander. Most of the nonhumans lived far longer than humans, though, and they outnumbered the human populations.

The Arrivals completed the major portion of the walk into Gallows without incident or real conversation. Chloe remarked on the cyns she saw, the homesteader shacks, the cacti that were like those at home as well as those that weren't. Seeing the Wasteland through her eyes reminded Jack of how beautiful and alien he'd found all of it in his first years. The rest of the group was caught up in the intensity of the Verrot in their systems—or their fear of Katherine's temper—so no actual conversation followed Chloe's stray remarks. Instead, the Arrivals were silent and quick as they passed across the stark landscape.

Once they were close enough to town that the buildings of Gallows had come into focus, Chloe muttered softly, "We are definitely not in Kansas."

In a sort of daze, she walked toward the front of the group. At a gesture from Jack, the rest of the group let her do so. This time, he smiled at her awe—and at her words. That particular phrase had been spoken by Hector and Melody at various points not long after their arrival here. It was a small thing, but it reaffirmed his belief that the Arrivals did all come from the same place. Photographs were a relatively new phenomenon in the world Jack had known. They'd replaced daguerreotypes, and he'd heard that there were people back east who had seen realistic-looking color photos. Since he'd been in the Wasteland, he'd learned from various Arrivals that photographs had evolved into *moving* photographs that, eventually, had sound. Movies didn't exist here, but it was interesting to think that the world back home had created such miracles.

They'd all had a few moments of awe when they'd discovered different parts of the Wasteland. Chloe wasn't going to have as much time to pause and adjust as the others had. She'd already had Verrot, been attacked by cynanthropes, met a bloedzuiger, and would soon know about Ajani. They could let her have a moment to wonder at the first town she'd seen in her new world.

Gallows was a little rough, but Jack and Katherine tended to like it because it felt like the world they'd left behind. The buildings were mostly a beige adobe and a sort of pink clay brick that was unique to the Wasteland. There were some wooden structures or wooden flourishes—signs of wealth out here—but the number of lindwurm farms made wood less than practical for everyday folks.

"There are places here that aren't so different from where you come from," Jack assured Chloe.

Melody snorted. "Doubt it."

"That *is* a dragon," Chloe murmured before glancing at Jack and asking, "Are there monsters you don't have here?"

"It's a lindwurm. There are a lot of farms out here." Jack paused. "But, yes, there are monsters that aren't here, and yes, it does resemble the fairy-tale dragons from home."

Someone inhaled sharply behind him.

Jack looked over his shoulder. "What?"

"Fairy tales?" Katherine repeated with a barely concealed laugh.

Jack scowled to hide his flare of embarrassment. "I read them to you often enough when you were a girl, so yes, Katherine, *fairy tales*."

His sister held her hands up in a placating gesture, and he noticed with relief that she was fighting a smile. He forced himself to keep scowling, though. Her softening toward him when she was in a temper wasn't the same as her being all right with him noticing it. He turned his attention back to Chloe. "We lack princes and princesses, if that helps."

Chloe smiled and said, "That's not what I think of when I think monsters."

He shrugged, but he didn't know what to *say*. He wanted to say something clever; he wanted to hear what she said next, what she thought, but he didn't want to say so with the rest of the Arrivals watching them. It was an unusual feeling to want to simply listen to a woman talk, and it left him feeling foolish.

Before the silence grew too uncomfortable, Katherine launched into a recounting of the other day's lindwurm wrestling. Her words were a tumble of sounds that Jack might've struggled to follow if not for the Verrot in his system. He wondered idly if he had sounded so breathless when he first drank it; he knew he certainly felt that harried. Still, she seemed almost like she was rushing unnaturally. He forced himself to concentrate on his sister's words as he watched for threats from the surrounding desert.

He didn't think he was nearly as reckless or obnoxious as his sister made him sound, but he'd grown used to her less than flattering assessments of him. Still, even in the midst of her recounting, he noticed that her voice was filled with pride. He glanced at Chloe, and she smiled at him.

" . . . fool thought he was back home on a horse instead of a lindwurm," Katherine finished.

"I could've let you handle it yourself," he interjected.

Katherine ignored him, and the others started throwing in their own lindwurm stories. Their words didn't sound to Jack's ears quite as harried as Katherine's did, or maybe he didn't know their cadences as well. Chloe listened to them with rapt attention, although he did catch her glancing at him a few times.

As they entered the town proper, Jack took a moment to adjust. Sometimes the transition between the natural rhythms of the desert and the discordant energy of Gallows set his nerves on edge. The others had stopped talking as they walked farther into town. Jack couldn't rightly call the Gallows Desert safer, but the wide-open spaces often made it easier to locate threats—at least the sort of threats on the group members' minds of late. Gray-robed monks and the always ostentatious Ajani would stand out from the desert landscape, but in town, they could blend a bit more easily with the locals. More important, they had more cover in town. The maze of buildings and carefully cultivated landscape of plants that really shouldn't thrive in the desert—and wouldn't if not for the stubborn efforts of the locals—provided ample places for monk or man to hide.

They'd only gotten as far as the less expensive stores on the periphery of the town proper when a bloedzuiger pushed away from a shadowed doorway of a milliner's shop. It didn't completely step into the light, but it moved close enough that it began burning. The smell of cooking meat was disturbingly appealing. Bloedzuigers might look nearly dead, but they were healthy, living creatures—merely ones with a different sort of biology.

Jack looked to the brand on its forearm, and after ascertaining that it was, in fact, one of Garuda's local pack, he stepped onto the planked porch. Chloe stayed with Katherine and Edgar, but Hector, Melody, and Francis accompanied Jack.

"Ajani was in town," Garuda said through the bloedzuiger. "I entered this one to speak to you, but would rather not feel the sizzle of such young flesh. Others of mine are waiting in the shadows to keep watch for you."

Jack nodded. "And the monks?"

"At least three of them were here. Not with Ajani, but I doubt that it is coincidence that the monks are here when he is. I would go with you, but"—the bloedzuiger eased closer to the shadows of the building—"I doubt you want to wait until sunfall."

"You've already done more than enough." Jack tipped his head in a bow of sorts and then rejoined the others, who were watching the street.

"Well?" Katherine asked.

"Keep alert. Monks *and* Ajani."

"Monks?" Chloe asked.

"Yes. They're demon summoners, not always the best shots, but great with spells." Katherine's words were dispassionate, but Jack was sure that everyone there, aside from Chloe, knew that she was looking for a few kills. She was surly on the best of days when magic users were involved, but she was worse when one of their own had died because of them.

"Demons, monks, and . . . what's an Ajani?" Chloe looked from Jack to Katherine and back.

Jack knew he'd have to explain, but he wasn't ready to do so. He had the brief urge to send Chloe and Katherine back to camp. If he thought his sister would go—or would've stayed—he would've done just that. "Ajani's just a man. A person just like us."

"We're *nothing* like that cocksucker," Katherine snarled. "None of us are."

"Right. A bad man. Got it." The expression on Chloe's face was as resolute as Katherine's was. Both women had guns at the ready, and Jack realized that there was no way either one of them would've listened to his order that they stay hidden away somewhere safe. He struggled sometimes with the notion that many women weren't as willing to be tucked away safely as he'd like. Apparently, they weren't even cooperative about staying out of trouble in the world he'd known back home so many years ago.

Hector tossed one of his knives in the air like a juggler as he walked. Francis looked more relaxed, but Jack had long suspected that he'd had more exposure to mind-altering substances than the rest of the team combined. Jack was confident of their combined abilities. Hector was skilled enough to fight in his sleep; Edgar was steadfast with or without Verrot; and Melody took an unnerving amount of glee in a kill.

"Let's hunt, then," Melody said.

And Jack didn't have the heart to try to correct her. He'd like to say it was anything other than a hunt, that they weren't out for blood, but he tried not to lie any more than was necessary. They wanted the monks dead both because of the threat they represented and because of Mary's death. As for Ajani . . . Jack had wanted his head on a pike for years. Attempts at goodwill had only forestalled the inevitable, and if Ajani really was behind Mary's death, the time for patience was past. There *had* to be a way to kill him, and they were going to find it.

# CHAPTER 19

Gallows wasn't like anything Chloe could've imagined. After walking through a desert where the cacti were somewhere between familiar and slightly off, she expected the town to be the same. The town, however, was a shade beyond unexpected. Squat buildings that looked like they were made of mud and stick stood next to taller, narrow buildings that were made of brick. There was little wood, and even less metal.

At the outskirts of town, the roads weren't much more than pathways where the sand and dirt were tamped down by too many feet, but as they walked farther into the town, the paths were covered by a red grass of some sort. It looked a bit like the grasses that grew at the edge of a marsh at home, long thin strips with pointed tips, but in a shade of red that was reminiscent of cardinals. The splash of color would look odd in the desert, but with the pinkish brick of the buildings, the effect was almost garish. The layers upon layers of plants seemed to keep the fine dust of sand from being quite as pervasive, but decreasing the grit in one area was nowhere near enough to make a difference. Chloe's whole body was coated by a layer of sand, and when she swallowed, she could taste a slight salty flavor from the minerals in the sand that drifted through the breeze.

Her companions looked like they could blend in here. Jack and

Kitty were both in battered trousers, nondescript shirts, and worn jack-ets. Hector and Francis looked much the same. It was only Edgar, with his stiff black shirt and black trousers, and Melody, who stood out a bit. Melody was the most unusual of the group. She had on what would look more fitting on a PTA mother or cubicle worker: a knee-length, sand-colored skirt and a powder-blue blouse with a white stone neck-lace that was reminiscent of pearls. Her hair was combed into some sort of almost formal-looking twist, and she appeared to have located some sort of pale blue eye shadow. In all, she looked almost sweet, if not for the holster on her hips and the fact that she was walking down the street with a shotgun in her hands humming a happy little song. Back at home, Melody could've been the office manager from hell; here, she appeared to be a woman clinging to whatever era she'd once known while still adapting to the weird world that was the Wasteland.

"Monk. Left. Got him." Melody fired almost simultaneously with her words. The blast of the shotgun seemed uncommonly loud in the quiet of the streets.

Chloe stared at the shotgun-toting woman for a moment and then at the dead monk in the street. She'd seen dead cyns earlier, but this was a person. The memory of the last dead man she'd seen threatened to surface, but she shoved it away and concentrated on the *now*.

"A little more warning, Melly." Hector shook his head.

"He saw us." Melody shrugged as she spoke, but she had a slightly mad look in her eyes. Chloe wasn't sure if it was from the Verrot or if it was Melody's natural response to guns, but she wasn't too inclined to ask. No one other than Hector openly criticized Melody, although Francis gave her a wary look.

If the monk had accomplices, they weren't anywhere in sight. Hector walked over and squatted beside the remains. He looked back at Jack, shook his head once to convey that the monk was dead, and then began searching the corpse.

That, more than the shooting, made Chloe look away. Shooting a known enemy before he could attack you made sense to her, but corpse robbing was on her list of unacceptable acts.

Francis noticed her reaction and stepped up beside her. He said quietly, "Hector's checking for clues. Jack doesn't stand for theft."

Chloe smiled at Francis in gratitude. He, meanwhile, seemed to be on babysit-Chloe detail. She couldn't really blame him. She wasn't sure what to do to help, and the rest of them seemed to have slipped into the kind of group behavior that spoke of habit.

She didn't know enough about any of them to have a real way to gauge their characters, but she instinctively trusted both Kitty and Francis. Hector and Melody made her uneasy, and the jury was still out on Jack and Edgar. Even if she didn't trust them, though, it wasn't like she had a list of other options. She'd woken up in a strange world with nothing but the clothes she'd been wearing. She had no skills she knew of so far that were marketable—other than being a fair shot. A degree in sociology, a hodgepodge of menial jobs, and knowledge of book and television trivia weren't much of a résumé here from what she could see. Hell, she wasn't even sure the locals needed résumés. So far, she'd only seen bloedzuigers, cynanthropes, and a dead monk. None of that predisposed her to thinking there were a whole lot of golden opportunities on her horizon if she left the group who'd found her in the desert.

Hector and Melody were talking in low tones beside the corpse. Jack, Kitty, and Edgar were scanning the area. They all looked like they were hyperalert, either because of the Verrot or the situation—or most likely both.

A few of the locals who were out of doors gave the group a wide berth, but no one seemed to be particularly alarmed by them—or by the corpse now bleeding on the red reeds on the street. Maybe death in the streets of Gallows wasn't all that unusual, or maybe the Arrivals weren't the only ones who had issues with demon-summoning monks. Chloe wasn't sure. What she did take comfort in, however, was the way the group was regarded. The local people—who looked mostly or entirely human in several cases—didn't look at them like they were villainous. A number of the Wastelanders were all looking in the same direction, though, and it wasn't at them. Chloe followed their gazes to see a pale blue mass about eye level, but at some distance away.

"Hey, Francis, what's that?" She pointed.

He glanced in the direction she'd pointed and called out, "Blight."

The mass was getting closer, and as it did, Chloe realized that it was a swarm of tiny pale blue insects winging their way. They were so close together that as they'd flown they'd given the illusion of a larger solid object. She'd think the insects were a beautiful surprise, except for the fact that the few Wastelanders in the street rushed indoors en masse. Doors slammed. Shutters were yanked closed.

"So . . . not good?" she asked.

"Not for natives," Francis replied. "We're mostly safe, though."

*Mostly* wasn't particularly comforting, but the rest of the group didn't look too alarmed. Kitty frowned, and Melody lifted her shotgun again. She cracked the barrel and slid in two shells, although Chloe thought that using a shotgun against bugs seemed a bit like overkill.

"Do they sting? Bite? What?"

"Stay behind me, and get moving," Francis answered.

A man stumbled out of a narrow lane between two taller buildings, and the swarm surged toward him. As their group backed away, Chloe found that she couldn't tear her gaze away from the sight of these delicate, winged things covering the man so completely that he was soon a whirring blur of soft blue. Instead of the scream she expected, she heard manic laughter.

"Come on." Jack had her arm and was pulling her toward a door.

He pounded on it with a fist and called, "Let a few of us in, or no one will tend to the swarm."

A few moments passed before the door opened, and Jack pushed her into a tiny shop. A quick look at the shelves revealed that it was a fabric store or possibly a tailor's shop. Kitty, Edgar, and Hector came inside too. Francis, apparently, was still outside with Melody.

"Stay in here." Jack looked at his sister as he said this, and then at Edgar, who nodded once in assent.

"This will work better than yours." Kitty held out a long-barreled gun, not quite a shotgun but longer than any pistol Chloe had ever seen before arriving in the Wasteland.

"Thanks." Jack took it and pulled open the door to leave. As he did so, at least a dozen of the winged things rushed inside the shop and separated, flitting around the shop in a chaotic pattern as if the bright colors of the fabrics were confusing to them.

He shoved the door closed again, not latched but closed enough that no more insects could slip inside the building.

The very tall woman Chloe assumed was the proprietress and the four other people inside all let out sounds of distress and scurried around in a chaos as frenetic as the insects'. Chloe wasn't sure if they were seeking weapons or shelter or both.

"Go," Kitty ordered her brother. "We've got these."

Jack nodded, yanked the door open, and hurriedly left.

A couple more insects flew inside.

The Wastelanders were now scrambling to unfurl swaths of fabric. They tugged down bolts of cloth in their panic. One woman had the presence of mind to help another, and together they draped a patterned, heavy fabric over themselves and dropped to the floor. A squat man crawled under a display after yanking the bolts out and tossing them aside.

Hector threw one of his knives at an insect that had touched down atop a bundle of bright pink cloth, killing it neatly. As Edgar walked to the back of the shop, he plucked the knife out and tossed it back to Hector. At almost the same time, Edgar swatted a bug out of the air with the barrel of his gun and then promptly squashed it with his boot. It was the most peculiar use of a gun that Chloe had ever seen.

Kitty and Hector moved so they were on either side of Chloe in opposite corners. Both had knives drawn. Neither looked at her, but Hector instructed, "They won't kill us, but they sting like nothing you've ever felt at home."

"And make you insensible," Kitty added.

"Great." Chloe looked around for a weapon. Spying a shovel that looked like it was used for scooping ash from the currently unlit fireplace, she snatched it and held it like a baseball bat. She might not be able to hit an insect with a gun barrel, but she could hit one with a shovel.

As she watched for insects, she asked, "Why are the Wastelanders hiding if the Blight isn't fatal?"

"The Stinging Blight can be fatal for *us*," replied one of the two women under the patterned fabric.

"Or cause madness," added another fabric-covered Wastelander.

"She's never seen the Blight. New to the desert," Kitty said.

Chloe wasn't sure why Kitty was implying that she wasn't new to the whole Wasteland, but she wasn't going to ask here and now. She stared around the shop. Hector nailed another insect. Edgar and Kitty had both thrown knives, and he'd already retrieved her knife and thrown it back to her. Chloe was starting to feel like she was of no use when an insect flew toward Kitty. It was directly in front of her, and she'd already launched both of her knives.

"Kit!" Edgar had lifted his knife but couldn't throw it without hitting her too.

Chloe stretched to the left and thwacked the insect with her shovel, hitting it in a downward motion and then stomping on it. The movement felt a little like a cross between volleyball and baseball.

"Thank you," Kitty said as she went forward to grab her knives.

They found a sort of rhythm after that. Chloe got the ones they couldn't kill with knives—those that were too close to the bystanders under their cloth shelters or too close to the Arrivals.

Finally, Hector announced, "There's only one left."

"You counted?" Kitty leaned against the wall, knife held idly in her hand.

He tossed one of his knives up like he was juggling a ball not a weapon. He caught the knife before answering, "Of course."

They continued to watch, but after several more minutes, the people under their cloth shelters came out, and Edgar returned to the front of the shop to stand between Kitty and the door. Chloe hopped up on the front counter with her shovel at the ready.

The missing insect didn't appear.

When Jack pounded on the door again, Kitty was the one to open it. Chloe didn't miss the way her eyes tracked over him. Kitty might grumble about her brother, but she was inspecting him the way a worried mother examines her young after a separation. Bits of insects and what she suspected to be insect blood clung to him. Several fuzzy wings were stuck to his hair. Kitty didn't seem to find anything alarming in his blue-tinged appearance.

"Francis brought along one of his experimental goops," Jack said by way of explanation. "The explosion of it was enough to eliminate most of the swarm. Melody's homemade scattershot took out a lot of them too."

"So deadly bugs and feral dogs . . ." Chloe fingered a bolt of violet fabric that looked like blue silk but felt remarkably sturdy. Nothing about this world was what she expected, and the more she saw, the more she thought it was far deadlier than she wanted to handle. She met Jack's gaze and said, "I'm not sure who I pissed off to end up here."

"Sweetheart, we've all asked ourselves that very same question." Jack nodded cordially to the Wastelanders.

The woman Chloe had assumed was the proprietress bustled over. She still looked around warily for the remaining member of the Stinging Blight, and one of her employees was prowling nearby with what looked to be a rubbish bin and lid. Hector was leaning by the door watching the store for movement, and Kitty was . . . Chloe frowned. Kitty was *shopping*.

Jack followed her gaze and then winked at her. "Ma'am," he said to the proprietress, "I believe my sister has selected a few items we would like to have delivered."

"To the inn?"

"To our camp out past the Forked Tongue," Jack clarified.

"No." The woman shook her head. "I'll hold your purchases here, and you can pick them up later when it's more convenient."

"Or we can just not purchase anything," Kitty called out without lifting her attention from the black cloth she was now examining.

Hector's knife went zinging by, pinning the remaining insect to a wooden changing screen. "Got it."

With a casual gait, Jack sauntered over and plucked the knife and insect from the wood. He folded the tiny dead thing into his hand and then tossed the knife to Hector, who caught it with the sort of careless ease that made it appear that the blade was attracted to his hand. Then he tipped his head in a brief bow, opened the door, and left.

"The black and this blue stuff," Jack said. "Katherine will tell you how much of each and sort out the delivery details. It seems only neighborly to buy a few things to compensate you for offering us shelter."

The woman sighed with what sounded like reluctance, but one of her employees was already gathering the items while another was writing figures on a sheet of paper.

"I don't suppose you can sew?" Jack said in a low voice.

Chloe's expression must have been as doubtful as she felt because he smiled again, and offered, "I'll teach you. Better to need to learn *that* skill and already be handy with a gun than the other way around."

# CHAPTER 20

When Ajani looked around the pathetic little settlement masquerading as a town, he wasn't sure whether he was relieved to have arrived there. The jerkily moving conveyance had stopped, but it had done so in *Gallows*. In time, he hoped to eradicate these primitive outposts. Fortunately, time was one of the things he had in excess. He hadn't aged a day in what he'd calculated as a touch over thirty years. Each importation tired him, and the toll of them seemed worse the last few years, but exhaustion was the only real burden his body had to absorb.

Daniel had gone ahead a few minutes ago to check the security of the house. Although there were servants aplenty inside, they could sometimes be persuaded to be disloyal. Until Daniel returned, Ajani waited with the rest of his people outside.

A young man stood waiting in the street outside his lodgings. "Sir?"

One of the servants opened the door with downcast eyes. Most of the local help weren't worth knowing. They didn't have the same loyalty that his imports did.

As Ajani exited his chair, the boy said, "They're in town, sir."

"Ashley?" Ajani looked behind him. "Reconnaissance, please. Take a couple of the others."

As soon as Daniel stepped outside and gave the all-clear sign, Ashley motioned to two of the others, and they disappeared.

Daniel stepped closer to his employer. Now that he was the highest-ranking employee here, he was tasked with being Ajani's right hand. All of the imports knew the rules. If one was given a duty but failed to carry it out, one wouldn't get another opportunity anytime soon. If one failed severely enough, one would forfeit eternity.

"The brethren?" Ajani asked.

"En route as ordered," the boy who'd been awaiting him answered.

Ajani allowed himself a smile of satisfaction. He'd arranged everything perfectly. Jackson's motley band would eliminate the brethren who'd been beckoned to meet with him, and then they'd be appeased, feeling as if they'd won something, which always made them easier to handle. There were more than enough demon-summoning monks in the Wasteland, so the death of a few of them would serve a dual purpose: thinning their numbers and making the so-called Arrivals more malleable.

# CHAPTER 21

An hour after their encounter with the Stinging Blight, Kitty was with Jack, Edgar, and Chloe walking down yet another street. They hadn't seen any other monks or Ajani, and she suspected the other half of their group hadn't either. Uncharitably, she wished she felt like she could trust Chloe enough to support Jack, so they could split into three groups instead of two. Until she was sure of the new woman, though, they'd work this way. The combined stresses of everything were making her irritable enough that Jack and Chloe probably wished they *had* split into separate groups.

"Maybe Garuda lied," Kitty suggested.

Jack spared her a look that spoke volumes. Common knowledge in the Wasteland was that the bloedzuigers didn't lie; it would violate their ridiculously detailed codes of etiquette. She and her brother had argued the matter often enough. He believed that etiquette prevented bloedzuigers from lying, but *rules*—especially rules of behavior—weren't reason enough for her to accept the notion that they couldn't lie. Rules were broken all the time, and Kitty simply didn't trust the monsters.

"Sometimes I swear you'd believe Garuda no matter what he said," she stated—as much for Jack's sake as for Garuda's. "I swallowed the nasty Verrot, which I hate, because the bony bastard said Ajani was around."

Inside her head, she heard the bloedzuiger laugh.

*"I told Jackson that the brethren have a benefactor,"* Garuda said.

His voice always felt like cornhusks rubbing together in her mind.

*"Cornhusks?"* he prompted. *"What is that?"*

Clearly, she wasn't concentrating on keeping her thoughts sorted into private and bloedzuiger-accessible. Over time, she'd gotten much better at erecting shields in her mind to keep Garuda from rummaging about in there, but despite her progress, she still felt her mental shields slip sometimes. If she hadn't had to drink Verrot, she'd not have to deal with this.

*"You should tell Jackson about your skills,"* Garuda said.

Kitty shook her head. Her gaze went to Jack and Chloe, who were speaking in low voices. Whatever she did or didn't do was *her* own business, not Garuda's. She took a deep breath, calming herself, focusing. Then she stopped walking and put a hand on Edgar's biceps. "Hold on."

*"I have never told Jackson about our little tête-à-têtes,"* Garuda said. *"You might not think me honorable, Katherine, but I've obeyed your request."*

Edgar gave her a curious look, but he stilled beside her all the same. Jack and Chloe were several steps away.

Carefully, Kitty envisioned Garuda and then began visualizing building a wall in front of him, a fortress of sorts that looked like it was made of heavy stones stacked atop one the other. When she reached his chin, she looked at him. He smiled at her, and she realized that he'd let her see him. She ignored the urge to look at his surroundings, forcing herself to stay focused on her task instead.

She tried to lift another mental stone to block his now-grinning face and staring eyes.

*"You get better and better at this, Katherine."*

"Kit?" Edgar had an arm around her waist. "Are you injured?"

*"You won't be able to lift that one,"* Garuda chided. *"Not unless you're even more a rarity than I know."*

"Fuck you."

"What?" Edgar slipped around in front of her, keeping his arm at her waist. He stared into her face, seeking some answer.

Kitty hissed, sounding even to her own ears too much like one of the monsters, and said, "I wasn't talking to you."

Garuda's pleased laughter filled her head. *"I find it pleasing that you have made so much progress, Katherine. Almost no one in the Wasteland can do this."*

*"Just bloedzuigers and me,"* she half asked, half said.

The old bloedzuiger didn't reply.

*"Garuda? Did I block you?"*

*"No."*

Kitty realized that Jack and Chloe were staring at her, and Edgar looked at her with a dawning awareness. She couldn't let her conversation with Garuda end just then. Hurriedly, she repeated her reply, this time clearly as a question, *"So just me and the bloedzuigers?"*

*"That is what you said."* This time Garuda's voice was guarded, which was telling. Kitty frowned. His evasiveness revealed a new truth: there was at least one other person or creature like her, and Garuda wasn't interested in telling her who or what.

"Katherine?" Jack turned and looked at her. "Did you want to split up?"

In the street beside her, Edgar spoke in a voice too low for Jack to hear. "Unless you say otherwise, I think we ought to stay with Jack."

*"Your mate is right."*

Although Edgar was not her mate or spouse or any such thing, bloedzuigers didn't understand partnership. At least, that was the answer Kitty clung to for not correcting Garuda. The alternative was admitting that she couldn't lie to the bloedzuiger inside her head.

"No." Kitty paused. There were too many individual conversations happening. "No, Jack. Yes, Edgar." In her head, she added, *You need to stop talking to me. I have to focus.*

She stepped away from Edgar, and in a moment she'd caught up to Chloe and Jack. Edgar kept pace with her, and a hasty glance at his expression made it abundantly clear to her that they would need to deal with the problem of her keeping this secret from Jack sooner than she'd like. It seemed increasingly impossible that her secret could stay hidden.

"Sorry, Jack. I thought I saw—"

Garuda interrupted, *"One of the newborns says two monks are out creeping up on the rest of your pack. He can see them from his shelter. Fell Road. Near the bakery."*

"Monks," she said.

*"I have told the newborn to assist them."*

"Where?" Jack looked around.

"Fell Road." Kitty took off running.

Edgar didn't hesitate to follow her. However, when Kitty looked back, her brother shot her a look that said there would be questions later, but he and Chloe followed as well.

When they reached the others, Hector was trying to get past a monk who appeared to be as competent with knives as he was. Both he and the monk were bleeding from several wounds. Melody was being held by two other monks. Her shotgun was on the ground beside her, but with two captors, she wasn't having much success at getting to it. Her tidy twist hung lopsidedly from the back of her head, and her face was snarled in rage as she shouted orders.

Francis was trying to respond to the garbled commands Melody called out, but he was struggling. Both sides of his face were red with his blood, and he had a ripped piece of his shirt tied over the left side of his head, covering his eye. He turned, and Kitty could see that his uncovered eye was bleeding too.

"Chloe, help Francis," Jack called. "One of you, check for others."

"I'll take Hector," Kitty told Edgar.

The division took mere moments, as if the words and actions were simultaneous, but even those few moments felt too slow. Their entanglement with the brethren had already led to one permanent death. Kitty couldn't bear the thought of the monks killing another of the Arrivals.

*"The brethren aren't what caused her death."*

Garuda's words startled Kitty. For a brief moment she'd almost forgotten that he was in her head, and she'd definitely forgotten to keep her shields in place. This time, however, she didn't regret it. There were hidden meanings in the old bloedzuiger's words, implications in the things unsaid that she wanted to ponder—just not when they were in the midst of an attack.

*"Later, you need to explain that. I don't want to get shot because you're talking,"* she told him as she continued toward Hector while searching the windows and doorways of the buildings that surrounded their location for other enemies.

This time Garuda remained silent, a fact for which she was grateful.

Like they did in most altercations in Gallows, the locals stayed away. The Arrivals were useful for solving a quarrel, caging a demon, or taking out monks, but they weren't accepted by the Wastelanders—and they certainly weren't *helped*. A familiar bitterness bubbled up in Kitty, but she did her best to squelch it.

The monk facing Hector retreated when he saw Kitty coming, and she had an unpleasant moment of having to decide between helping Hector and pursuing the monk.

"I'm good," Hector said, even as he swayed a little on his feet. "He's almost as hurt as I am."

She had to trust his judgment. After a quick glance to see if anyone else needed backup, she took off after the monk. He darted around a corner, his robes tangling around his legs as he tried to turn quickly, and Kitty was certain that she had him.

But then Melody screamed, "Jack! Down!"

Everything in Kitty's world skidded to a halt at the sound of those two syllables. She spun around and ran back to where Hector still leaned against a wall. As she lifted her gun, she saw Jack drop, and Chloe—who was kneeling on one side of Francis while Melody knelt on the other—calmly and cleanly emptied every chamber into the monk who'd had his gun trained on Kitty's brother.

The monk fell, his gray robes flooding red.

Simultaneously, Jack fell backward. It was his shoulder that bled, though, not his chest. Melody stayed with Francis, who was trying to get to his gun despite Melody telling him, "He's fine, Francis! Stay *still*."

"I can still shoot even if I can't see," Francis insisted. "Just tell me where to aim."

"No!" Melody slapped his hand away from his gun. "Jack's fine. Everyone's just fine, Francis! Behave yourself."

By the time Kitty could reach Jack, Chloe was at his side. With a resolve that unnerved Kitty as much as it assured her, the recently arrived woman tore Jack's shirt open to examine the wound.

"Clean through," she said as Kitty joined them.

"Stop." Jack tried to push himself to his feet, using his good arm for leverage. He glanced up at Kitty and snapped, "Damn it, Katherine! If you're going to stand there, you could at least help me up."

Kitty couldn't bring herself to mind his surliness. She crouched down. He put an arm around her shoulders, and in a moment they were standing.

*He's alive. He's not dead. He's just a little hurt,* she told herself. *He's not dead.*

Already, Kitty could see that Chloe was right: the injury wasn't severe, and with the Verrot in his system and the odd healing powers that the siblings shared, Jack would be fine. No doubt it still hurt like a bitch, but pain alone wouldn't kill a person.

"Where's Edgar?" Jack asked.

The fear she'd felt at hearing Melody scream Jack's name flashed over her again, but before it could settle in her bones, she saw Edgar coming toward them. Her gaze swept him from toe to top, and when she met his eyes, he was doing the same to her. She let out a breath in relief.

"No survivors," Edgar said as he approached. "I got the one that was running from Kit."

"I can't see out of *either* eye now. Someone care to tell me what's happening?" Francis snapped in an uncharacteristically angry tone.

With more effort than she'd have liked, Kitty pulled her gaze from Edgar. "We're all fine, Francis. Jack's got a flesh wound. Hector's a little worse for wear."

"And I hardly got to kill anyone," Melody complained.

"Sorry, Melly." Hector limped over to Melody and Francis. "You shot a monk when we arrived."

"True!" Melody perked up. "Who wants to grab a drink?"

Chloe frowned at her. "Jack's shot. Francis"—she gestured in his general direction—"is *blind,* and you want to—"

"I'm not traipsing across the desert right now, Jack," Melody interrupted, pointedly turning away from Chloe. "I was up early, hiked out here in the heat, dealt with Blight and monks. I'm going to a tavern."

For a moment the guise of sweetness that Melody tried to wear slipped so obviously that Kitty remembered again why she wouldn't share quarters with the humming woman: she was unstable and mean.

Melody glared in turn at Chloe, Kitty, and Jack, but she wasn't fool enough to glare at Edgar. The last time she'd gotten too confrontational, he'd lost his temper. Jack had made him promise not to shoot her again, but Melody didn't know that.

Hector draped an arm over her shoulder. "The monks are dead or gone. A break wouldn't hurt."

*"My newborns can watch,"* Garuda said. *"If you want to tell Jackson, he'll feel better."*

Quietly, Kitty told her brother, "Let them go. Hector will keep an eye on her. We'll catch up in a minute." In a split instant, she made a decision she'd avoided for years. Maybe she was being silly, but seeing her brother bleeding—even from such a tiny injury—made her want to do anything she could to ease his worries. She whispered, "Garuda says his newborns will keep watch from the shadows. He'll . . . let me know if there are any monks—"

*"Or Ajani,"* Garuda interrupted.

"If there are monks or Ajani nearby," she finished, still in a whisper.

Jack turned his head to stare at her, and she met his gaze without squirming much. They were both silent, but the next move was his, so she waited.

"Jack?" Hector prompted.

"Go to the Gulch House. We'll be there soon. " Jack glanced at Chloe and said tersely, "Go with them. Keep Francis safe."

Once they'd all left, he stepped back from his sister and asked, "Now, how *exactly* will Garuda tell you?"

# CHAPTER 22

Jack watched his little sister debate how much truth to tell him with the same transparent expression she'd once worn when she'd stolen the candy he'd been hiding to give her for her birthday. He knew she was weighing out how much to admit and trying to suss out how angry he'd be.

As he waited as patiently as he could, he took in the faces of Wastelanders who were watching them from their windows, the blood that was spilled in the sandy street, and the ache that was quickly dulling in his arm. The Verrot he'd consumed, from the bottle he'd shared only with Chloe, had given him far more of the bloedzuigers' traits than he was used to having. Healing was not usually part of the package. A little speed was normal, as was the ability for Garuda to find him, but the speed at which he was healing this time was unusual.

Finally, Katherine sighed, swallowed, and in a slightly trembling voice said, "I can talk to him in my head."

"You can . . ." He took a moment. There were only a few possibilities here. Either his sister had lost her mind, she'd developed some new skill, or she was lying to him. Carefully, he prompted, "Ask Garuda how many bloedzuigers were w—"

"Two," she interrupted. "He says that's a foolish question, though, considering how many bottles of Verrot you brought to the camp. A wiser question would be what happened before you drank from the newborn?" Katherine scowled at him then. "Apparently, he isn't sure you'll want to tell me *that,* though, because he fears it might lead to other questions about 'drinking from the source.'"

"I see," Jack muttered—and he did. He saw that his sister had hidden something major from him and that Garuda was up to something.

Jack considered Garuda a friend, but he also knew that the bloedzuiger was angling for something. There was a reason he'd hinted at a topic that would lead to Jack's admission that he'd kept secrets from the others. Perhaps it was simply Garuda's way of pointing out that *both* siblings were keeping secrets.

"Did you drink from that bony bastard, Jackson?" Katherine poked Jack in the chest, and as he flinched away from her, he realized that his bullet wound was already nearly healed.

Before Jack could answer, Katherine snapped, "Well, you *are* a bony bastard . . . I don't care if you like my etiquette."

"Katherine, just hold on a sec—"

"You drank from a bloedzuiger *right after* it drank from Garuda? No wonder you were so high. Idjit." She stomped away.

Jack looked to Edgar for help.

"Kit?" Edgar said.

Katherine turned. Edgar's level voice stalled her next burst of temper before it could begin. "Why don't we walk toward the Gulch while you two argue. We should hire out a few rooms for the night. Francis and Hector would probably appreciate a rest, and the monks are dead. You and I can stand watch."

"I know what you're doing." Katherine folded her arms and stared at Edgar.

But there was no one more capable of facing down an angry Katherine than the calm gangster who had loved her all these years. Edgar just grinned at her. "Of course you do. If you prefer, Jack will stand watch, and we can drink or enjoy some privacy." When she narrowed her eyes and opened her mouth to argue, he said in a low voice, "We are putting on a show for the locals. Is that what you want here?"

All of the steam left Katherine at his words. She stepped closer to the men, smoothed down her skirt, and said, "I'm still angry."

"Because I kept a secret, Katherine?" Jack met her gaze. "One like Garuda being able to talk to you like you were . . ." His words faded midway as he realized that he was about to say precisely the *wrong* thing.

Katherine's temper didn't start up this time. She stared back at him with what looked suspiciously like teary eyes and finished his sentence: "A bloedzuiger."

At that, she walked away from them, headed toward the Gulch House. Edgar gave Jack a look that said that there was an increasingly short distance between here and a fist. Edgar had consumed Verrot too. He might cope with the rush better than some folks did, but he was still a lot closer to volatile today than he usually was.

"Did you know?" Jack asked.

"Not until today," Edgar said. "You know Kit doesn't like being different than us. Any of this magic stuff bothers her." He strode forward to keep pace with Katherine.

Jack lagged behind them a little. Katherine needed a few moments to calm herself, and Jack needed a minute to think about the reality that his sister *and* Garuda had been keeping a significant secret from him. It was no wonder that she'd had such an objection to Verrot—and always made herself scarce after drinking it.

In his head, he called out, *"Garuda?"* and immediately felt foolish. If Garuda could talk to him mentally, he would've done so by now.

As they walked the not quite half mile to the Gulch House, Jack tried to work out why it bothered Katherine that she could do something that was such an asset to them. Whatever this was that let the bloedzuiger talk to her, it was likely tied to her ability to work Wastelander magic. Her magic had helped them almost as often as Hector's skills with blades and Francis' affinity for medicine. Katherine was unique among them. Rather than take pride in that, she resented it, and Jack didn't understand.

They'd almost reached the inn when Jack decided it didn't rightly *matter* if it made any sense to him. What mattered was that he told his little sister what she needed to know. Quietly, as if that would mean Edgar couldn't hear his words, Jack told her, "You're better than the rest of us. I wish you hadn't thought you had to hide this, but I know that of all of us, you're the one I'd trust enough to handle the burden of this."

Katherine darted a glance at him as if to read a lie in his expression.

Keeping his voice pitched low, Jack continued, "So Garuda can hear me? He can pass messages to you?"

"It's like he's right here," Katherine admitted. "I hate it."

Jack shook his head. "You could've *told* me, Katherine. We could've . . . I don't know, but I hate that you hid it from me. Don't you know by now that you can lean on me?"

"More than enough people lean on you . . . Garuda reminds me to tell you that Verrot still makes me stronger and faster. He says I respond *exactly* like a bloedzuiger." She paused. "He thinks I could drink from the source because of that; he *has* thought it for years. He also says that's why he killed you that time." She frowned, and when she spoke again, there was a knife's edge to her voice. "He *killed* you?"

At that, Jack admitted, "I don't know that he meant to. He—"

"Garuda didn't," Katherine interjected. "He says to tell you, 'I would never injure you carelessly.' Apparently, he didn't mean to kill you, and he's glad that you recovered." She gave Jack a sharp look.

"Right, then," Jack drawled. "I drank from Garuda. Not much, mind you. It killed me."

"I'd have noticed you missing for six days, Jack."

He took his sister's hand and made her stop for a moment. "I woke after only a few hours."

When Katherine didn't reply, Jack felt himself looking to Edgar. It wasn't that he didn't trust the man, but he wasn't keen on sharing secrets he'd guarded for good reason. One of the things Jack had learned long ago was that the Arrivals all clung to old superstitions even when they didn't realize it.

Without hesitating even a moment, the big man shrugged and said, "Weird shit happens in the Wasteland. You two are all I trust here, so no matter how much you've hidden, I don't think it matters."

The realization that Garuda was listening to their entire conversation hit Jack then, and in that instant he understood part of why the effects of the Verrot made Katherine so unhappy. Jack called Garuda a friend, but he wasn't sure he'd want the bloedzuiger—or anyone, for that matter—hitching a ride in his head, seeing all that he did, hearing all that he heard.

"Garuda, we need to meet to discuss this," Jack said as he stared into Katherine's eyes, as if by the sheer intensity of his will he could find the gaze of the bloedzuiger who watched them from his hidden den.

Katherine opened her mouth to speak, but Edgar's voice silenced anything she or Jack would've said. All Edgar said was, "Ajani."

Both Katherine and Jack turned. The man himself was nowhere in sight, but several of his guards were watching them as they neared the Gulch House. One of the guards, Ashley, nodded at them, and then she walked away from them to parts unknown.

Garuda had been right: Ajani was here, and he was obviously anticipating their arrival. Better here in public than someplace where there were no witnesses. Jack had plenty of faith in the Arrivals, but since Ajani's people never stayed dead, altercations with them were more than a little tense. Melody was a hair-trigger shooter on the best of days, and when it came to Ajani's guard, she was a shoot-first, never-ask-questions woman. Edgar's rarely glimpsed possessive streak inevitably came out of hiding after Ajani unsettled Katherine, and that left Hector and Jack as the only reasonable ones—except that Hector preferred a fight to a conversation and Jack had a burning need to kill Ajani. If he could be killed, Jack would've done so by now, but Ajani was clearly not a native Wastelander because, like the Arrivals, he didn't stay dead. *Witnesses are for the best.* When the Wastelanders watched, Jack found himself striving for more self-control, and right now that was the best plan he had.

# CHAPTER 23

By the time her part of the group had settled into the tavern at the Gulch House, Chloe had started to feel calmer, like the Verrot high was a quiet hum of energy inside of her rather than an ongoing urge to run-fight-explore-screw. The sensation was akin to an inferno shrinking to a small campfire. She could stir it back up, or she could let it burn steadily.

Being in a tavern was like being home for Chloe: drinking establishments had a feeling of sameness everywhere in the world she'd known at home, and that was holding true in the Wasteland. The low light, battered tables, and suspicious glances were a familiar sight—even if the faces of some of the creatures or people giving her the once-over were truly foreign. A waitress with a physique that would draw approving looks in either world had delivered a round of water and some sort of oblong cactus fruits a few minutes ago, and Chloe was studying the fruit to figure out how to handle it without injuring herself.

"Watch," Hector directed as he withdrew a knife that looked reasonably clean from somewhere on his body. It wasn't a throwing knife, but what looked to be a chef's knife of some sort. He made two diagonal incisions in the fruit and flipped the two ends open with the tip of the blade, exposing the soft part of the fruit. Then he pointed with the blade. "There. That's the edible part. Tell Jack you need a cutting blade."

"Thank you." Chloe took a piece of the fruit and ate it, buying herself a moment before looking at Melody, who had watched the whole process. The smiling woman had been studying her as they'd walked and then as they'd settled in at the tavern to await Jack, Kitty, and Edgar.

When Chloe finally lifted her gaze to meet Melody's eyes, Melody asked, "What did you do at home? I was a wife and secretary."

"I'm not married," Chloe offered. Beyond that, she didn't feel much like sharing. She also didn't feel like getting into a pissing contest with the displaced, gun-loving, hostile ex-housewife. She tried for a friendly smile.

Melody matched the smile, but she tapped her perfectly arched fingernails on the table as she watched Chloe eat. Hector cut up some fruit for himself and Francis, who was holding a bloodstained cloth to one of his still-bleeding eyes. The two men seemed content to let the women sort out their relationship, and Chloe couldn't blame them. Melody didn't seem like someone most people would want to confront. She might look like someone's vision of an average—if overgroomed— woman, but it didn't take a genius to realize that there was a lot of crazy under that polished exterior.

Hector and Francis had moved on to discussing lodging arrangements; the bits of conversations Chloe had heard so far seemed to boil down to the fact that Jack would decide whether they stayed or went back to camp. Francis wasn't going to ask to stay in Gallows. Clearly, the pecking order was pretty much Jack at the top, Kitty and Edgar as lieutenants of a sort, and then the rest of them. Maybe Melody was simply trying to decide where Chloe fell in the order of things.

"You shot that monk pretty easily," Melody said conversationally.

Chloe nodded. "You did too. Different monk, same ease, from what I could see."

Abruptly, Francis and Hector stopped talking; Melody's nails tapped faster.

"You didn't shoot him like it was new to you." Melody paused, both in her words and her tapping, let the moment stretch, and then continued: "The shooting, I mean."

With a shrug, Chloe allowed, "I'm comfortable with guns."

The tension spiked, and Chloe wondered briefly if the men would get involved if the crazy woman attacked her. If they stayed out of it, she was pretty sure she could handle herself. *I think.* Melody had the added benefit of enjoying violence with a sort of cheeriness that Chloe didn't get. On the other hand, Chloe was still feeling a pleasant excess of energy. She wouldn't guarantee her success if it came down to a showdown, but she wasn't ruling it out either. Bending to bullies wasn't anywhere on her to-do list, not now, not ever again—even over something simple like answering questions she didn't want to address.

"We're all killers, Chloe." Melody's nails began tapping again on the table in rapid succession like tiny bullets. "Before you arrived here, you were already a killer."

"So Jack said." Chloe leaned back, purposely casual in her posture and tone.

The look Melody gave her was far from casual. "So how many people did you kill?"

"Melly." Hector jammed his knife into the table. "Don't go starting shit."

"I'm just making conversation." Melody's gaze didn't waver. "You show me yours; I'll show you mine. How about it, Chloe?"

"Thanks, but I'll pass." Chloe kept her voice light. Talking about *that* wasn't something she did. *Ever.* She sure as hell wasn't going to play a game of who's-got-the-biggest-dick with the hostile housewife. "I'm more of a new-world, clean-slate sort of woman, you know?"

"Not really," Melody said.

Before things could become even more confrontational, Jack, Edgar, and Kitty walked into the tavern. A small bit of worry that Chloe hadn't realized she was holding evaporated at the sight of them. She felt instantly safer now that the gun-toting siblings were in the room. Francis seemed like an decent guy, but he was mostly blind. Melody was batshit crazy, and the jury was out on Hector.

Kitty said, "Ajani's going to be here any minute now. A few of his lackeys were out there."

"Take Francis to the room," Jack ordered.

"We don't have rooms," Francis said.

"Get them." Jack looked around the tavern and then at the others. "You three stay inside."

Melody nodded; Francis shrugged. Hector walked away, calling to the waitress who'd brought their fruit. Edgar withdrew his gun and glanced at Kitty, who merely murmured, "You know the answer, so don't bother asking. I'm with you."

Jack stood staring at Chloe, and she tried not to squirm under his gaze. She didn't think she'd done anything wrong, but he was watching her in silence. Finally he said, "You should . . . come with us."

"Okay." Chloe didn't know what was going on, but she figured she would stand beside the people who'd taken her in, especially as their group was three fighters down. With a comfort she wouldn't have expected a couple of days ago when she was still back in the world that had been her home, she pushed aside the material of her skirt and slid her gun from the holster on her thigh.

"You won't need that right now," Jack said quietly. "Ajani's here to talk . . . well, lie, really."

Chloe pointedly looked at visibly armed Edgar and raised her brows in question.

"He's protective of my sister," Jack said.

A few of the patrons moved to the windows, but no one reacted much beyond that. Kitty bowed her head and whispered some words. Despite his earlier injuries, Hector looked longingly at them as he returned to help Melody steer Francis toward the stairs that led to the upper floors of the tavern. "If there's shooting, I'm coming out," he stated.

Melody smoothed back her hair. "I'll be sighting down from the upstairs window even if there *isn't* shooting."

"There won't be shooting," Jack told them. "Go."

He led the rest of their small group outside. They stopped on the small walkway in front of the inn. The walkway was made of some sort of stone or rock, and over the top was a small roof of what looked like dried cactus and hardened mud that created a shelter to protect them from the elements. In the street just in front of them a man sat in an ornately decorated sedan chair. The little bit of him that Chloe could see made her think of sweeping historical movies. At home, she would say that he was dressed from another era. Here, however, she couldn't tell if he was in costume or if he was simply in the habitual dress of people who lived in another part of the Wasteland.

The sedan chair was the sort of conveyance that spoke of arrogance and wealth regardless of Ajani's attire. It was a vehicle of sorts, like a carriage, but without wheels or horses. Instead, it had long poles so that servants could lift and carry it. Chloe couldn't imagine how awkward she'd feel being carried around in a heavy enclosed chair, but maybe this mode of transportation was normal for some people here. She hadn't been in this world long enough to know. All she'd seen of the Wasteland was a bit of desert and a little of the town of Gallows, which seemed to be teetering on the edge of wilderness. The desert town might be atypical. Perhaps there were more civilized cities farther away.

Ajani pulled back one of the white curtains of his vehicle and was unabashedly watching the group of Arrivals. He had light brown hair, blue eyes, and plain but attractive features. He wore a well-cut blue shirt in some sort of lightweight fabric. The buttons that lined it appeared to be gray stones. Nothing about his clothes or features was very striking, but with what she'd learned so far about the Wasteland, Chloe could surmise that he had more than a little money.

The servants had the slightly cagey look of criminals trying not to look as dangerous as they really were. There were about a dozen of them, mostly men, and all of them bedecked in gray trousers and jackets that appeared to be a cross between livery and a military uniform. Carefully tailored clothes didn't do anything to hide attitudes, and as Chloe looked at the men and women surrounding the sedan chair, she wondered if there would be yet another altercation.

*If today is typical of life in the Wasteland, I'm going to be exhausted all the time.*

Ajani gestured to his entourage.

One of the servants opened the door, and the man stepped out of the enclosed box. "Jackson." He nodded, and then he bowed to Katherine. "Miss Reed." His gaze flicked to Edgar, but he neither nodded nor bowed. "Cordova."

Chloe stilled, realizing that she hadn't even known the surnames of the Arrivals. She'd fought next to them, killed with them, and she only knew their first names.

"I don't believe we've had the pleasure," Ajani said, drawing her attention back to him.

Kitty let out a rude sound, and Chloe looked at her. Kitty rolled her eyes and tilted her chin toward Ajani, and Chloe felt some of her tension fade. Kitty's disdain made the man in front of them seem less like the monster Chloe had expected.

She looked back at him, not yet speaking, and waited.

Ajani waited only another moment before prompting, "What do they call you?"

"Who's asking?"

A flicker of amusement passed over his expression, but then he bowed from the waist. "I am Ajani, Miss . . . ?"

"Chloe."

He nodded. "Thank you for allowing me to call you by your familiar name."

For a moment she felt somehow tricked. At home, it was her surname she'd guarded. There were a lot of Chloes in the world, but there were fewer Chloe Mattisons. She'd kept the Mattison part of her name to herself when meeting strangers, better to prevent their looking up her address, number, e-mail, or any number of other things. The Internet was filled with information she'd rather not discuss, but plain old everyday "Chloe" was not as easy to research. She shrugged rather than reply to his implied question.

"Would you like to walk?" He gestured at the street behind him. "Or perhaps go for a ride? I suspect you're exhausted from your journey."

"Just say what you came here to say, Ajani," Jack said. The hard edge in his voice shouldn't have thrilled Chloe like it did, but she had a lifetime of bad choices in men to thank for that.

"Did Jackson explain that you have options?" Ajani didn't look away from her. "I know you've only just arrived in this world, and it's probably overwhelming. No doubt Jackson swept you up, took you to his merry band of misfits, and they've done their best to make themselves seem less . . . crude than they are. Let me show you another possibility."

At this, Jack stepped up beside Chloe protectively, but he said nothing.

"A life of deprivation isn't for you. I can offer you a better set of circumstances." Ajani gestured at the servants standing near him, all of them attentive. "They all come from your world too, but they've chosen to work for me. I'd like you to do so as well."

Kitty, apparently, wasn't as willing as Jack to let the man say his piece. "What Ajani isn't saying is that going with him means signing on as one of his thugs."

"Ah, Miss Reed, as subtle as ever." Ajani gave Kitty a look that was both patronizing and creepily affectionate, but he didn't refute the accusation. "My offer for *you* to join me, my dear, still stands. You deserve a life of adoration, of being treated like a treasure."

"Piss off, *dear*." Kitty pointedly rested her hand on the butt of the revolver at her hip. "I'd rather be permanently dead than spend a minute alone with you."

Ajani tsked at her and then caught Chloe's gaze. "And you? Would you like to see what the rest of this world has to offer, or are you going to stay in the desert hiding behind Katherine and Jack's skirts?"

Chloe didn't feel like she knew enough about the Arrivals to make a forever decision, but she wasn't particularly impressed with Ajani either. "I'm not sure I'm staying in the desert, but I'm not accepting your offer just now either. It seems doubtful that those are my only choices. Maybe I'll become a seamstress."

The look Ajani gave her was unreadable. "They'll tell you horrible things, have you think that I'm a heartless wretch." He stepped closer and leaned in. "I feel it only fair that I should be allowed to tell my side. Is that too much to ask, Chloe?"

"Today? Maybe." Chloe didn't back away. She tilted her head up and locked gazes with Ajani. "Today I've met cynanthropes, bloedzuigers, and the Blight. I'm tired to the bone."

Ajani held her gaze for several moments before a wide smile came over his face, transforming his mildly attractive features into something alluring. "You lie well."

"Excuse me?"

"You only just arrived, and you're out fighting already. You should be so thoroughly exhausted that you can't even walk into Gallows, much less quarrel in the streets with this rabble." Ajani looked at Jack then. "Verrot, I presume?"

Jack shrugged.

Ajani returned his attention to Chloe. "You liked it. Everyone does. I can get it for you too, Chloe. You could have that and so much more."

The very mention of unfettered access to Verrot made her hands curl into fists at her sides. She wondered if it was addictive, if she'd crave it, if she could enjoy it without consequences. It still coursed through her body, a longer high than anything she'd known in her life, but at the moment it was causing her to feel a lingering hum, not the all-encompassing rush she'd felt when she ran through the desert with Jack.

Her face flushed at the memory of kissing Jack. If Jack hadn't put a stop to what was happening, she'd have been naked in the desert with him. Very carefully, she didn't look at him or at anyone else. Let Ajani think she was flushing because they were talking about Verrot. She licked her lips before saying, "It sounds like you're trying to bribe me."

Ajani laughed a little, but even in this he was controlled. "No. I'm trying to entice you to choose a better life."

"And they're all letting you do it, although it seems pretty obvious that they don't like you." Chloe looked over at Edgar, who was the most murderous looking of the group; Kitty was a close second. Jack was the only one who seemed relatively calm about the whole thing.

Then Chloe added, "Here's the thing, Ajani: I don't know you or them or much of anything. All I can say for certain is that I'm not making any decisions today other than whether to sleep first or eat first. Later, you're welcome to convince me or bribe me, and they're free to spin tales of your flaws. Right now I don't care."

For a moment she thought he might press to continue the discussion, or that the others would. Jack tensed as Ajani looked to his servants, but despite the spike in tension, no one did more than glare.

After several seconds, Ajani stepped away and bowed. "Until another day, then, Chloe." He looked at Kitty and bowed to her as well. "Miss Reed . . . Jackson. Cordova."

Then he returned to his sedan chair, and Chloe watched as he and his servants left. Theirs was a strange, slow procession through the town compared to the bloedzuigers' and cynanthropes' impossible speeds.

Once he was several buildings away, Kitty turned to Chloe. "You don't have to trust us, Chloe. It's good to be suspicious, but I'll tell you that there are a few truths you'll learn in the Wasteland. One of the ones I figured out well over two decades ago is that trusting Ajani is deadly. He might not look like a monster, but he's the one thing in this world I would call unredeemably evil."

Chloe tried to weigh her answer carefully. Kitty had nursed her, and the group had been nothing but kind to her. "I'm not inclined to believe him, but like I said, right now I need to rest."

After a terse nod, Kitty and Edgar went inside the Gulch House, leaving Chloe outside with Jack. He leaned against the wall, and she stepped a little closer to him so she didn't have to raise her voice to be heard.

"Rest?" His tone was doubtful, and his gaze was fixed on the departing sedan chair rather than on her.

She didn't reply.

"Verrot isn't usually as strong as what we had last night or yesterday or whatever day that really was, but unless you're used to it, the odds of sleep this soon after taking it aren't good. And after taking Verrot *that* strong . . . ?" Jack turned his head and gave her a wry smile.

165

Chloe nodded. "I don't know that I could sleep, but a little down-time would be good."

"Alone or with company?"

More than a few times in her life, Chloe had made drink-influenced choices that, luckily, hadn't resulted in anything worse than hazy memories. She was lucky that she'd avoided sexually transmitted diseases or assault. When she'd gotten sober she'd promised herself not to end up in situations where drinks influenced her decisions. She didn't think Jack posed any kind of *physical* threat, but he had the potential to be a very bad decision of another sort.

"I don't know you, or much about this world," she hedged.

"True." Jack motioned toward the tavern. "If you want some of those questions answered, I'm willing to answer them. Hector hired out a few rooms."

Chloe glanced at Ajani's increasingly distant figure and then at Jack. "Is that what you meant? Just talking?"

The look Jack gave her spoke more clearly than words. "You seem a lot more clearheaded now than you were in the desert."

"Enough so that I'm not going into a room with just the two of us."

He was quiet for a moment, and she wondered if she'd offended him. She was on the verge of clarifying that it wasn't that she thought ill of him at all when he stepped closer to her.

"Sometimes all I want is to have a few hours when I don't have to think about monsters, including Ajani, or wonder why we all ended up here," Jack said in a low voice. The dangerous undertone that she'd heard in his voice earlier was nowhere to be heard now, but what was there instead—raw honesty—was even more tempting.

"I get it," Chloe admitted. She'd lost herself in various ways over the years. Unfortunately, bottles and bodies only delayed fears; they didn't provide answers. At the same time she couldn't shake that sense of instinctual protectiveness she'd felt in the street. She liked Jackson Reed, trusted him more than she could explain, and she wanted to spend time with him. Maybe it was a latent cowboy fixation or just a response to the way he looked. Regardless of the reason, she wanted to find out more about him, but she wasn't about to let herself tumble into bed that easily, so she gave him the only answer she could just then.

"Talking would be good."

# CHAPTER 24

Seeing Ajani always made Kitty feel like her last reserve of goodwill was going to vanish. By nature, she wasn't a violent woman; she took no pleasure in the things she'd had to do to survive. Sometimes, she thought that was at the core of her issues with her brother: he saw their unnatural state of undying as a call to action, a greater purpose in life. She still wanted the same life she had wanted back in California, a home and family. Unfortunately, to have that here would mean turning her back on her brother—the only family she had—so she fought at Jack's side. None of it meant she found any joy in killing.

But she was quite certain that she *would* take joy in killing Ajani. The way he looked at her made her feel like something slimy was falling onto her skin; he brought back memories of the sort of men who walked into the Swinging Door Saloon back home. Then, she'd hoped that they wouldn't turn their eye her way. Men like him were why she had kept a tiny pistol tucked into her corset and a pair of sheathed knives hidden under her skirts. Being alone with Ajani was one of her only personal terrors. Aside from her fear of losing Edgar or Jack, it was her single greatest fear—and Edgar knew it.

He stood beside her in the darkened tavern. "I'd kill him if there was any way that he'd actually stay dead."

She wasn't going to lie and say that she was okay with Ajani's attention. As she'd stood outside, she'd thought back on Daniel's warning, and she wondered if she *should* share it with Edgar. Something different hovered at the edges of Ajani's standard flattery and taunts. It unsettled her.

When she and Edgar reached the tiny alcove under the steps, she paused. Quickly, before she could remind herself that it was a bad idea, she pulled Edgar to her and kissed him. She meant it to be a simple kiss, a thank-you-for-understanding-the-words-I-don't-say kiss, but he pulled her closer. One of his hands splayed across the small of her back, holding her to him, and she realized that her arms were wrapped around his neck. She melted into the kiss with a body memory of how right this was and a sliver of desperation at the realization that it had been so long since she'd been in his arms.

When he pulled away, she wished she could retreat to the distance she'd insisted on imposing between them during the past year, but she couldn't. She was wrapped around him, and he was staring at her like she was his universe. Even though they were in a tavern, they were sheltered from view. Half desperately, she wished they weren't, as if a bystander could ever help her find the self-control that threatened to vanish in the next heartbeat.

"I'm sorry," she whispered as she stepped out of his embrace. "I shouldn't—"

He kissed her softly, a quick affectionate brush of lips, and then said, "Liar."

She turned away so he couldn't see her expression. "It was a mistake."

Instead of answering, he kissed the back of her neck. When she didn't tell him to stop, he began tracing the bone lines of her corset with his fingers. Both blouse and corset were between his skin and hers, but she still felt like there were lines of fire where he touched.

She leaned back, knowing that he'd close the scant gap between them. "I can't survive you dying again," she told him in a shaky voice.

He didn't bother trying to argue with her, to chastise her for what they both knew was fear and foolishness. He held her still with a hand on her hip. Then he lifted the other hand to thread his fingers into her hair and tilt her head to the side. As he kissed and nipped her throat, he slid the hand on her ribs between her breasts and to the side. "I'm alive. You're alive with me. This"—he bit lightly on her pulse—"and this"—he pressed his hand over her heart—"are racing. That's your heart, Kit. Do you feel it?"

She pressed back against him. "I feel something."

He half laughed, half growled. "You see? We're both alive."

Instead of answering, Kitty turned in his arms and kissed him again. This, the freedom of being in his arms, of his lips against her, of his body pressed to her . . . this was what made life worth living. "You don't argue fair."

"Wasn't arguing." He put an arm around her and started walking. "I love you. You love me. You'll come around, or . . ." He let his words fade.

They ascended several steps without his completing his sentence. Kitty waited, but Edgar said nothing more.

By the time they reached the second floor, she prompted, "Or what?"

His expression as he looked at her was one of confusion, as if he had no idea what she meant.

With a little huff of irritation, she started up the next flight of stairs. Midway up, she stopped and asked, "You said I'd 'come around or,' but then you stopped. So what's the 'or'?"

"There isn't one." Edgar gave her a cocky grin, the sort he'd once used when he'd first arrived in the Wasteland and decided to seduce her. Back then, she'd been so determined to be able to bed down with a man with no complications that she'd deign to see Edgar only when she felt like it. She'd taken up with Daniel, both to prove that she could and to convince herself that she wasn't in love with Edgar. In the process, she'd destroyed her friendship with Daniel, but it had still done nothing to discourage Edgar. He'd ignored every rule she'd imposed with a steadfast determination that she didn't know how to resist, and after a couple of years, she'd stopped pretending they were casual. When she'd pushed him away a little over a year ago, she was surprised that he agreed.

After a moment of trying to ignore her curiosity, she gave in and asked, "What changed?"

"One of us has to be reasonable, Kit."

*"Reasonable?"*

"Reasonable," he repeated as they stepped onto the third-floor landing.

As they started down the narrow hallway, she didn't reply.

Hector had dragged a woven cactus-wood chair into the hallway. He sat with the chair tipped back on two legs, one boot-clad foot propped on the railing. His arms were marked with dried blood, as were his trousers and shirt. A short-barreled shotgun rested in his lap, and one of his omnipresent knives was being tossed into the air.

"Ajani's gone," Edgar told him.

"Figured." Hector nodded, catching the knife.

Kitty forced herself to focus on business for a moment rather than shove Edgar into a room and explain that she was, in fact, perfectly reasonable. She thought about her decision in regard to him, and concluded that just because she'd given in and kissed him now and again but hadn't gone any further didn't mean she had stopped being reasonable. Admittedly, she sometimes looked for excuses to kiss him, and she'd been watching him more and more lately. That was inevitable: they had years of history. It was only to be expected that she'd have trouble keeping her resolve. She tapped her foot impatiently, and then caught herself when Edgar and Hector both gave her a surprised look.

With a wide grin, Hector tossed the knife again and caught it before prompting, "So are you two—"

"No," Kitty snapped.

"That explains the mood." He shot Edgar a sympathetic look. "Sorry, man. I thought the Verrot might solve that."

Edgar said nothing, and his expression revealed nothing. Despite her temper, Kitty was grateful for that. Sometimes she hated how little privacy any of them had.

"I figured I'd best stay here till you or the boss arrived." Hector offered a wry smile. "Melly's feeling the effects of the Verrot and just . . . you know how she gets. She's in the other room. Maybe we'll go out now that Ajani's gone. She's likely to pick off lizards or Wastelanders from her window if we stay up here all night."

Edgar nodded.

Hector motioned at the next three doors, the only ones past him in the hallway. "She's in the next room. There's one for Jack, and another one beside it. Then"—he pointed at the door beside him—"someone can bunk with Francis. He can see out of the bloody eye a little, but it's not healed enough that he should be alone. I can stay with Melly or with him depending on—"

"We'll let you know," Edgar interrupted before Hector could ask whether Kitty would room with Edgar or Chloe. Renting all four rooms seemed more extravagant than Jack usually allowed himself to be, but Chloe was still a wild card. Mary had been content to bunk with Jack, Kitty, or Francis. Edgar used to room with Kitty, but he mostly went wherever Jack told him—unless it was with Melody. They'd all accepted her into their group, but no one but Hector was ever willing to stay with her. Her particular brand of crazy didn't bother the knife-juggling carny overmuch.

Kitty felt a wash of worry at the thought of Francis' injury. They got hurt often enough in their line of work, but frequency didn't negate pain. Francis was the most sensitive of the group, the one who helped her tend the others when they were hurt; it seemed unfair that he was the one most often injured. Guilt and anger tangled into her worry: guilt that she was only now able to check on him, and anger at Ajani for coming around when she had more important matters to tend.

Edgar tapped lightly on the door to Francis' room. Kitty followed, calling out, "It's us," as they entered the room. Like every room she'd seen at the inns in Gallows, this was a small, worn-looking space. It was illuminated by bright light from a small, uncovered window across from the door. On a narrow cot barely long enough for him was Francis. His arms were folded under his head; his legs were extended and crossed at the ankles. At first glance it looked like he was staring at the ceiling, but his eyes were closed.

"I'm not healing right."

"What?" Kitty went over to the bed and sat down beside him. She peered down at his face. Blood and tears seeped out from one of his closed eyes and trailed down his cheek onto a rag that had been folded and tucked against his face. "Maybe it feels a little slower than usual, but—"

"I can't see much more than I did when it first happened," Francis interrupted. He winced a little as he opened both eyes. "You're a hazy shape, Kitty. Eyes heal faster than this."

"But Hector said . . ." Kitty started to object, but her words dwindled as the blood started to flow faster.

Francis closed his eyes again and then lifted the rag to swipe away the blood, smearing it across his face in the process.

Edgar went to the doorway, opened it, and told Hector, "We need a washbasin."

After Edgar closed the door, Kitty said quietly, "You lied to Hector?"

At that, Francis smiled. "This from the woman who lied to me to get out of camp just yesterday?" He reached out a hand, which Kitty caught and squeezed, and then he said, "If things don't make sense, I tell you or Jack first. Those are the rules, Kitty."

Mutely, she nodded, and then realized that Francis' eyes were closed. "You're right," she said quietly.

She looked up at Edgar. "Maybe we can get more Verrot. Francis didn't take much." She tried to reach out for Garuda in her mind, like searching for a thought or memory that was at the edge of clarity. When she felt him, as if he were opening his eyes and looking back at her, she said to both Garuda and Francis, "If Verrot doesn't work, we can see if there's a native remedy or something. This should be healing. We need to find out why it isn't."

*"It has to be some sort of poison,"* Garuda said. *"Further proof that the monks are working with Ajani."*

Now that she was concentrating on reaching out to the bloedzuiger, she wondered whether the doorway he seemed to have into her mind, which he seemed to be able to enter or exit at will, worked both ways, and she could enter into or exit his mind just as easily. Today was one of the few times that the existence of this mental doorway wasn't completely unwelcome. She told Garuda as much, and although she couldn't see him, she knew he was happy to hear it. Now that she wasn't resisting him so much, their mental connection seemed even more powerful.

*"I have been experimenting with toxins of late. I will look for those that would create his symptoms, as well as those that the monks are known to have used in the past,"* Garuda offered.

Kitty didn't want to refuse the help he offered, but she had to ask, *"Why are you being so nice to me?"*

*"Because you are unusual, Katherine. When one lives for centuries, the unusual is intriguing as nothing else can be."* He paused, and she felt like she could feel him smile. *"And because you want to kill Ajani almost as badly as I want him dead. It makes us allies."*

At that, Kitty couldn't help but smile. She still didn't particularly like the bloedzuiger's presence inside her mind, but this time, unlike the times they'd communicated this way in the past, she felt like Garuda's being there was an asset.

Once she felt Garuda slip out of her mind, she told Francis, "I have a few ideas. We'll figure it out. Maybe not today, but if your body doesn't heal from this naturally, we will find other options. I can try spellwork too, if necessary."

Eyes still closed, Francis nodded.

"I promise I'll do everything possible." Kitty brushed his hair away from his face with her fingertips and then took the rag up again to wipe the blood from his cheek. As she did so, she glanced at Edgar.

Without her needing to say anything, Edgar understood. "I'll find Jack," he said. "He was still outside with the new woman."

"Tell Hector to stay with Melody if you see them," Kitty added as Edgar went to the door. She wasn't going to break down sobbing; that wasn't a luxury she allowed herself very often. Instead, she sat beside her friend, wiping the blood from his face and thinking of solutions—and a few stray thoughts on exactly how much she wanted to hurt any of the people who were responsible for Francis' injuries.

# CHAPTER 25

From the moment that Edgar and Kitty left her alone outside with Jack, Chloe had heard that wiser inner voice reminding her that getting involved with Jack was a superbly bad idea. *You know nothing about him. He already said that* all *of them are killers.* What did it say about him that he was the one in charge of a group of murderers? Being with him would not only be a violation of the very rational edict against sleeping with the boss, but in these circumstances, it was also a whole new level of wrong: she wasn't clearheaded, wasn't even sure when she decided that she was on board with this he's-the-boss plan. She'd never been particularly renowned for having good sense.

They'd walked through the dusty desert town for a few moments, but when Chloe saw Jack wince and rotate his arm, she felt a flare of guilt. "You were shot. How did I forget that?"

He shrugged with his uninjured shoulder. "It's mostly healed, just tender."

Chloe stopped. "Do you—I mean, do *we* usually heal that fast?"

"Depends."

"On?"

"I have no idea." Jack smiled at her, and her stomach felt like the Blight was swarming inside her, as if hundreds of tiny wings were taking flight at once.

For a few moments they walked in silence, and then she said, "If you want to go back . . ."

"Because of the bullet? Or because you're feeling a touch less skittish?" Jack asked.

In some way, his bluntness was a refreshing change from most of the people Chloe had known back home. When she hesitated, trying to find a way to be forthright in return, he prompted, "Chloe?"

"Right. I'm not saying I trust you, *any* of you really, but if you had intentions, I don't think you're trying to . . ." She looked away, feeling the uncharacteristic urge to blush. "I mean, you seem like a gentleman, despite everything. You were the one who stopped the two of us earlier."

Jack gave her what she was coming to think of as his serious stare. It was the look that came over his face when he was weighing out his words, as if the act of speaking were something that merited more consideration than most people these days ever used. After a pause he said, "I have decidedly *un*gentlemanly hopes, but there are places aplenty to hire satisfaction if I wanted to." He motioned to an intersection of streets in the distance. "There are creatures of all sorts who work in the flesh trade here. It's not so different from when I was in California . . . except in the variety. There's things here a far sight stranger than anything I could've imagined as a younger man."

With a start, Chloe realized that the cowboy attitude toward brothels was a bit more casual than the one she'd known during her time. At home, there was often a wink-and-nudge behavior that implied that there was something dirty about sex. Using the services of a prostitute wasn't something most men would even admit to considering, much less doing. In the West, in the world Jack had known, however, women would've been scarce, and brothels were simply places that provided a service for a fee. She suspected that it was much the same here.

But even as she was thinking that, Jack said, "I haven't been to them in a while. There was a woman in my bed until recently, but she died."

"Your 'dead packmate' that the bloedzuiger mentioned?" Chloe prompted.

He nodded. After a moment he said, "Mary. Her name was Mary. She was from 1989, but she'd been here for a few years. This wasn't the first time she'd died here, but this time she didn't wake up."

"The bloedzuiger called me a replacement." Chloe didn't quite phrase it as a question, but it was one all the same.

"When one of us stays dead, someone else arrives." Jack's expression grew clouded. "There's no telling when it'll happen, why it happens, how to stop it. We were watching for you. That's how we found you so fast. I get a sense of when I should be expecting a new Arrival."

"So Mary died, and then . . . I arrived." She realized that they'd stopped walking and were standing in front of a store. Inside the store, three people who looked like the extra-thin sort-of-humans who had been at the tavern watched them with open curiosity. Chloe smiled at them politely, but their stares made her uncomfortable, so she turned back toward the Gulch House.

Jack kept pace with her. After several steps, she asked, "And Ajani?"

"I don't know if he gets a sense of Arrivals or if he just has spies. We don't know much about his doings until a few years before we arrived here. No one knows how old he is, how he got his money, what he wants. All I can say is that he makes the same offer to everyone—work for him, and he'll keep you alive and wealthy. Some people say yes." Jack didn't look at her as he spoke: his gaze was fixed on the street in front of him. "Melody went with him briefly a while back, but after a few months, she returned to us. I'll admit to wondering if she told him you were here, but it doesn't much matter. He always finds out."

Chloe let all of this settle into the increasing clarity she was finding about her new situation. It wasn't clarity of the oh-that's-logical variety, but it was information that fit together to help her start to make better sense of the situation. "So she—Mary—was in your bed, and I'm the replacement for her there too? Do all the new women—"

"No." He gave her a hard look. "Mary and I were friends of a sort. After a time, we got so that we enjoyed a bit of comfort together. I hadn't planned for what happened earlier. It *did* happen, though, and..."

They'd reached the Gulch House. She stopped and prompted him, "And...?"

"And I'm not sorry it did. Mary and I... we were friends who enjoyed each other, but I don't see the sense in much else. You interest me, and I like the look of you." He sighed and rubbed a hand over his face, as if he could wipe away the weariness and the stress.

She didn't know what to say. She wasn't looking for anything either. "I just got out of a relationship," she said carefully, "and I've got a long list of bad ones before that."

Jack nodded.

"That murder bit?" she continued. "It was a man I'd been seeing... Jason. He did some things, hurt me. One night I was drunk, and I decided to stop him from hurting me again..." She let the words fade away. For years, talking about *that* hadn't been wise. Even though she was in an entirely new world now, the long-held habit of silence was still hard to shake. She could've avoided that last night with Jason; she decided to kill him instead, to put an end to it before a night came when she *couldn't* escape. She hadn't ever once said that aloud. Her testimony in court wasn't a full lie, but there were some omissions and a bit of careful shading of the facts. The whole truth would only have made sense to someone who'd understood what Jason was capable of doing. The well-dressed men and women in the court weren't going to be able to fathom what a man like Jason was like. She'd known that—just as surely as she knew that Jack might know it too. After the cyns in the desert and the monks and everything else in Gallows, she knew that Jack hadn't ever led a sheltered life. He was a realist, so she told him what she wouldn't tell Melody in the tavern. "Some men don't let go. I made sure Jason wasn't going to hunt me down some night."

Jack held her gaze for a moment, but there was no judgment in his eyes. All he said was, "If you want to keep walking, we can. If you want someone else to keep you company right now, I can get one of the others."

"No." She shook her head. "But being inside an actual room would be nice."

She waited for him to ask her to clarify, but he didn't. He nodded and opened the door for her.

Once her eyes adjusted from the bright sun to the shadowed room, she realized that none of the others were in the tavern. Jack asked a few questions of people, and then he led her farther into the building and out another door into a small, enclosed yard where they found the proprietor. The fenced-in space reminded her of a beer garden, a space where people could enjoy the sunlight or smoke. So many places at home were all no smoking now that some bars seemed to have bigger crowds outside than in. Here, smoking was apparently *not* banned. The garden seemed mostly to be a space for customers to play some sort of games, none of which she recognized. On various tables, faded game boards were painted. The man Jack sought came toward them, and in a few moments they had directions to the location of their rooms.

Once they were inside again, Jack pointed out, "I don't know what the others are doing. They could be out, or in the rooms." He paused, motioning her to what appeared to be a wood-and-mud staircase. "I can knock, find Katherine or Melody, and you can—"

"I trust you, Jack," she said softly. "I'd like to come to your room."

He was silent as they walked up to the third floor.

On the third floor, he pointed to an empty chair in the hall. "Edgar and Katherine are up here, or Hector would be on guard still."

"Do you need to check in with them?" Chloe asked, surprised by the sense of disappointment she felt.

Jack looked at her with that serious expression again, and then said, "I'd rather not. My sister is a bit temperamental, and right now she's liable to take her anger all out on me." He gave Chloe a sheepish smile. "I wouldn't mind postponing that."

Chloe nodded, and they made their way to the last room, the one the innkeeper had called the "spacious" room. When Jack opened the door, she had to shake her head. If *this* was the spacious room, she half suspected they'd all be sleeping standing up against a wall in the other ones. The bed was admittedly wider than a twin, but much smaller than the queen bed she had in her apartment in D.C. A privacy screen hid what she assumed would be a toilet of some sort. The walls were bare. The privacy screen itself was a little more interesting: a painting of a forest covered the whole thing. The bed linens were deep green, and a worn but serviceable green rug was spread on the floor beside the bed. The rug was irregular in shape, and as Chloe looked at it, she realized that it was made of feathers of some sort.

Jack noticed where her attention was directed and said, "It's soft, but doesn't get dirty. The pelt is damn near water repellent, so they hold up well in inns." He crouched down to touch the rug. "I still can't get over some of the things here. I have a couple of these. I try to keep one at each of the camps."

Chloe kicked off her boots and went over to stand on it. "Wow." She wriggled her toes in the feathers and closed her eyes for a moment, enjoying the sensation. "That's better than any fur I've felt."

"Better than any back home at least," he agreed.

Chloe glanced down at him. He was smiling up at her, and aside from the fact that they were discussing a rug made from a bird, she could almost think they were two average people having a normal conversation. Sure, he still looked very much the cowboy, and he'd healed from a serious gunshot wound in a matter of hours. She'd tried her damnedest to find normal back home, though, and it had never made her feel what she felt here in the decidedly abnormal world with a man who'd been born a century before her.

Jack stood, and the already tiny room seemed even smaller. "I'd offer you a seat, but I'm not sure whether the rug or the bed is more comfortable."

"You can't tell me that bed is as soft as the rug."

"I *could,*" he drawled. "Sadly, lying's probably not going to get me into your good graces."

She poked him in the side, and he let out a sound that seemed suspiciously like a laugh.

"You're *ticklish*?" She shook her head and reached out again.

"Chloe," Jack started in what she suspected was to be a warning. It was too late, though, because she already had her fingertips on his side.

"Yes?"

"I am not," Jack said, but he grabbed her wrist to stop her from tickling him.

She lifted her gaze to meet his. For a moment they were motionless. Then she snaked out her other hand and tickled him again.

His laughter made him seem like a different person, just a regular man—a sexy-as-hell one, but not one who had the sort of edges that made her remember to be cautious. Earlier in the desert and a few minutes ago outside, Jack had been intense. In a fight, he'd been deadly. During all of it, he'd been in control. Suddenly, though, the far-too-serious cowboy was replaced with someone far more captivating: he was *real.*

When Jack grabbed her other hand, Chloe started backing away.

Her legs bumped up against the bed, and she let herself lean back, pulling him down on top of her.

He released her hand and caught himself so he didn't fall on top of her. Even so, he covered her with a not unwelcome weight, and she admitted that there was something altogether perfect about having a man as strong as Jack up against her. She wasn't one for the oversize gym rats at home, but she appreciated the rocklike hardness of a body toned by hard work.

Unlike in the desert, she was clear enough of mind now to make a sound decision—although if she were totally honest with herself, she'd admit that she'd made the decision before they even entered the building. She liked him; she'd felt a clarity of purpose in him when he was in danger. She wanted him to be okay, to be around to talk to; she wanted to be beside him. With the hand he was no longer holding, she reached up and trailed her fingertips over his face.

"What are we doing here, Chloe?"

She didn't want to say all of those things she was thinking. She just wanted to feel him. The thin layers of her skirt and his trousers seemed far too restrictive. She arched her hips upward against him and watched him go still.

In one swift movement, his hand released hers and clasped her hip, holding her motionless, keeping her from repeating the action. "Those ungentlemanly thoughts I mentioned? This isn't helping with them." He stared down at her. "Tell me yes, or tell me to stop."

Chloe tugged him down to her and kissed him. His fingers dug into her hip with bruising pleasure, but he didn't move beyond kissing her. So she stopped kissing him long enough to say, "That's a yes."

"Thank God." He released her hip and pressed down into her, at the same time reaching up to cup her face with one hand as he kissed her again.

Too soon he pulled away, but only long enough to remove the gun holstered at her hip. "Not comfortable," he murmured. He unfastened his holster too, and after a few practiced moves, he'd unarmed both of them and put their weapons safely on the floor.

Absently, she noticed that he'd locked the door when they came into the room and that the weapons were still within easy reach, but then he ran one hand up the length of her still-exposed leg while he tugged off one of his boots.

Before he could remove the second boot, she'd grown impatient and pushed him down on to the bed—which was definitely not as soft as the rug.

All of her doubts had vanished, or maybe just fallen into silence at the feel of Jack's body against hers. There wasn't an *un*toned muscle on him, and his kisses were the sort that spoke of confidence and skill. Even if this was a mistake, it was feeling very much like the sort of mistake that included several orgasms.

Between kisses, they'd shed both of their shirts, and her skirt was bunched up at her waist. His trousers were unfastened, but he hadn't yet yanked off the second boot. She was about to insist he remedy that when he murmured, "Your lack of undergarments is still distracting."

Chloe swallowed and started to apologize, but her words were lost in a gasp as Jack slid down her body and lowered his mouth to demonstrate one of the benefits of forgoing undergarments.

After the first orgasm rolled her eyes back and her hips upward, she ordered in a decidedly languid voice, "Less trousers. More naked." She exhaled and tried again, succeeding at a slightly firmer tone. "More naked *now*."

He laughed and nipped her thigh. "Yes, ma'am."

But before he could comply, someone knocked on the door.

"Jack?" Edgar called. "I need to talk to you."

Chloe started to pull away, but Jack clamped his hands tighter on her thighs. He lifted his head, glared at the door, and said, "No."

She wasn't sure whether he was saying no to her moving or to Edgar.

"Jack!" Edgar repeated in a louder voice. "Are you awake?"

"Hold on. Mary and I are—" Jack cut himself off midsentence.

Chloe's sharp intake of breath made him look at her, and she saw the regret in his expression. It didn't come close to halting the wave of embarrassment and stupidity she felt washing over her.

In a low voice he told her, "I didn't mean . . . Damn it."

Carefully, Chloe rolled out from under him and looked for her missing bra and shirt. She forced her embarrassment to stay out of her voice and said only, "Go see what he needs."

Then she turned her back to him as she hurriedly re-dressed.

"Chloe." He put a hand on her shoulder, but she didn't look back at him.

"Jack?" Edgar called again. "You need to see Francis." There was no mistaking the seriousness in his voice.

He squeezed her shoulder. "Chloe . . . just . . . I'll be back as soon as I can. Just stay here."

Chloe didn't reply. There weren't any words that either of them could say that would make her feel less like a fool, and she knew that he couldn't stay to talk anyhow. She also didn't want to walk out of the room with him. Truthfully, she wasn't entirely sure *what* she wanted to have happen at this point, but she knew that Jack needed to look after his team and check on the injured man.

He lingered for a moment; the only sound in the room was their breathing. He obviously had no idea what to say to her. His hand dropped from her shoulder, and she wasn't sure whether that was better or worse.

"Go on," she said.

Jack scowled and called, "I'll be right out." Then he stepped in front of her. "I'll be back as soon as I can. It was just habit, Chloe.... I *know* who I'm here with." He caught her face in his hand and held her steady as he looked into her eyes. "Chloe? Do you hear me?"

She nodded, took a deep breath, and tried to smile. She didn't answer. What else could he say? He obviously wasn't over Mary, and she wasn't interested in being the stand-in for his dead lover. She'd told him the secret she'd held for years. She'd bared more than her body to him. *This was a mistake. We were high, and we made a mistake.* It was Alcoholics 101: bad choices when fucked up. She'd feared as much when they were in the desert; she just hadn't expected to be proven right so quickly.

Jack left, closing the door quietly behind him, and she could hear low voices as he and Edgar discussed whatever crisis had befallen Francis. For a moment Chloe sat on the bed. Then, when the voices had departed, she picked up her boots and her gun. She holstered her gun, carefully opened the door, and stepped outside the room with her boots still in her hand. She couldn't bring herself to stay in Jack's room. She knew she probably should, but she couldn't. She didn't know which room was *hers* either—or if he expected that she was going to stay with him.

Maybe she was overreacting, but she'd felt more at ease with Jack than with anyone else in the group, and now, because of a stupid decision, that had changed. She wasn't looking for forever, but she wasn't starting out her life in a new world with a one-nighter in which she was a stand-in. Attacks by monsters, drinking addictive blood, killing a monk... it was all more than a little overwhelming. Somehow, though, the fact that she'd started her time in a new world with the exact same bad taste in men she'd proven to have in her old world was the final straw in a whole truckload of fucked up. She needed some air.

Once she saw that the coast was clear, Chloe pulled the door shut carefully so as not to make any noise and crept down the hall as quickly and silently as she could. She just needed to get out of Jack's room and think. Staying here would lead to a stupid argument or trying to ignore being called another woman's name. Neither option was one she could accept.

# CHAPTER 26

Jack couldn't say he wanted to stay and talk to Chloe, but he knew he'd have to and only hoped that she wasn't too angry—or worse yet, *weepy*—when he returned to the room. He wasn't going to go all namby-pamby with emotions or anything, but he figured he owed Chloe a little more explanation than he'd offered. Unfortunately, he didn't exactly have an explanation beyond what he said: Mary was the only one in his bed the past couple years, so it was an honest mistake. She'd only been gone a little while. He'd meant it when he told Chloe he didn't expect her to replace Mary in his bed just because she was here. Hell, it wasn't like Mary had replaced someone either. It just happened that Mary was his friend, and Chloe was . . . he wasn't sure what. He liked her in a way that he hadn't expected, and it had nothing to do with replacing Mary. The timing was a bit awkward, and if not for the Verrot, he suspected that he'd have been better able to resist his interest, given them time to get to know each other first. Regardless of the timing, though, he felt something unexpected and *good* for Chloe. Back home, in another world and another life, he'd have thought about courting her, but this wasn't that world.

*And I'm not that man anymore.*

Even though he couldn't court her, he still wanted . . . something.

He couldn't believe that his interest was just a result of Verrot and grief. He knew it wasn't—he also knew he couldn't start figuring out what he and Chloe were doing until he tended to whatever Francis needed.

Edgar shoved aside the chair that leaned against the wall outside the door and opened the door to Francis' room. It was a tinier version of Jack's, and one he'd slept in from time to time over the years. Not a whole lot ever changed in Gallows. The rooms to let were all pretty familiar by now. Like a lot of the rooms at the Gulch, this one had two narrow beds, a privacy screen, and a small stand with a washbasin. Several folded cloths were stacked next to the washbasin.

He and Jack stepped inside the confining space only to be greeted by his baby sister aiming a pistol at them. Edgar held his hands out in a placating gesture and opened his mouth to apologize.

Before he could speak, Katherine snapped, "Knock or say something when you open the door. Goddamn monks and Ajani and his thugs are all roaming around town. I could've shot you."

"Sorry, Kit," Edgar rumbled.

Francis laughed. "Somebody's in her mother-bear mode."

With a sigh, Katherine lowered the gun and reached over to pat his shoulder. "Well, you're a good cub."

"*Some* of us aren't lousy patients," Francis teased her. Then he turned his head in the direction of Edgar's voice. "Jack, are you here too?"

"Right here." Jack looked at the blood leaking out of one of Francis' closed eyes. Upon closer inspection, he could see that it wasn't just blood. The liquid was too watery, as well as being more pink than red. "Does it burn? Hurt? What can you tell us?"

"Both eyes hurt, but this one feels like it's on fire." Francis paused as Katherine wiped his cheek again, and then he added, "I'm not healing at all, Jack. Kitty wants to believe it's just a little slow, but even without the Verrot, I should've stopped bleeding by now. The other one shouldn't be still blinded either. Something's wrong."

"Hush! You'll be fine," Katherine murmured. "We just need to figure it out. Garuda's on it, and God knows you have enough herbs back at camp. We'll brew something up, get some Verrot into you, and you'll be as good as new."

"I hope so," Francis said in a wavering voice.

Katherine's expression was more openly worried than it usually was when one of the group was injured, but Jack figured that was because Francis couldn't see her.

As she wiped Francis' blood streaks away, she lifted her other hand and held her index finger in front of her lips with a "shhh" gesture.

Jack nodded, letting her know that he understood, and then he gestured to the door.

"Are you all mouthing words at each other or staring at me in silence?" Francis prompted. He turned his head toward them, eyes still closed, and added, "If you're not going to talk about plans in front of me, go somewhere else and do it. I need help, not pity."

"Francis . . ." Katherine started, but her words faltered.

After a moment, Francis sighed and said, "It's okay, Kitty. Go talk to Jack. Edgar?"

"Still here," Edgar affirmed from where he stood learning against the wall. He glanced at Jack, who nodded in affirmation, before offering, "If Jack's with Kit, I'll stay here. I can't imagine Melody is much comfort with Verrot in her."

Francis snorted. "Why do you think Hector was in the hall? He needed to keep an eye out for trouble, and we all thought I might start randomly throwing knives if she was in my room much longer."

"Katherine and I will figure this out," Jack promised.

"Of course we will," Katherine murmured in the voice that Jack expected she'd have used with her own children. Carefully, she folded a rag and covered Francis' eye with it.

Without asking, Edgar ripped a strip of fabric off of another piece of cloth and handed it to her. As she'd done for so many years and to so many people, Katherine nursed Francis, tying the cloth to his eye so that it would keep the seeping blood, tears, and pus from dripping down his cheek. Jack watched her with the sudden awareness that part of her bond with Francis was simply that he shared nursing duties with her. She'd had a lot of years where the nurturing of the Arrivals was all on her shoulders, and Francis alleviated some of that burden—much as Edgar had shared Jack's own burden of keeping order or stepping into the worst of the fracases.

Katherine didn't look up from the knot she was tying to hold the makeshift bandage in place as she asked, "Where is Chloe?"

Jack wasn't about to admit anything to his sister, not because he'd done anything *wrong* per se, but because what had happened with Chloe wasn't anyone's business. "She's resting in my room."

"In *your* room?" Katherine's lips pressed together.

"You were with Francis, and she doesn't really know Hector or Melody and—"

"And you've been looking at her like she's a snack you intend to consume since she arrived," Katherine interrupted. "Seriously, Jackson, we don't even know if she's going to stay with us or join Ajani. You're right that she shouldn't be left alone, but until we know more about her, keep it in your pants."

There were a dozen different things Jack could tell his sister, but the sad truth was that she was right. Everyone who arrived in the Wasteland was a killer of some sort or another, and he knew better than to ignore that detail. The smart thing to do was to focus on work. That was how he'd kept his sanity the past twenty-six years: concentrate on the mission first, last, and always.

Katherine glared at him, as if daring him to tell her she was wrong, and Jack had the fleeting urge to do just that. Arguing wouldn't help either of them just then, though, so he changed the subject. "Let's talk to Garuda before we do anything else. If anyone knows what could be wrong, it's him."

Katherine's face took on that faraway look that Jack was already associating with conversations that she was silently having inside her mind. *How in the hell did I miss that all of these years?* She looked at Jack and said, "We could meet him tonight."

Jack nodded. He didn't admit it aloud, but he was grateful that they had a way to quickly reach the bloedzuiger. Garuda knew more about the Wasteland than anyone else Jack had met in all of the years he'd lived in it. If it was a poison that was causing Francis' condition, Garuda could find out what it was. If it was some sort of magic, he could direct them to the answers. Moments like this were why Jack found Garuda's friendship so invaluable. He dealt fine with killing things, but he wasn't sure what to do when one of the Arrivals was dealing with an injury that their peculiar biology wasn't healing. He'd been in the Wasteland longer than he'd been in the world he'd been born to, and he'd become accustomed to their healing abilities. "We can discuss other options too. Maybe send Melody and Hector back to camp to get the rest of the Verrot."

"Sure." Katherine glanced back at Francis, but didn't move.

Edgar walked to the door, opened it, and grabbed the chair that was in the hallway, presumably from Hector having been stationed there. Instead of closing the door, he looked at Katherine. "I'll take care of him, Kit. Go on."

Katherine kissed Francis' forehead, and then, gun in hand, stepped outside. Once she and Jack were in the hall, she asked, "Do you want to talk in one of the other rooms or . . . ?" She motioned toward his room.

"Yours will work. We can move Chloe to your room later if you aren't rooming with Edgar." Jack wasn't sure what he'd do if Katherine *was* staying with Edgar. He could order her to room with Chloe, but he'd much rather give Edgar and Katherine their space if they'd finally sorted out their drama—and even if Chloe wasn't feeling very forgiving, Jack would still rather share space with her. The floor of the room wasn't that hard, and he held hopes that they could get back to where they were before he'd screwed up. None of that emotional nonsense was anything he felt like discussing with his sister, though, so he asked, "Did you tell Garuda everything?"

"I did." She opened the door to the tiny room where she'd be sleeping. "He's been over toward the Divide, but he'll be here soon."

Jack followed her into the room and closed the door behind them. "Does he have any other ideas?"

"Poison." Katherine dropped to the floor with the sort of bone-tired motion that she didn't usually allow herself. "Monks. Ajani . . . or maybe the 'natural collapse of unnatural physiology.' That's the extent of the ideas Garuda had." She gave Jack a quiet look of desperation that reminded him far too much of their early years in the Wasteland, when the whole world was alien to them.

Jack responded the same way that he had all those years ago. He looked at his sister and tried to sound like he knew what he was doing. "We'll give him the Verrot. We'll talk to Garuda, and if we don't get anywhere, I'll go back to Governor Soanes. Either he knows something or . . . is involved. I'll figure it out, and everything will be fine."

And then he hoped to hell and heaven both that he wasn't lying.

# CHAPTER 27

When Chloe reached the ground floor, she half expected to see one of the Arrivals in the tavern, but none of them were in sight. Maybe they were all together dealing with whatever crisis had necessitated summoning Jack. Maybe some of them were out doing God knows what. All Chloe knew for certain was that if she stayed in the tavern, she'd be sampling whatever local liquor they had, and while that was a tempting idea, she'd already had Verrot—which hadn't exactly been a consequence-free experience. For that matter, neither had her bender back in D.C.; drinking there *or* here simply wasn't a good idea.

Somehow the fact that she had been in bed with Jack only minutes ago seemed more surreal than anything else that had happened since she'd woken up in this strange world. Unfortunately, it also seemed *less* surprising. She'd long ago stopped trying to pretend she was attracted to good men. Her dating record was a series of bad and worse decisions. She could blame a few of them on drunkenness, but the rest were some sort of quirk of biology: nice guys didn't attract her—or find her attractive. If substituting her for a dead girlfriend was the worst thing Jack did, he'd be one of the least awful of her mistakes. Bobby had failed to mention that the packages she'd picked up from his friend were kilos; Michael had forgotten to mention that when he said "ex-wife" he meant "wife who was all too happy to stab a girl for screwing him." Allan had spent more years in prison than he had in school. Isaiah was a great guy—up until he got so strung out that he half dragged, half carried her through a parking lot to an ATM so she'd withdraw money for his fix. They all seemed nice when she'd met them, often a little rough around the edges, but she was more comfortable with guys who filled out a pair of jeans. Men in suits, on the other hand, usually made her nervous. She'd only dated two suits: the first one was Jason, whom she'd killed; the second one screwed her boss and sent Chloe out on the bender that led to ending up in the Wasteland. In jeans or suits, the men she liked were trouble through and through.

"You'd think I'd get a goddamn clue," she muttered.

She stood motionless at the foot of the stairs. Maybe it was the Verrot wearing off, or maybe it was being in a weird new world, or maybe it was falling into a bed with another in the list of bad choices, but she just wanted to run away and hide. Running would attract even more attention, though, so Chloe smiled at several of the people in the low-lit room. Then she straightened her shoulders and walked purposefully toward the exit, ignoring the watchful gazes of the tavern dwellers. There were those who looked like men and others she wasn't sure how to identify. She didn't know exactly what defined a man. The large-eared, short, stocky beings who stood in the darker shadows and the slightly willowy ones who stayed near the few windows all looked mostly human until she let her gaze linger. Small details became more obvious with a closer look, and soon she wasn't sure which was the more unsettling: the "slightly other" creatures or the vastly different ones like the bloedzuigers. Somehow, she'd come a world away from the home she'd known, yet here she was feeling the same flash of hurt and anger.

And as she had experienced at home, she found herself needing to walk in order to clear her head. This time she wasn't looking for a tavern at the end of the walk. That was progress. She'd clear her head, and when she got back to the inn, she'd pretend none of the nonsense with Jack had happened. That plan made better sense than the path she'd been on before she and Jack were interrupted.

Chloe stepped outside into the full desert sunlight and blinked against the brightness. The harshness of it reminded her that she didn't know enough about the desert to set out across it. The Wasteland was filled with monsters, and the few bullets she had in her gun weren't going to get her very far. Maybe she could stay in town; she'd just need to find someone willing to hire her so she could earn enough to afford food and shelter. She needed to find her feet. That meant finding some independence, and *that* required a job.

She stepped into the street and started walking. She didn't have a lot of skills that seemed likely to be useful here—modern technology wasn't something she'd seen any evidence of so far—but she could carry a tray or push a broom. She was walking down a different street than the one she'd traversed with Jack a few hours earlier, but she'd yet to see a sign advertising work. Much to her relief, she'd also not seen Hector or Melody.

At the next intersection, Chloe found a man strolling toward her with a friendly look on his face. He smiled but didn't bow his head in that almost old-fashioned way of so many people here.

She smiled politely as he approached.

"You're Chloe, right? Kitty's friend? I heard she was in Gallows with someone new." He held out his hand. "I'm Daniel."

Chloe hesitated, but then shook his hand. "Hi."

"Is Kitty still in one of the shops?" Daniel looked at the nearby buildings before lowering his voice conspiratorially and adding, "She does have a habit of getting caught up in her shopping sometimes. I've spent a good number of hours standing in the street just like you wait-ing on her to decide between things, only to find that she'd bought both rather than choosing one." He laughed quietly.

Chloe smiled. "I'm not sure where she is right now. I was just taking a walk."

Daniel frowned a little before offering, "May I escort you, then?"

"I'm not going anywhere in particular," she hedged. Daniel seemed nice enough, but she wanted to be left alone.

"First time in Gallows?" he pressed.

She nodded.

"It's not always safe for strangers to be out on their own here. I can show you the high points until Kit's free. Come on." He turned and started traveling back in the direction he'd just come from. When she didn't follow him, he queried, "Unless you were meeting someone else . . . ?"

"No."

After a slight pause, he smiled cheerily at her and added, "Then here we are." He pointed toward a market of some sort. "That's Billbee's. They specialize in local produce, but sometimes they carry luxuries from out past the Divide. Fair prices." He pointed at a dark-shuttered building that she'd have assumed was closed. "That's Mill's place. He handles money lending around here. Privacy guaranteed, but the rates are absurd."

Chloe was struggling to be friendly. Daniel seemed like a nice enough man, and he certainly wasn't hard on the eyes. Maybe he'd be a nice distraction from the confusing way she felt about Jack. She flushed guiltily at that thought. Daniel was a friend of Kitty's, and he was of-fering to help her, and she was coldly thinking of him as a distraction.

"Chloe?" Daniel prompted. "Are you all right?"

"It's been a difficult couple of days," she admitted.

Daniel paused, as if he were considering the situation. Then he suggested, "Join me for a meal? I'm staying at the edge of Gallows, and my host has a comfortable sitting room and a wonderful cook."

"I don't know." She folded her arms over her chest. Partly, she thought that a harmless distraction was exactly what she needed. It had been a lousy few days, and a good meal with a friendly Wastelander sounded nice. Unfortunately, that didn't mean she could trust this guy that easily. "I'm not very good company today, and I'm sure you have better things to do."

"Better than time with a beautiful woman?" He laughed softly. "There aren't too many things better than that, especially in the Wasteland."

"I'm not . . ." She shook her head. "I don't know you."

"We can go ask Kitty or one of the others about me. Better yet, if you want, you go, and I'll just wait right here," Daniel offered.

For a moment, Chloe considered it. Going back, though, wasn't something she was ready to do just yet. "I wanted to look around at jobs. I just got into town, and I should concentrate on getting settled," she hedged. It wasn't an excuse, not completely at least.

Daniel smiled at her. "I've lived here for years, Chloe. I can help you with that one too."

"Why?"

"You're a friend of Kitty's, and Gallows can be rough, and none of the Arrivals are here with you." He seemed like a nice enough man as he implored, "Join me, please? You look like you could use a friend, and I know what that feels like."

"Okay," she said quietly, deciding to trust her instincts. "An actual meal sounds nice, but I need to let them know where I went."

"Of course!" Daniel looked around, and then he beckoned a man over to them. "Could you take a message to"—he glanced at Chloe—"the Gulch House, I assume? That's usually where Kitty stays."

Mutely, Chloe nodded.

"Tell Katherine Reed, the Arrival woman, that her friend Chloe is joining me for dinner," Daniel said. He glanced at Chloe, smiled, and then added, "Oh, and let Kitty know that she's welcome to join us as well."

They were in a desert where a harsh sun beat down and the simple act of breathing caused sweat to trickle down Chloe's skin. Despite that, Daniel offered her his arm, a gesture as out of place in the desert as everything else about him. After a moment's hesitation, she took it. The material of his shirt felt like silk of some sort, slithery soft under her hand.

As they walked through the dusty town, Chloe weighed her words carefully. She had only one gun and a few bullets, and she was walking through a strange town with a man she'd only just met. She'd already given her trust too easily to the other man she'd met here. "I don't trust you," she said levelly. "I'm agreeing to dinner, but that doesn't mean we're friends or anything—or that I'll be giving up my gun."

"That's logical." Daniel gave her a sympathetic smile. "You should keep your gun. This is a dangerous world."

Chloe nodded, feeling both appeased and foolish.

"I know you're one of them," Daniel continued. "Gallows is a small town, and anything to do with the Arrivals elicits interest. What year are you from?"

"Two thousand and thirteen," she murmured.

He nodded. "Things there are probably a lot different there than here. I think it was easier for the others. This world is more familiar to those who lived in harsher times."

"Some things are timeless," she suggested, thinking about the way she felt for Jack, the way the natives looked at her and the other Arrivals, the simple need to find food and shelter no matter when or where a person was.

"I can't imagine it's been easy," Daniel murmured.

A trio of women and one creature of indeterminate gender waved and called to them from a balcony.

"Do you know them?" Chloe asked.

"They're doxies," Daniel said conversationally. "Not one of the worst of the brothels, but one that caters to unusual appetites."

"Oh." Chloe looked again at the four beings. Nothing about their dress or the building confirmed his claim, but nothing disproved it either.

They walked in silence until they reached a building that was much nicer than anything else Chloe had seen. Where the other structures all looked weathered, this one looked like it had been recently constructed.

"Here we are," he said. "Would you like to eat first or enjoy a hot bath? The servants can prepare one for you, and I suspect you might enjoy washing away the sand."

Chloe blinked at him. "This is your home?"

"No. I'm just staying here."

As they approached the building, a servant opened the door. Just inside the door another waited to remove their shoes and wash their feet. At the same time a third servant brushed their clothing off, and the servant who'd opened the door swept the dust outside. Chloe didn't know whether this was ostentation or practicality. If she and Daniel kept their footwear on, they'd track dirt and sand everywhere.

One of the servants said, "We prepared your bath."

Daniel caught Chloe's gaze. "Why don't you take it? I'll wait for you in the conservatory." When she hesitated, he added, "You'll feel refreshed. Then we'll dine, talk, and relax. Maybe Kitty will even arrive by the time you join me."

The temptation was hard to resist. After the hours of fever and the fights, an actual soak in a tub would be wonderful. She'd bathed in the tent, but it hadn't been a proper shower. "Thank you," she said.

And just like that, she was whisked away by yet another servant. As she followed the silent woman through the darkened hallway, Chloe had to admit to herself that this was a vast improvement over both the camp where she'd been staying and the Gulch House.

# CHAPTER 28

Kitty and Jack had very little luck coming up with a plan beyond "research cures." They debated and discussed as Jack alternated between pacing and sitting. All the while Edgar remained with Francis, and neither Hector nor Melody returned to the inn. Unlike the rest of the Arrivals, Melody wasn't particularly quiet unless she was hunting—which meant that they all always knew when she returned. It wasn't Melody or Hector who had Jack so jumpy, though. Only a fool would mistake his uncharacteristic tension for normal post-conflict or even post-Verrot agitation. Whatever was going on with Chloe had Jack as jittery as a june bug. Kitty was trying not to pry, but while they discussed options, Jack's gaze darted to the door every few minutes in hopes of hearing a knock that wasn't coming.

"So we wait on Garuda," he said again.

"Yesss," Kitty stretched the word a bit more than she meant to, and then added, "And if Hector isn't back soon, you and I or Edgar and I can head out to camp to get the Verrot."

They'd discussed that exact thing not two minutes ago.

"Right. That's good." Jack looked at the door again.

"That's *it*," Kitty snapped.

"What?"

"Your attention is not on business," she pointed out. When he remained silent, she leaned back in her chair and asked, "Do you really think she's sleeping?"

"No." He focused his attention on Kitty, looking as guilty as she'd ever seen him.

"What did you do?"

For a moment he said nothing. He didn't squirm, that wasn't Jack's way, but he did come to his feet and pace the length of the small room. He looked out the tiny window down at what Kitty knew to be an uninteresting view of the dusty street.

Finally, with his back still to her, he said, "I called her Mary." He glanced over his shoulder at Kitty and clarified: "It wasn't like I called her Mary when I was talking directly *to* her, but Edgar knocked and I said that 'Mary and I' were busy."

Kitty tried to hold her brother's gaze, but he looked away. So she pointed out, "She's just arrived, and even if she *had* been here awhile, it's not a crisis to call someone the wrong name usually." She watched him tense, so she continued: "Now, I can see a woman being upset if, say, she'd been intimate with someone and *then* or dur—"

"No." Jack cut her off. He turned to face her, crossed his arms over his chest, and scowled. "It wasn't during, and we hadn't had . . . *relations*. We just . . . Damn it, Katherine, it's not something a man discusses with his sister."

Calmly, Kitty suggested, "It might be something that you want to discuss with Chloe instead of letting her stew on it."

This time, he did squirm. His expression was troubled, and he darted another look at the still-closed door and then back at his sister. "I was trying to let her have some space."

"Coward." Kitty grinned at her brother. Seeing him off-kilter was rare, so she couldn't help but take a moment's amusement from it.

"Fishwife."

Kitty laughed. "Spineless fop."

"Hoyden." Jack's tension had visibly lessened, and a thread of a smile curled his lips.

"Do you want me to talk to her?"

He gave Kitty a grateful look. "Would you?"

"You'll still need to tell her you were an ass, and that you ought to have known better. You probably ought to beg, but at the very least, rustle up some of that gambler's charm you used to know how to use." Kitty patted him on the arm, and then she went to find Chloe.

It was a little ridiculous that a man Jack's age could find a bit of muslin so scary, but he'd never had a real relationship. There were women he rolled around with, women he'd rented, and women he'd called friends of a sort. Kitty couldn't remember ever seeing him act like a fool over one, though. Part of her approved of it, but the rest of her hoped she wouldn't have to shoot Chloe. The woman seemed decent enough so far, but decent enough wasn't exactly the same as deserving-of-Jack.

Kitty tapped on the door of the room that Jack always rented. She called out, "Chloe?"

When no one answered, she tried again in a louder voice. "Chloe, it's Kitty. Are you awake?"

There was still no answer, so Kitty turned the knob and found the door unlocked. Out of years of habit, her hand went to her gun. *Just in case.* She repeated herself as she walked into the room, "Chloe? It's Kitty."

A quick survey proved that it was empty. A slower look verified that nothing of Chloe's remained in it either. After Kitty looked around to assure herself that there were no signs of struggle or anything amiss, she left the room, pulling the door closed. Logic said the other Arrivals would have heard if anyone were outside the rooms they'd rented.

Francis' quarters were only a couple of doors away, and Chloe would've had the sense to raise a ruckus if someone *had* managed to creep in quietly.

With a sinking feeling, Kitty returned to Jack. When she walked into her room, he looked past her to the hallway, his gaze clearly seeking the absent Chloe.

"She's not there," Kitty said.

In an instant, Jack was on his feet and out the door. He didn't race down the stairs, but he moved quickly enough that Kitty had to scurry to keep up with him. Chloe wasn't in the main drinking room or in the attached courtyard. None of the other Arrivals were in sight either.

Outside, Jack stopped and scanned the street. None of their people were there either. His expression was one of worry, not anger, and Kitty hoped that Chloe hadn't wandered off and gotten herself into trouble. In many ways, she was safer here than in the desert. Many of the Wastelanders were unlikely to start trouble with one of the Arrivals, but they didn't know Chloe yet. They might think she was simply a Wastelander they didn't know, a stranger passing through town.

As Jack started prowling the streets, Kitty kept one hand loosely at her side in case she needed to draw. The thought of the joint threats of more monks and of Ajani's people made her more than a little uneasy, but it wasn't like they had backup handy. Edgar was with Francis; Melody and Hector were who knows where. Typically, with Jack at her side, Kitty wouldn't worry overmuch, but between the dangers out there, the poison that was currently blinding Francis, and Jack's unexpectedly emotional state, she wished she could summon the other Arrivals to her side. She couldn't, but there *was* someone she could call on for help.

*"Garuda?"*

In Kitty's mind, she felt the doorway to Garuda open up. He'd been being very courteous about keeping it closed, and she suspected that her conversations with him—and her confession to Jack—had made the old bloedzuiger behave better than he usually did. Typically, he was a nuisance when she'd taken Verrot.

*"Is someone else injured?"* Garuda's normally calm voice was less carefully modulated, and Kitty could hear the worry. *"It's not Jackson or your mate, is it?"*

*"No."* She smiled despite herself before adding, *"Or me."*

Garuda tsked at her. *"Of course it's not you. I'd have known."*

Kitty filed that detail away. *"Chloe is missing. Has any of your pack seen her?"*

*"No."* After a heartbeat's pause, Garuda said, *"They are seeking her now."*

As Kitty waited for more information, she continued walking alongside Jack. They'd reached one of the brothels that never seemed to completely close. It was early for business, but that didn't stop the girls from hanging over the balconies or from the windows watching for anyone ready to be parted from his or her money. The business wasn't something that made Kitty uncomfortable, but she didn't like how eagerly the brothels tried to recruit Arrivals. Wastelanders might not find them acceptable to date or wed, but they'd pay premium for a taste. That attitude made Kitty froth at the mouth—which was precisely why Jack insisted that the Arrivals not accept free pleasure from the prostitutes *and* why he wouldn't allow any of the team to take on any side work at the brothels. If they were on the team, they were expected not to sell their flesh, and if they had need of comfort they couldn't find in camp, they paid for their business at the same rate as the locals did.

Of course, his attempt to have the Arrivals treated like the Wastelanders treated each other only served to make him more desirable to the brothel girls. He tipped his head to them when they called out, "Jack!"

Kitty shot them a quelling look, but they only waved and smiled.

"If you're looking for your new Arrival, she took off walking with Daniel," one of the girls called out.

"Willingly?" Jack's shoulders visibly tensed.

"Looked like it," the girl said.

In Kitty's mind, she heard Garuda confirm what the girl was saying. Quietly, she murmured to Jack, "Garuda says the girl is right."

Jack didn't reply, but a look of fury crossed his face. Whatever Chloe had said or done, she seemed to have caught his attention in a way no one else had—and right now Kitty wanted to kill her for it. Jack was the together one, the person who kept them all sane in this crazy world. He was the calm in a sea of chaos, and because of Chloe he was hurting. Kitty felt betrayed and more than a little unsettled.

*"A lot of the Arrivals talk to Ajani,"* Garuda reminded her. *"Daniel is simply expediting the process."*

*"Please don't be reasonable right now,"* she implored. *"Find me the cure for Francis. I'll handle Jack."*

As Garuda retreated, another of the women bent forward over the railing, offering a generous view of her bosom. "I could make you feel better, Jackson."

"Not today." Jack looked in the direction of Ajani's local residence.

"Jack?" Kitty put a hand on her brother's forearm. When he looked at her, she said, "Maybe Daniel didn't take her to—"

"Katherine . . ." Jack started in that lecturing tone of his.

But Kitty wasn't in the mood for his high-and-mighty act. She held up a hand. "If Daniel took her to Ajani—which admittedly, makes sense—she'll make a choice. We don't even know that she went there. Daniel might just find her . . ." Her words dwindled; there was no good way to say that the woman who'd been warming the sheets of her brother's bed might find Daniel's companionship enjoyable. Cautiously, she added, "Whatever she decides, it's not *your* fault."

The hurt in her brother's eyes was far too similar to the way he'd looked when Mary hadn't woken up, and Kitty decided right then that she'd be putting a bullet in Chloe next time their paths crossed if the woman *did* decide to work for Ajani. Hell, she might do it as well if Chloe opted to become Daniel's lover. No woman worth anything would choose to work for Ajani or screw Daniel when Jackson wanted her. It seemed downright ridiculous that he'd gotten so smitten after only a few conversations and a bit of rough-and-tumble, but as Kitty looked at his face, it was pretty damn clear to her that he had.

"Francis needs us." She felt a twinge of guilt for forcing her brother to focus on Francis, but she didn't know what else to do.

Jack was silent.

"Please? If you go into Ajani's house, he can come into ours," she added. "He can come after me."

Her brother looked at her. "I'd never do anything to endanger you."

"Then come back with me now," Kitty pleaded.

He nodded. Years ago Jack and Ajani had come to a gentleman's agreement on the protocol for dealing with the Arrivals. It wasn't quite the extreme etiquette that bloedzuigers followed, but it was awfully near to it. Unlike most of the Arrivals the past few years, Jack was from a time when a man's word mattered. Ajani was . . . well, no one knew for sure what he was or where he was from, but whatever his history, he had abided by the agreement. Ajani might not be willing to share anything about his history, but he kept his word the way Jack did. If Chloe was in any of Ajani's houses by choice, there was nothing Jack could do about it—just as the reverse was true.

After another moment in which he looked like he was struggling for self-control, Jack turned and headed back toward the Gulch House. "Tell Edgar we're headed out to camp to get the Verrot. Tell Garuda we'll see him in the desert."

# CHAPTER 29

Jack steadfastly walked back to the Gulch House to gather his gear before heading out to meet Garuda. As he'd stood in the street with his sister, he'd considered throwing everything away—over a woman he'd only met a couple of days ago. It was completely illogical. There were rules, ones that had been in place for over two decades, ones that Jack couldn't violate without throwing safety so far out of reach that there would be no return. Ajani wouldn't meddle with the Arrivals if they sided with Jack, and if they went with Ajani, Jack wouldn't interfere. He and Ajani had agreed not to use force or coercion. In truth, those rules aided Jack more than Ajani. If not for the gentleman's agreement they'd made, Ajani could attempt to take Katherine by force. Even with the rules in place, Jack and Edgar still did everything they could to keep Katherine from being out and about on her own.

And Jack had just left her standing in the street when he'd turned back toward the Gulch House. He glanced over his shoulder and, with no small amount of relief, saw Katherine walking toward him.

"I'm fine," he lied when she caught up with him.

She smiled, but she still looked worried. "I know. It's just a lot to deal with lately. We'll figure it out. Francis will be fine, and we can do the job with one less person anyhow." When he didn't respond, she added, "Chloe might not even choose Ajani, Jack. Let it go."

"I know you trust Daniel, but he's not our friend." Jack didn't quite understand how his sister managed to hold on to her tenderness for Daniel, but he wasn't having a great deal of luck understanding his own emotions just then. It wasn't that he loved Chloe; he didn't even know her well enough to *like* her all that much. All he could say was that he felt a spark, and after so many years of thinking he wasn't even capable of such a thing, he was eager to find out what could come of it.

"Daniel's not evil," Katherine said quietly. "I'm not saying he's good, or even that he meant anything other than to take Chloe to Ajani. I'm just suggesting you be a little patient."

"I know, but Chloe was out there alone because I fucked up. First the Verrot, then the . . . what we almost did when we were in the desert." Jack didn't want to meet his sister's eyes, so he resumed walking. "And then after we were about to . . . finish what we started in the desert, I called her another woman's name. What reason did she have to *stay*?"

"In the desert *and* here? I know you were upset over losing Mary, but . . ." Katherine's words faded, and she shook her head at him.

They walked silently for a minute before Jack said, "I didn't love Mary. I wanted to. Hell, *she* wanted me to, but I didn't. Whatever Chloe is, she isn't a replacement for Mary."

"So tell her that when you see her even if she's in *his* house," Katherine suggested. "That's not breaking the rules. Daniel does it; Ajani does it. They both tell me to join them all the damn time. You just have to be willing to swallow your pride and say your piece in front of whoever's there."

"They'd love that, wouldn't they?" he said bitterly.

"It's either that or accept that she's in Ajani's house now, and as long as she's there, if she warms anyone's bed, it can't be yours."

The thought of Chloe in Ajani's or Daniel's bed was enough to make Jack stop midstep. He didn't turn back, but the thought of shooting Daniel was powerful enough that his hand dropped to where his gun typically would be—and he realized that he'd actually gone outside without a weapon. When he'd heard that Chloe was gone, he'd walked out unarmed.

Katherine, who fortunately *was* armed, stepped in front of him. "If she stays, she's as dead as Mary to us right now."

"Like Daniel?" Jack said, regretting the words the moment they were said.

"Exactly like Daniel." Katherine looked pointedly at his empty hand. Even when he'd been falling-down drunk, he didn't go outside without a gun. Worry over a woman had made him do so. "Either way, you can't do anything about it tonight, and we don't have time for you to be off your game. Not now. I'm going to get the Verrot and meet Garuda. Get your gear, or I'll tell Edgar he's going with me while you stay here and babysit Francis."

Jack walked in silence the rest of the way to the tavern. She was right: they couldn't violate every safety precaution they'd put in place over the years; there was no way he would endanger his sister like that—but no amount of logic quashed his furious urge to knock down Ajani's door and carry Chloe out of that house. He'd lived half of his life focused on the mission, on the good of the team, on doing the right thing. Wanting something—wanting *someone*—for himself was new.

A little while later, when they were not quite halfway between Gallows and the camp, Jack and Katherine found Garuda standing calmly in the Gallows Desert. As was typical in meetings with the bloedzuiger, an escort was with him. In this case, only one of his pack stood waiting for the customary greeting. It was an odd tradition, but many years ago, Garuda had explained it as a ritual of respect. The conflict between one of his representatives and his guest established power dynamics, but Jack was well aware that Garuda adjusted the fights for his own reasons. The old bloedzuiger had been known to use the tradition to remove a troublesome newborn or to establish his authority over the guest, so Jack had expected to find a young newborn that could be quickly dispatched before they moved on to business.

When he realized that the accompanying bloedzuiger appeared to be one of Garuda's older, more articulate ones, he looked around for another one to fight. There were no others in sight and no cover behind which they could hide.

"You want me to fight him?" Jack asked.

"No," Garuda said.

Jack held his hands out to the sides in a questioning gesture. "I'm not in the mood for games today."

"Traditions are not games, Jackson," Garuda chastised softly, and then his gaze went to Katherine. "Katherine."

She stepped past Jack. "I'm ready."

Clarity hit him then: they'd been speaking when he couldn't hear them, and his sister was apparently intending to fight one of the oldest bloedzuigers Jack had met.

"What in the hell are you two playing at?" Jack reached out to grab his sister's arm, but she moved out of reach in a blurringly quick move.

"Stand aside, Jack," Garuda all but hissed. "Katherine summoned me here, so she will attend to the pleasantries."

"If you think I'm letting my sister—"

"Shut it, Jack," Katherine interrupted. Slowly, looking like she was warming to the idea, she smiled at Garuda and then said, "And, you, don't talk while I'm fighting."

Garuda lifted his shoulder in a shrug, and then gestured to the bloedzuiger, which promptly launched itself at Katherine.

She dodged almost as quickly as it had sprung, and Jack gasped at the sight of his sister moving at such a speed. He'd thought that he was long done with being surprised by the things she could do, but as she kicked and punched the creature in front of her, he found himself amending his beliefs.

"She didn't fight that way in Gallows," he murmured to Garuda.

The bloedzuiger only nodded. His attention was fixed on the fight in front of them. Abruptly, he tossed a blade toward the fighters, and Katherine snatched it out of the air without even looking.

She frowned as she glanced at the knife and then snapped, "Are you trying to kill me?"

"No. It was a test," Garuda said bluntly. "You can read him, Katherine. Through me, you can anticipate his movements." He stepped closer to the fight and ordered the bloedzuiger, "Faster."

"I'm not here for tests," Katherine growled. At the same time, she'd stabbed the knife through one of its wrists, grabbed the other arm, pulled it over, and stabbed it too, pinning the bloedzuiger's arms together.

It tried to strike her with its pinned hands, but Katherine caught them and forced them upward and then back, bending the bloedzuiger's body into an arc. She continued propelling its arms until it was forced to fall onto its back, and then she slammed her boot-clad foot into the bloedzuiger's jaw, forcing its head to the side and holding it to the ground.

"Call it," she ordered.

"The needs of etiquette are met," Garuda said softly.

Katherine took a step toward him, and for a moment Jack wondered if he'd need to intervene. His sister looked like she might turn her attention from the creature she'd just incapacitated to the bloedzuiger who controlled it.

"I've never known another creature capable of doing what you do." Garuda's tongue snaked out to lick his lips in what Jack hoped was an absent-minded motion. If not, the bloedzuiger was trying to provoke Katherine.

"I'm human," she objected.

"You're more and more like one of my own," Garuda added, seemingly goading her in word even as his tone stayed even.

Katherine narrowed her gaze at him. "Just because I react peculiarly to your blood doesn't mean I'm a monster."

Garuda sighed. "I am not a monster, Katherine."

"In my world—"

"You aren't in another world," Garuda chided. "You're in *this* world, and your body acts more and more like one of us. Your proximity to me when you've had Verrot, and your acceptance of our connection, make it even more so. You are one of only two in this world who can do such things."

"Two?" Jack interjected. "Who is the other?"

Garuda met Jack's gaze. "Ajani."

Katherine's eyes flashed. *"Ajani?"* She raised her hand and pointed at Garuda. "He reacts to Verrot like this, and you didn't think to *tell* me before now? Or at least to tell Jack?"

As she reached out to shove her finger at Garuda's chest, he caught her hand. "Being like my kind does make you kin to my pack, but it doesn't mean I accept insults, Katherine." Keeping her hand in his with no apparent effort, even as she struggled, Garuda added, "There is a protocol that must be observed. I could not tell you until such time as it was necessary."

He glanced at Jack then. "You are both temperamental beings, and had you known, I'm not sure what the consequences would have been."

"Ajani is why you forbade your pack and your associates to provide Verrot, isn't he?" Jack asked. When Garuda nodded, Jack continued, "No other being in the Wasteland responds to Verrot like Katherine and Ajani do. Has anyone done so *before* now?"

"No." Garuda stared at Jack, although he did not volunteer any more information. The bloedzuiger followed the rules of his kind even now. That didn't mean, however, that he wasn't staring at Jack as if he would *will* the very thoughts into his mind if he could.

He didn't need to, though; Jack saw the answer. "You don't think Ajani is from this world."

"That would be my belief," Garuda said evenly. "I've thought as much for some time, but until Katherine revealed her secret to you, there was no proper way to provoke that thought in your mind. There are rules. *He* might not understand them, but you do, Jackson."

Katherine's gaze darted between them. "I might have some of your traits, but I better not be going to develop *that* one. Speak plainly. How go'damned hard is that?"

Garuda stiffened visibly. "For my kind, I speak as plainly as I can without violating etiquette."

"Kather—"

"You're right," she interrupted Jack. "I'm sorry."

The bloedzuiger Katherine had fought walked over at that point and held out a bottle of Verrot to Katherine. "We brought this to you. For your packmate."

Garuda beamed at them, his unpleasantly red lips curved in one of the most joyous smiles Jack had seen on the bloedzuiger. Garuda looked from his fellow bloedzuiger to Katherine with an expression of almost paternal pride before saying, "The medicine and the Verrot will heal your Francis. There was doubt as to your worthiness, but you've proven yourself." He glanced at the other bloedzuiger. "And you've earned the right to the desert territory, Styrr."

The creature, Styrr, bowed. "I will protect her and the territory with my life." As it straightened, its gaze was fastened on Katherine. "I hope you do not die in the coming fight."

Jack waited for his sister to say something inflammatory, but she merely bowed in return and murmured, "Me too."

# CHAPTER 30

Kitty looked to Garuda's newly promoted bloedzuiger and then to Garuda himself. She wasn't sure how she felt about the idea that there were consequences to her resistance to admitting that she reacted peculiarly to Verrot. It made her wonder what else she didn't know because she didn't understand the rules of different Wastelander cultures. The miners made sense to her because they reminded her of people she'd known in California, but she'd not made much effort to understand the bloedzuigers. In truth, she wasn't entirely sure she even understood the human Wastelanders.

"Do you believe Ajani sent the brethren after us?" she asked.

Instead of replying, Garuda caught her gaze and in a voice that was both in her mind and audible to others, he asked, "Are you kin to my pack, Katherine?"

It felt like his words echoed, stretched out in tendrils to reach bloedzuigers throughout the Wasteland, and Kitty felt her mind tangling with those threads, connecting to them in an instant that could vanish or last forever. "I am."

The threads of connection snapped into place, and she realized that Garuda was allowing her access to several hundred bloedzuigers. As long as she had Verrot in her system, she could reach out to all of those minds. In the complete clarity that Garuda allowed her, she understood too that this was a level of access that was granted only to the eldest of his kind.

"I cannot say for certain," Garuda said in answer to her question about the brethren, but then he added to his answer privately in her mind: *I would speak to Governor Soanes. Listen to the pack; see what they have witnessed.*

And she did. No one could show her proof of Ajani consulting with the brethren, but there were snippets, brief flashes of images that flooded her mind quicker than she thought she could process them. Vaguely, she noticed that she'd dropped to her knees as the images began to resemble a linear narrative.

*Ajani visited the governor. They stood speaking in the street, and then Ajani turned his gaze to the bloedzuiger who watched them.* In the vision, she was and was not that bloedzuiger. Ajani's gaze was fastened on her. *On us, on the pack.*

"Katherine?" Jack shook her.

*The brethren came to the governor; four of them went into his office in a procession of gray robes.*

"What did you do?" Jack had an arm around her, but it felt like she could and couldn't feel it all at the same time. He wasn't speaking to her—except he was: she was connected to the entire pack. She wasn't hearing him beside her, but through Garuda.

*"That's why his arm feels weird,"* she told Garuda.

*"Focus on the knowledge"* was all Garuda said.

Kitty pulled her gaze away from what she saw through his eyes and returned to the pack's memories.

*"Stay away from Miss Reed," Ajani snarled, looking far more monstrous than she'd ever seen. A man knelt in front of him, held in place by two guards. She couldn't see his face, only his back, but she had a sinking feeling that she knew him.*

*Ajani turned to a third guard. "Make him suffer, but I want him healed before we go to Gallows."*

As she watched, she tried to remind herself that it was a memory, that it wasn't happening at that very moment, but she wished she could close her eyes as the guards beat the man. She heard the sizzle of burning flesh, the screams, the blows, and she watched him pass out from the pain. When they released him, he tumbled back, and she saw his face. Even through the blood and swelling, she knew him.

"Daniel," she whispered aloud.

*"He disobeyed his master,"* Garuda said.

Kitty forced herself to search the other threads, to look for connections between Ajani and the brethren, but she found none. She saw the monks with the governor on one other occasion, but she didn't see them with Ajani. There were brief flashes of Ajani, but they were rare. Finally, the connection with the whole of Garuda's pack receded, and she understood that Ajani knew that the bloedzuigers watched him, that he only showed them what he wanted Garuda to know.

*"I don't understand why he . . . why me?"*

*"Because Ajani knows that you are as he is, Katherine."*

*"Why?"*

"I don't know," Garuda said aloud. The connection was severed, not only to the pack but also to him, and she felt a wash of pain that was not hers.

Kitty realized that what had just happened was unprecedented—and had left him exhausted. Garuda was remaining upright only by sheer will.

From the ground where she knelt, she stared up at him, trying to find her voice. The transition to speech was oddly discomfiting. "I saw," she said, "and I have a question for the governor."

Jack glanced from her to Garuda. "Care to fill me in?"

"What Katherine shares with you is her choice. There are rules that allow me to speak to my kin, but not to you." Garuda glanced at the wrist of the bloedzuiger beside him, and the creature held it up to his master's lips without hesitation.

As Garuda drank, he watched Kitty, and for the first time she saw something beautiful in the way the other bloedzuiger was replenishing Garuda's energy. It seemed natural—and caring. As always, the magic had left her feeling shattered, but this time she also felt vaguely intoxicated. Her mind replayed the final moments of her connection with the pack, and she realized that Garuda had pushed some energy her way before he'd severed that connection. She smiled at him, realizing how wrong she'd been about him. He'd given her enough strength to return to Gallows.

Jack was unaware of what Garuda had done and offered his hand to help her up. She stood and leaned against her brother as she told him, "The monks worked for the governor, and Ajani visits the governor." She paused, weighing the words yet unspoken. "He . . . Ajani knew that the bloedzuigers watched him, and he let them see that much."

Telling Jack about Daniel's torture was necessary, but she couldn't unman him by sharing more details than were absolutely essential. She settled on saying, "Ajani tortured Danny because of me."

"He what?" Jack asked.

"Tortured him. Burned, broken . . ." She tried to push the images away. "Danny was right to warn me, Jack. We don't stay dead, but if Ajani had me, I'd find a way. I'd have to. I couldn't . . . survive the kind of things he did to Danny. Things he did because of me."

Garuda pulled his mouth away from the other bloedzuiger's wrist. "No. Not because of you." He dabbed his mouth with a cloth. "Ajani did that because he wants them to fear him. Your Daniel knew the cost of speaking to you."

She glanced at Garuda and murmured, "Thank you . . . for everything."

He dipped his head in a brief bow.

"I'm going to kill him," Jack snarled.

"Ajani or the governor?"

"Both of them, all of them, I don't know." Jack made a sound of frustration. "If the monks are working for the governor and Soanes is meeting with Ajani . . . And as much as I don't like Daniel, I'm not going to stand by while he gets *tortured*. Daniel was one of us. He might not be now, but no one should be tortured—especially for looking out for you."

"Oh, I'm fine with killing Ajani," Kitty said. "If we knew how, I'd have done it years ago, but we owe Governor Soanes a chance to explain before we go jumping to conclusions."

The shocked expression on Jack's face was almost amusing. "*You're* recommending caution?" He looked at Garuda. "Is this your doing?"

"Katherine may be feeling the remnants of the calm I sent her way as I broke our connection," Garuda admitted in what Kitty now understood to be an embarrassed tone.

"I can read bloedzuigers' emotions," she said softly, shocked by how very wrong she'd been. "I didn't think you even *had* emotions."

Garuda laughed, a sound that wasn't any less odd because it was spoken aloud rather than in her head. "Why do you think newborns are so base? It takes time to learn to master emotions when they are so intense."

"You and me? We're going to have a long chat. I will get answers. A *lot* of them." Kitty shook her head at him. "Bet on it."

"If I hadn't been trying to do just that for years, I might be appropriately intimidated," Garuda joked.

*He joked?*

"I'm sorry," Kitty said steadily, meeting his eyes as she spoke. "I've been a bitch to you for so long."

"Fear makes us all do stupid things time and again." Garuda gave her an affectionate smile.

Kitty shook her head again and told Jack, "Now that this bony bastard gave me answers and medicine for Francis, we should go tend to things." At his surprised expression, she added, "If this calm isn't faded by the time we reach the governor, you'll have to be the difficult one for a change."

Garuda bowed to Jack and then turned to Kitty. "I will have a gift for you should you decide to resolve the matter of Ajani's obsession with you. I believe we may have finally found a toxin that could solve both of our troubles. Simply speak through Styrr." He motioned to the bloedzuiger who had just nourished him.

She glanced at Styrr, and the bloedzuiger dipped his head in a slight bow.

Garuda continued, "He is assigned to the area now and will adhere to your commands, Katherine. Tell him if you need me or the pack, and we will come to your aid. Once the toxin is ready, he can tell me where you are so I can bring it to you." He withdrew two vials. "This is the medicine you need to add to the Verrot and give to your injured packmate. Styrr knows the correct mixture."

"Thank you." Gratefully, Kitty took the vials. "I am *sorry* for not understanding for so long."

"I know," Garuda said, before glancing in turn at Styrr and at Jack. "Keep her safe." Then he was gone, leaving the Reed siblings alone in the desert with the newly promoted bloedzuiger who was stationed in their region.

And for the first time since she'd woken up in the Wasteland, Kitty felt like she might truly belong in this weird world. She felt the echo of the connection to hundreds of bloedzuigers, the fury over Ajani's actions, and the certainty that he did not deserve the ability to connect to the bloedzuiger pack.

# CHAPTER 31

When Kitty and Jack walked into Francis' room with Styrr in tow, Edgar barely acknowledged the bloedzuiger or Jack. Kitty knew that he didn't mean any disrespect to Styrr, but her newfound bonding with bloedzuigers made her want to encourage conversation. Later, perhaps, they could do that. Right now her focus was on helping Francis.

"We're here," she told Francis. "With medicine and Styrr, one of Garuda's people."

He nodded, but didn't sit up or speak. A bloodied cloth covered his eyes, and Kitty tried not to gasp as she looked at him. By now, he should've been well into healing—especially with Verrot in his system. Instead, his wounds were still bleeding like they were newly made. He looked weak and listless from the continued blood loss.

"I'll prepare the treatment." Styrr went to the table and poured some of the Verrot into a mug and tapped out the medicinal mix into it. "He should drink first. It will help."

Kitty poured Verrot into a second mug and carried it to the bed where Francis reclined. "I'm going to help you sit up so you can drink."

Behind her, Jack and Edgar were speaking in low tones as Jack brought Edgar up-to-date on the events that had transpired in the desert. He finished with, "I'm going to update Melody and Hector. We're headed out within the hour."

A tense silence filled the room when Jack left. Both Styrr and Edgar were watching Francis. His hands were shaking as he lowered the now-emptied mug. "Who's still here?" he asked.

"Edgar, me, and Styrr . . ." Kitty answered.

Styrr brought over the Verrot that was mixed with medicine, but didn't hand the mug to her. "May I?"

Kitty took the empty mug and put it aside. Then she told Francis, "Lean back. I'm going to hold your face steady while we treat your eyes."

"Do you need help?" Edgar asked.

She shook her head, and then she cupped Francis' face in her hands. Blood and tears still trailed down one of his cheeks; her fingertips were wet with them as soon as she touched his skin. Her own eyes threatened to fill with tears. "Go ahead," she told Styrr.

The bloedzuiger said, "It will hurt."

"It already hurts," Francis said, but as he opened his eyes, he pressed his lips together determinedly. Like all of them, he'd known his share of pain during his years in the Wasteland. Dying wasn't usually a painless experience—nor was waking up after death.

With a steady hand, Styrr poured several drops into one of Francis' eyes. The medicinally treated Verrot caused the eye to open wider, and a harsh cry of pain escaped Francis' lips. His body thrashed, and Kitty wasn't sure if she could hold him steady. She managed not to let go of his head, and she could see that he was trying not to flinch away. He'd bitten the inside of his lip so hard that blood trickled from the corner of his mouth.

And then Edgar was beside her, holding Francis down. Once he stopped writhing, Edgar released him and grabbed a holster from the dresser. "Open your mouth," he ordered. Francis obeyed, and Edgar shoved the leather belt into his mouth.

"Steady," Kitty whispered. She nodded at Styrr, who poured drops of the mixture into Francis' other eye. It soaked into the tissue of the eye as if it were being absorbed by a dry cloth. Both pupils widened so completely that they seemed to consume the irises. No color remained beyond black and red, and Kitty swallowed against the sight of her friend's disturbingly discolored eyes.

"Again," Styrr said quietly.

They repeated the process in both eyes, and then Francis fell into a state that appeared at first to be death, but was only unconsciousness.

"He'll need to drink the next two days, but the eyes will only need to be treated once more." Styrr walked over to the chair that Edgar had been sitting in when they'd arrived, and sat down. "I will need your assistance in the morning. Then you may go, and I will watch over him while his body heals. He'll not wake for several hours."

"But he's alive," Kitty said. "He's healing, not dead."

Styrr nodded.

"Then we'll have to wait to go after the governor until the morning," Kitty pronounced. "I'll tell Jack."

For a moment, Edgar simply stared at her. "No."

"Excuse me?" She frowned at him. Now that she'd treated Francis, and left him under Styrr's watch, she could turn to the next task. That was simply how things were done. "Jack's not at his most calm right now. I'm not going to let him go alone, so he can wait and—"

"No," Edgar repeated. "They can still go now, and you will wait here with me. Francis needs you, and Jack will be fine with the others. You're barely upright after whatever happened in the desert; you're not going."

"Bullsh—"

"If you go, I'm done, Kit. Ajani is apparently more obsessed than we thought, and he's probably working with Soanes, and Jack says you were insensible after whatever you and Garuda did in the desert.

You stay here tonight, or . . . I won't stand by while you do something stupid." Edgar walked out, closing the door behind him.

For a few minutes, Kitty stood still in shock. She was exhausted. She couldn't lie and say otherwise, but that didn't mean that she liked being given ultimatums. Still . . . if the situation had been reversed, she'd have been just as irate as Edgar was. If he—or Jack—had tried to walk into a potential confrontation when they were on the verge of collapsing from exhaustion, she'd have been livid. If they'd had as many threats staring them down as she did, she'd have been ready to cosh them over the head to keep them from leaving. She couldn't expect either of them to treat her differently. Jack was so off his game that he wasn't telling her that she needed to rest, but Edgar hadn't missed a beat.

*And he's right.*

After making sure that Styrr had everything he needed, Kitty went after Edgar. She walked into his room without so much as knocking. She stopped just inside and shoved the door shut behind her. Edgar was removing his shirt and continued to do so as if she weren't there. He didn't speak or acknowledge her presence as he dropped the shirt in a bucket of sudsy water. He remained silent as he retrieved a second shirt and carried it to the stone slab that now rested on the table. Two crude irons were heating in a bucket of hot coals, and next to that was a wide basin of cold water. How exactly he managed to persuade the inns he stayed in to allow him to have such fire hazards in his room she never understood.

He stood in his trousers and nothing else, but in true Edgar fashion, he gave her the same look he would've given if he'd been fully dressed. Then he turned his attention to the shirt in his hands. He spread it out and picked up one of the irons from the bucket of coals. Without looking at her, he asked, "Did you need something?"

In all of the years they'd spent together and apart, he'd never sounded dismissive. It frightened her. "Forgiveness?" she asked.

Edgar lifted his gaze from the shirt he was pressing. "For what? Hiding things from me? Trying to go out when you're exhausted from magic?"

She folded her arms over her chest and stared at him. "Fine. I may be willing to admit that I was being a *little* unreasonable."

He turned the shirt over and slid the heated iron over it. "Is that all? You push me away for *months,* but I'm supposed to be fine with you being careless?"

For a moment, she was tempted to walk away, but that reserve of calm that Garuda had given her kept her from running. "Yes. No. I don't know what you want me to say."

"Yes, you do," he corrected.

Quietly, she said, "I'm not going with Jack tonight."

"That's a start." He continued ironing his shirt for a few moments before saying, "Let me know when you're ready to talk about the rest. I'm tired of this, Kit, so if you're not here to set things right, there's the door." He gestured toward it with the iron.

Kitty turned away, feeling only marginally better than when she'd come into the room, but before she opened the door, she stopped herself. This was absurd; *she* was absurd. She spun back around and walked over to Edgar.

"Maybe I overreacted to your death last year. I just . . ." She felt tears threaten and blinked to keep them away. "You were dead, and all I could think about was spending forever without you. I know you don't believe it, but I *know* it, Edgar: I won't die for real. I can't stand the thought of being here without you, unable to die, miserable forever."

Edgar lifted the iron and deposited it into the basin of cold water. It hissed and steamed. "So you thought both of us being miserable now was better?"

She said nothing as he retrieved the second iron and dipped it into the cold water. She watched him as he ladled the water onto the coals, and then moved the bucket to the hearth, where it would not cause harm if it were to tip over. He didn't speak either, waiting in that implacable way of his for her to answer his question. They'd had conflicts enough over the years that she knew his patience far outlasted hers.

"You're not going to make this easy, are you?" she asked softly.

Edgar shook his head. "If I wanted something easy, I wouldn't be in love with you, now would I?" He motioned to the door again. "Are you answering me or leaving?"

Kitty turned her back and went to the door—and locked it. Then she turned to face him. When she did, she caught the flash of hurt in his expression: he'd obviously thought she was leaving. "I thought that if we stayed apart, I'd stop loving you, so that when you died next time it wouldn't destroy me."

"It destroyed me every time you died too," he said quietly.

Kitty walked back to him and laid her hand flat on his chest. "I'm sorry. I figured I could learn to be apart from you, and then I wouldn't love you, and then . . . when you leave me, it won't hurt as much."

"How has that been working out?" Edgar covered her hand with his.

"It hasn't."

"So you're telling me you still love me?" he prompted.

"You know I do. I always have." She stared up at him and asked, "Can we go back to how things were?"

"No."

Of all the things in her life that had surprised her, this topped the list. He'd spent almost the entirety of their time apart trying to convince her that they should be back together, and now that she'd come to him and said he was right, Edgar was rejecting her. Kitty started to back away, but he wouldn't release her hand.

Instead, he wrapped an arm around her and splayed his other hand across her lower back.

Slowly, the confident smile he'd worn for so many years spread over his face, and then he said, "I don't want to go back."

"But—"

"Swear to me, Kit," he interrupted. "Swear you won't leave me again."

"I won't," she whispered.

"And the next time I ask you to marry me, you'll say yes."

"Edgar . . ."

Carefully, Kitty started to back away, extricating herself from his embrace as she moved.

At first, he let her. Then he swept her up into his arms. "Say it," he demanded. "I've been waiting for eleven years for you to say yes."

"Edgar, I'm not the marrying type."

"Bullshit." He started to lower her to the ground. "I mean it, Kit. I'm not going to let either of us be destroyed again when we can and *should* be together. Marriage or nothing."

She wrapped her arms around his neck. "You'd turn me out?"

"When I ask you to marry me, you'll say yes," he repeated.

"It's not like there are even proper churches here—"

"*Marry me.*" His lips were all but touching hers, but when she tried to kiss him, to end the discussion by distracting him, he turned his head. Gently, he whispered, "Just say yes, Kit."

"Yes," she promised.

Edgar caught her lips in a kiss as he carried her the few steps to the bed, lowered her to the mattress, and began unfastening her dress. When he pulled away and slid behind her, she objected. "I can just lift—"

"No. I've been this long without you. I want to see you *and* touch you." He slid her dress down over her shoulders until it pooled at her waist. Then, with the slow expertise that had made her insensible so many nights, he caressed her and dropped kisses over her skin as he unfastened her corset so very slowly.

"I can help with the hooks," she offered.

He laughed and slid his hands around to cup her still-covered breasts. "I like my way better."

"You mean torturing me?" She reached back to cup him through his trousers. "There are consequences to that."

He pressed into her hand and lowered her corset. "Thankfully."

Kitty wasn't sure whether to laugh or cry by the time they were both undressed. Even after all of the nights they'd spent together over the years, the reality of Edgar still surpassed her memories. She arched and sighed as he kissed, licked, and nipped trails over her skin. Then, finally, she exhaled in a moan and he slid inside her where he belonged.

"I love you." He half breathed the words.

"I love you too." She lifted her hips to urge him to move.

He didn't. Instead, he stared down at her and asked, "Will you marry me, Kit?"

"You don't play fair," Kitty complained.

Slowly he withdrew himself almost completely and then with torturous slowness moved forward. "Tell me again that you'll be my wife."

"I will. I'll be Mrs. Edgar Cordova," she swore.

"Again," he demanded.

And as long as she swore it, he kept moving.

Afterward, she was draped on top of him, feeling better than she had since . . . well, the *last* time she was naked in his arms.

She dozed off, and when she woke up, he was watching her with a look of complete satisfaction. She lifted her head and stared at him. "Would you really have stopped if I wouldn't swear to marry you?"

He laughed. "No, but you aren't ever that pliant, so I figured I'd get your promise while I could." He pulled her up to him and kissed her tenderly before adding, "I know you, doll. You don't break your word."

Still straddling Edgar, Kitty sat back on her feet and stared down at him. "Don't think I'll suddenly get all domestic and obedient."

"I don't *want* obedient." Edgar gripped her hips and lifted her so she was raised up on her knees. Then, staring up at her, he removed his hands and said, "I just want you."

With a happy sigh, Kitty lowered herself onto him. Her eyes fluttered shut at the sensation, and she exhaled before saying shakily, "That works for me."

# CHAPTER 32

Jack was relieved that Katherine wasn't waiting for him in the hall. He'd hoped that Edgar would convince her to stay here, but he hadn't actually *expected* it. Even when she was exhausted, Katherine was far from cooperative when she set her mind to anything. Feeling too much like he'd be sneaking out—and that she'd follow on her own—he stopped at Francis' room and went inside.

Neither Edgar nor Katherine was there, and Francis seemed to be sleeping soundly. Styrr stood, not quite leaning against the wall but near it, watching Francis. The bloedzuiger acknowledged Jack with an almost imperceptible nod.

"How is Francis?" Jack asked.

"Recovering." Styrr smiled. "He is in a healing sleep. I will stay here with him and guard Katherine."

"Where is she?"

"She has gone to her mate. He was vexed that she wanted to travel. They argued, but she is now acquiescing to his logic."

"They argued here?"

"No," Styrr said. "In another room. My hearing is more acute than yours. I would hear if she were in danger. I can guard her and this one"—he gestured to Francis—"without being in the room where she is."

Jack nodded, as if the idea of hearing whatever Katherine was doing in another room wasn't unsettling. He considering telling Styrr not to mention his "acute hearing" to her, but bloedzuigers didn't lie outright, so Katherine would find out sooner or later. "Right," Jack said. "I'm going to head out then. If she returns . . ."

"I'll tell her you've gone."

Once the small party of Arrivals had reached the privacy of the desert, Jack told Melody and Hector, "It looks like Soanes is working with Ajani, the brethren, or both."

"Why?" Hector asked.

Melody sighed and ran a hand over the short-barreled shotgun she carried like an infant in arms. "We'll ask him."

Jack almost felt bad for the governor, but then he thought of Mary, who was dead, and Francis, who was blind. If the governor had been working with the monks or Ajani, he'd need to answer for that—and Jack wouldn't be feeling too much guilt over unleashing Melody to get those answers. He tried to live a righteous life, but doing the right thing sometimes included a few ugly moments.

It was hard to tell whether it was because of Melody's enthusiasm for the potential violence ahead, the lingering Verrot in their systems, or Jack's own eagerness to understand what was going on, but they traveled to Covenant at a remarkable speed. By the time they'd reached the governor's offices, Jack's temper was no more in control than it had been when he'd stood in the desert with Katherine and Garuda.

Although Jack had been there a few days prior, he didn't recognize the man who waited inside the reception area. On some level, Jack wondered if he was more comfortable with bloedzuigers than with humans, but it wasn't all humans that he found unnerving. Ajani and Governor

Soanes were on the list of those he found unsettling; Garuda was on a very short list of beings he trusted.

The man, a person of both miner and human heritage by the looks of him, scurried over to Jack and held out his hands. "Mr. Reed."

For a moment, Jack looked at him in confusion. He didn't remember any custom that involved shaking both hands, nor did he have a coat or hat to hand the man. He didn't extend his hands, and the man, who seemed to be some kind of assistant of the governor, stood there at a loss for a moment.

After an awkward pause, the man said, "This is not a good time."

Jack weighed his words for a moment. "It'll have to be."

"I'm sorry, but the governor is indisposed." The assistant moved to stand between them and the door to the governor's office. In his hand, he clutched a key ring with oversize brass keys. "You can't go in."

"That's not a very wise plan," Melody murmured in a voice that Jack knew meant that she was moving into whatever less stable place she went to mentally when the prospect of violence was upon them. Hector, usually the only voice of reason she would hear once she was in her zone, didn't speak to caution her. He simply withdrew one of his knives and smiled. Every member of the team had strengths, but when it came to coercion, Hector and Melody were well matched. Hector's silent intimidation complemented Melody's obvious madness.

A loud crash sounded inside the office, and Jack stepped forward. "Open it."

The assistant shook his head. "It would be *more* unwise to open that door, Mr. Reed. I won't do it."

Hector and Melody came to stand behind Jack, one on either side of him. "I like bad ideas," Melody murmured gleefully. She lifted the short-barreled shotgun. "Can I open it?"

Hector said nothing.

"I'm not necessarily here to kill him," Jack reminded her.

Melody sighed, and the gun barrel dipped. Then she lifted it and aimed at the assistant. "What about him?"

Jack met the assistant's gaze. "Depends on whether he's going to try to stop us."

"I warned you," the man said, but instead of trying to stop them, he handed Jack the key ring and walked past the Arrivals without another word.

"That didn't sound promising," Hector took the keys from Jack's hand and walked to the door. He slid the key into the lock and turned it. In his other hand, he held a knife at the ready. "Muzzles up, kiddies, he said as he yanked the door open. He stepped to the side as he did so, giving Jack and Melody a clear shot into the room.

Jack stopped short at the sight that greeted them, trying to make sense of the contents of the room. It looked like the governor had re-decorated. The walls were partially coated in what looked like fresh red paint; after the split second of shock, Jack's mind filled in the correct interpretation. *Not paint, but blood.* A monk stood beside the gover-nor's chair, which had been turned so that its back was to the door. In the chair, the remains of Governor Soanes slumped to the side.

As Jack's mind finally allowed him to process the sight and scent of the room, he realized that the governor was long dead. Viscera hung all around the room like some sort of macabre party decoration, and the unpleasant scent of violent death permeated the air. Whether or not the governor had been working for the enemy—and if so, why—wasn't something that he would be able to answer.

"Demon-filled," Hector said, not taking his gaze off the possessed monk.

"He ate the governor," Melody added in what Jack could only de-scribe as a petulant voice. "Damn it! I had *plans*."

She emptied both barrels. The blast went through his chair and through the governor's body, but the demon-possessed monk simply stared at them. Melody's shots didn't hurt the demon inside, and monks never reclaimed their bodies once they allowed possession. Demons wore the bodies until they were bored or the bodies were too broken—unless the bodies were anchored. Then the demons could be injured or killed.

Jack withdrew the pistol on his right. The rounds in it were filled with salt and small bits of brass. They weren't as effective as spellwork, but they could anchor the demon to the body.

"Open fire," Jack said levelly.

Hector had switched to a handful of throwing knives with brass bands that he'd had made for such occasions, and Melody packed her own shells with "a little bit of this and that" so she could use her preferred gun against most of the Wasteland monsters.

As Melody fired, Hector released two knives in quick succession.

The demon-possessed monk moved more like the thing inside of it than like a human, darting serpent-quick and leaping agilely to avoid their attack. It seemed more interested in evading them than in attacking, which wasn't all too surprising. It had a body and had obviously already completed the job of silencing the governor. Once it was free of them, it could go enjoy having a physical form.

Melody drew a pistol from her hip and emptied all six rounds.

Hector launched several more knives.

The creature shrieked twice as both knives and bullets hit it, but with so much blood covering it, there was no clear indication of where it had been hit. If they could anchor the demon to the body with brass, they could permanently kill the demon. If not, they could hopefully at least destroy the monk's body.

As they all tried to anticipate which way things would go, the monk evaded most of their shots. The sight of the bleeding monk darting around and contorting his body into improbable positions to avoid their bullets and knifes was odd. So far they were successfully stopping it from escaping, but that only lasted a few moments. The creature knocked Melody onto her back, leaving a bloody handprint on her chest, and fled.

Hector rushed after it.

Jack reached a hand down to Melody, who scrambled to her feet as quickly as she could and raced after the monk too. As they burst out of the building, Jack saw Hector rounding a corner.

"Melody!" Jack pointed.

The three Arrivals followed the creature and saw it scurry up the side of a building, leaving dark handprints as it went. Hector grabbed a window ledge and continued pursuit. Still on the ground, Melody broke the barrel and reloaded. Jack scanned the rooftops.

After several moments Hector dropped back to the ground, and Melody lowered the gun.

"It's gone," Jack said. Free-ranging demons were fast enough to be a mile away by now, and a strong enough monastic host and a possession-experienced demon wouldn't be much slower.

"Well, that was unexpected," Hector said.

"Fucking demons," Melody grumbled.

# CHAPTER 33

Chloe had spent a quiet evening talking to Daniel. Kitty hadn't appeared, so late that night, Daniel had sent another courier to the Gulch House. Chloe hadn't really expected Jack to come after her, but she'd sort of hoped he would. It was foolishness: she wasn't sure what she'd say if he *did,* but she still wanted him to. She wanted some sort of explanation that would return them to that moment before he'd called her his dead lover's name. Admittedly, Chloe also felt like she was coping somewhat better than the last time she'd had an awkward separation—at least she hadn't crawled into a bottle like she did when she'd caught Andrew screwing her boss.

"I'm sure they're just busy," Daniel said consolingly as he led Chloe into a sitting room. "Kitty isn't the most considerate of women." He gave her a sad grin. "She's wonderful, of course, but not always thoughtful or particularly refined in her social graces."

"You know her well, then."

"We've known each other for a long time." He motioned to a servant, who brought in a tea tray and set it on the table. Once the servant left, Daniel continued, "I consider her one of the finest people in the Wasteland, but that doesn't mean I forget that she has faults. Her temper is horrible, and she is quick to the trigger."

"Not a bad thing around here, from what I saw today." Chloe poured herself a cup of tea. "The desert and the town both seem to be filled with trouble."

"True." Daniel looked at his empty cup, grinned, and poured some tea for himself. "Times have changed in your world, I see."

"Sorry," she said sheepishly. "My social graces aren't very refined either, are they?"

"And your temper?"

Chloe gave Daniel an innocent expression and sipped her tea. He laughed, and she shifted the conversation to mundane topics, happily telling him about the world she'd left behind. The next hour was peaceful and comforting. Then the courier returned.

Daniel accepted the message, read it, and handed it to her, saying, "Kitty and Jack had to tend to business. They'll be back in Gallows in a few days."

Chloe read the message, which said little more than that. It mentioned that Melody and Hector were still in Gallows, but they would be headed out to their camp in the morning.

"Do you want to stay here tonight? I'm sure my host won't mind," Daniel offered. "It's more comfortable than the inn."

"I don't know," she hedged. "I think my room there was paid up."

"If they didn't leave funds for you, I can help. You *are* Kitty's friend, so it's not as if I couldn't find you." His voice was teasing as he offered her money, but she still felt her lack of independence keenly. She had no money, nowhere to live, and no job. If the Arrivals chose to cast her out, the only other person she could turn to was Daniel.

"Chloe?" Daniel prompted.

"I've only just arrived here, and it all feels pretty overwhelming," she admitted, feeling strangely dismissed by the Arrivals. On the other hand, going to the camp without either Jack or Kitty wasn't appealing.

"If you're sure your friend won't mind, I'll take you up on the offer. I should probably head back in the morning."

"Or wait here until they're back," Daniel countered. "I can escort you to the camp then." When she opened her mouth to object, he held up a hand and added, "You can think about it tomorrow. Honestly, Chloe, you're very welcome here."

She gave him a suspicious look, but she didn't have any reason to distrust him. "When did you see Kitty last?"

"She and Jack were over in Covenant after Mary died," Daniel answered. "Right before you arrived, I expect." He returned his teacup to its saucer and glanced at the doorway, where the same servant who had brought them their tea was now standing.

"Dinner is served."

"Let's get you some decent food, Chloe." Daniel gestured for her to follow the servant to the dining room. "Everything will be clearer after a good meal and some good sleep."

Chloe wasn't sure that clarity would be so easily found, but she didn't have a better plan for her evening.

Over breakfast the next morning, Daniel suggested that she might enjoy his host's library while he went out to take care of an errand. It wasn't a very welcoming room, seeming more out of place than any other room she'd seen in the Wasteland, but it was filled with books and scrolls detailing history, creatures, and geography. The sheer extent of information made it easy to overlook how uncomfortable the chairs were and how stiff the decor seemed.

That's where she was later that afternoon when Ajani opened the door to the room.

"I trust you slept well, Chloe," he said by way of greeting, closing the door behind him.

She stared at him. Details clicked into place in less than pleasing ways. Daniel's "host" was Ajani. She was in the home of Jack and Kitty's enemy. No wonder they hadn't sent much of a message back to her. *They also didn't come after me.* They'd been fine with his coming to talk to her, and they'd chosen not to come to her when she was at his house. She felt like a pawn in a game no one had explained.

"I see Daniel didn't mention me to you," Ajani continued as he walked farther into the room. He made a small expression of regret, but Chloe wasn't sure if it was genuine. When she remained silent, he added conversationally, "He's been hoping to find someone to fill the void Miss Reed left in his life, you know. He was devastated by her rejection so many years ago, but he hasn't ever brought a woman home since then."

"He lives with you?" Chloe managed to ask.

"Now and again." Ajani walked toward her. "He likes his freedom, so he does keep quarters away from me, but when I'm in the same town as the Reeds, I prefer to keep him close." A look of irritation flashed across Ajani's face. "His affection for Miss Reed sometimes affects his judgment, and of course, both Jackson and Cordova do like to shoot Daniel."

"They shoot him?" Chloe repeated.

Ajani waved his hand as if brushing away an insect. "He recovers, of course, but I find it inconvenient when he's dead."

Chloe realized she was nodding, as if death were inconvenient, as if the pain of bullets were insignificant, as if it were not troubling to hear that the man with whom she'd recently been naked often *shot* the man with whom she'd shared breakfast.

Mutely, she walked to a chair and sat. Ajani took the seat across from her. They were silent in this very stiff room, surrounded by books, and discussing death.

"My staff tells me that there was an altercation with one of those demon-summoning cults," he said after another moment's pause. "Some of the natives can be such nasty, blood-spilling creatures. That little group of riffraff you were with isn't much better, though." He shuddered delicately. "I can't imagine living in the primitive conditions they prefer. Sometimes they seem not much better than animals bedding down in a stable."

"They seem to share a mutual dislike of you," Chloe pointed out. She didn't add that she wasn't seeing any reason to like him either. He was arrogant and condescending, but then again, the Arrivals all had their share of flaws. Although Chloe felt that she would trust Jack or Kitty over anyone else she'd met here so far, she wasn't so naive as to trust anyone's blanket condemnation after only a few days of knowing him. She was here now, so she'd talk to Ajani and form her own opinion.

"Daniel tells me that you are seeking a job," Ajani began. "I have positions available."

She shook her head. "I'm not interested in being a bodyguard or whatever your people are."

"I see." He folded his hands together and looked at her. "I could find a place for you at one of the better brothels instead."

Chloe snapped her gaze to him. "*Excuse* me?"

"You said you wanted a job. I'm offering to help you make arrangements if you aren't interested in a position that requires weaponry skills. Some women are more comfortable with gentler skills." Ajani's expression didn't suggest that he thought he was being insulting. If anything, he looked like he thought he was being considerate.

"I'm pretty sure I'll pass on being a whore. Thanks."

He obviously missed her tone completely because he shrugged slightly and said, "The accommodations at some of the upscale establishments are quite comfortable."

After a speechless moment, Chloe tried to remind herself that she was now living in a different world, but her temper seethed. "I'm a lot more comfortable with fighting than fucking for money, but I was thinking more that I could get a job at one of the shops or something."

Ajani tsked at her. "The natives don't *hire,* especially not one of the Arrivals. They pass their trades on to their young. Your options are limited. The houses typically pass on their trade too, but the Arrivals are enough of a curiosity that you'd be a good earner."

For a moment, she expected him to laugh, to tell her he was joking, to explain that somehow she had other options. He didn't. Instead, he continued: "I could have Daniel take you on a tour of the nicer brothels. There are several where you could—"

"No," she interrupted.

Ajani gave her a patronizing smile. "Are you opposed to the number of clients you'd need to entertain in the brothels? Or are you a virgin?"

"Yes. No. I mean, I understand that there are conventions here, but where I come from . . ." She shook her head. "I just don't think I can do that."

"The position of mistress is currently vacant." He looked at her much the way she'd seen people examine produce at the market. "You're attractive, and I do understand not wanting to kill . . . or bed the natives."

"You're offering me a job as your mistress?" She stared at him with a mix of amusement and horror.

"Yes. I prefer not to frequent the brothels as I prefer not to share, especially with the natives." Ajani made a moue of distaste before smiling at Chloe. "It's merely a job, my dear. The lovely Miss Reed continues to refuse my offers, so, until she acquiesces, the position is yours if you want it."

"Until Kitty . . ." Chloe couldn't hide her shock. When Ajani smiled at her, she realized that he thought she was shocked that Kitty refused him—not that he'd thought he stood a chance of convincing her to live with him. Chloe had only known the brash woman a bit over a day, but she was already certain that Kitty was never going to accept that offer.

"I would find you another position when she accepts," Ajani said.

Chloe wasn't sure if Ajani was evil incarnate, but she was beginning to think he might be insane. "I'm flattered, but I don't think I'd make a very good mistress."

Ajani nodded. "You think on it for now. I will speak with Daniel. If he wants to keep you, I could also consider offering you a position in one of my homes if he wants to surrender part of his salary. Perhaps as a maid or something." He stood then and nodded. "There is one other option, but you'll need to be tested. So, until we decide what to do with you, I'm afraid it's for the best that you stay here in the house."

Chloe wasn't sure she was hearing him correctly. "To be clear, are you saying I can't leave?"

"Until we do a few little tests, I'm afraid so." He smoothed down his already unwrinkled shirtsleeves. "We have always allowed the Arrivals to make a *choice*, you see, but I'm wearying of patience. You will be my guest until we determine whether or not you have what I'm seeking or if you are better employed in another way."

Fear filled her as memories of Jason and the things he'd done before she'd killed him overwhelmed her. Chloe's voice was a breath of sound at best when she asked, "What sort of tests?"

"Nothing scandalous. Simply reading some passages for me." Ajani patted her on the shoulder.

She couldn't move, couldn't think beyond the fact that she was trapped. Smiles didn't change the truth. Jason had smiled too. He'd smiled after he'd hurt her, smiled when he'd left her in restraints, smiled when he'd sat in front of the door with a gun. Her body shook from both the remembered fear and the current anxiety, but her legs wouldn't move. She had thought that years of training with guns would prevent her from ever feeling this powerless again, but in that moment all of the familiar terror returned and consumed her.

"Once we see the results, we'll decide what to do with you," Ajani continued, seemingly oblivious to her trembling. He paused. "Just to be clear, Chloe, I had the staff remove your pistol from your quarters, and they've all been instructed as to the rules. It's an unfortunate situation, but please know that Daniel negotiated the best possible terms for your stay with us. My original plan involved killing Jackson, Francis, and Cordova. They'd have woken, but I understand that it is still unpleasant to die." He held her gaze as he added, "And there *are* job opportunities that will be open to you even if you fail the tests. If not for Daniel's speaking up for you, this entire situation might have been very unpleasant for you. You should thank him."

"I should thank Daniel," she repeated dully.

"Yes, my dear." Ajani smiled at her. "And perhaps ask him about the punishments that I've had to mete out to those who disobey me or resist. It may help you to be more cooperative."

Chloe clutched the side of the chair, trying not to let her growing panic consume her. The man in front of her was evil, and the happy expression on his face confirmed her earlier suspicions that he was mad as well.

*I survived before,* she reminded herself. Today, though, that reminder wasn't quite as comforting. She was in a new world, the captive of a madman, and the only people who knew where she was either thought she'd sided with their enemy or were themselves in his employ. Oh, and he couldn't be killed. There wasn't any way she could see this going well for her.

# CHAPTER 34

When Jack and the others returned, Kitty and Edgar were sitting with a significantly improved Francis. Styrr had been standing quietly at the window, watching the street below. He looked at her, said, "They are here," and then he resumed watching the street.

Kitty couldn't say she was surprised. The bloedzuiger had been unfailing in his guard duties, but he was not particularly talkative. When he did speak for anything other than basic reasons, he directed his remarks only to Kitty.

Francis had slept for the majority of the time that Jack and the others were away. The medicine seemed to send his body into the opposite of a Verrot alertness, but it worked, and that was all that really mattered. Francis hadn't recovered full sight, but he could see hazy images in both eyes, and more important, the bleeding had stopped. Healing always took far more time than being broken.

"Soanes is gone," Jack said when he walked in.

Melody made an unhappy noise. "Nothing but bits by the time we were there. Demon-filled monk made a mess of him, and then didn't have the decency to stand still so we could at least torture him since he killed the governor before I could interrogate him." She huffed. "In my day, monks were monks, and monsters were on the television or in books, where they belong. Demons being inside of monks is just *rude*."

While Melody was talking, both Hector and Jack looked down at Kitty and Edgar's entwined hands. Jack nodded once at Edgar; Hector just grinned. Yesterday, she would've had a hard time not commenting on their reactions, but today she was too happy to bother. She rolled her eyes at Hector and turned her attention back to Melody, who was gesticulating and lamenting "the intolerably bad manner of demons and monks and corrupt governors."

"Melly?" Hector interjected.

Melody blinked like she was trying to refocus on the world around her, and then she patted her hair, smoothing it back in case any tendrils had escaped their assigned places. "Yes?"

"We could hunt," he suggested. "Maybe the bad-mannered monks came here."

Melody looked as happy as a girl accepting a bouquet of freshly picked flowers. "I *would* like to kill something . . ." she murmured, before abruptly turning her attention to Jack. "Hector and I are patrolling."

Jack nodded, and Hector ushered the manic woman out of the room.

Once she was gone, Styrr murmured, "She is very much like a young bloedzuiger . . . but she speaks. I am quite grateful that our newborns do not speak."

Francis laughed, and both Jack and Edgar smiled.

"Katherine?" Styrr said. When she looked at him, he continued, "Garuda asks that I tell you that the toxin he has prepared seems to be ready for use. The pack told him that speaking to the governor did not work, so he suspects your pack will soon seek Ajani. Is this true?"

"Maybe. What is the toxin?"

"It will kill Ajani," Styrr said mildly. "However, it cannot be administered by anyone native to the Wasteland."

"I am not native," Kitty said.

"True," Styrr replied, as if he were thinking. "Perhaps, for your protection—as kin to my kin—you might like to have it if you are going to see Ajani. It's not something we could offer to anyone not kin, but it would not be pleasing to the pack should you be injured."

Everyone in the room was silent for a moment, and then Kitty replied very politely, "Yes, I think I would like that if it's of no trouble."

Styrr bowed his head.

After a moment of stunned silence, Jack said, "If we have a way to kill Ajani, I'm going after him tonight. Tell Garuda to bring the poison."

"This is a gift we can only offer to kin." Styrr looked at Kitty, not Jack, as he said this.

Jack was the one in charge; he had always been the one who made decisions. It wasn't a burden Kitty had ever wanted to shoulder, but she'd also seen how near Jack had been to falling apart over Chloe. Maybe having someone else check his decisions wasn't an entirely bad idea right now.

She glanced at her brother, but he was staring out the window, seemingly lost in thought.

Kitty turned to Styrr. "*Could* Garuda bring it now?"

Merely a moment had passed before Styrr said, "He will be here shortly."

# CHAPTER 35

Jack knew that he couldn't go anywhere until Garuda arrived, but he was struggling with the delay. Knowing Chloe was with Ajani made everything feel more urgent. Jack wasn't going to leave her where she was in danger. She'd gone with Daniel and was in Ajani's clutches because of *his* mistakes. It wasn't just about Chloe, though: Jack had wanted Ajani dead for years.

Edgar went to find Melody, and Hector rejoined them, while Jack and Katherine started to plan.

"Styrr will stay with Francis," Katherine said. She glanced briefly at the sleeping Arrival and then at the bloedzuiger, who nodded his assent.

"We should go in teams." Jack had thought often enough about attacking Ajani over the years that he knew what he wanted without a lot of discussion.

"I'm with you and Edgar," Katherine said.

Jack gave her a bland look. He had a different idea in mind, but he'd rather wait until Edgar was back before he said anything. All he said for now was, "Hector and Melody always fight well together." He glanced at Styrr and added, "Maybe some of the bloedzuigers could join us."

When the bloedzuiger in the room didn't answer, Katherine repeated Jack's statement and added, "Could they?"

"That is not my decision," Styrr said.

The door opened and the three remaining members of their team entered the tiny room.

"So we're going to get the new girl back?" Hector asked.

"And I get to kill people," Melody added in a cheery voice. "No rules, right? I can shoot anyone *but* the new girl. I was cheated earlier, so I shouldn't have to follow rules this time."

"Not Chloe, and no servants unless they shoot at you," Jack corrected. "But aside from that, no rules."

Melody hugged Jack. "You're a good boss. Come on, Hector." She spun toward the door, paused to glance over her shoulder, and said, "I just need to grab a few things. We'll meet you there."

"I go in first," Jack told Hector. "Keep her on a leash until I'm in."

He nodded and followed Melody out of the room.

Once the door closed, Katherine leveled a stern look at him. "You meant until 'we're in,' didn't you?"

"Why don't I go solo?" Jack started. "You and Edgar can stay—"

"Don't even try to finish that suggestion," Katherine interrupted. "I stayed here while you handled the Soanes trip. I'm not going to sit this out because Edgar and I are . . . together."

"Engaged," Edgar interjected.

Katherine blushed. "Yes, *that*."

Edgar kissed her and then told Jack, "Kit's right: we're going with you. Killing Ajani is a good way to begin our new life together."

Jack looked at his sister and the man he considered the most reliable of the Arrivals. He could order them to stay behind, but doing so would be foolhardy. More to the point, they were both resolved enough that he didn't expect that they'd listen. They obeyed orders well, as a rule, but this wasn't an ordinary situation. "Fine. Gear up."

After Jack restocked his bullets, he headed to the main tavern room to meet back up with Katherine and Edgar. He claimed a table and ordered several items to share while they waited on Garuda. The food at the Gulch House wasn't ever reliable, so ordering a variety increased the odds of finding a meal that was neither overcooked nor undercooked.

The three of them were more than halfway through the mess of food they'd ordered when Garuda arrived. His presence in the Gulch House tavern caused a bit of a commotion. For longer than the Arrivals had been in the Wasteland, he'd been the oldest bloedzuiger, and thus a creature of influence and power. As he made his way to their table, a hush fell over the room.

Garuda ignored it. When he reached them, he bowed his head in greeting. Jack and Edgar nodded at him, but Katherine stood and embraced him, leaning in and tilting her head as she did so. Garuda's posture matched hers, although the tilt of his head was far more pronounced.

They both stepped backward, still in unison, and the overall appearance was that of a dance.

"Kin to my pack," Garuda said quietly.

"And guest of my mind," Katherine replied.

They both frowned briefly as they took their seats. Murmurs rippled over the room. Every inhabitant of the room was watching the exchange of greetings between the bloedzuiger and the Arrival.

"I didn't know that you knew that tradition." Garuda watched only Katherine. For all the acknowledgment he gave to the rest of the table or the room as a whole, the two of them might as well have been alone.

"Neither did I," Katherine admitted shakily. "It was instinct."

Garuda reached out and patted her hand. "It was a good instinct. Our kin bond was witnessed by all of these"—he waved his other hand in the general direction of the room—"beings. The word will spread that you are as my pack, and they will know that to injure you is to offend the whole of the pack."

Jack met Garuda's gaze. "Do you have it?"

Garuda folded his stick-thin fingers and bent his hands toward each other, creating the strange illusion of his hands as insect wings folding together. "There are rules of diplomacy." He looked to Katherine expectantly.

After a moment, she prompted, "Will you offer aid to the kin of your pack?"

"I will," Garuda said with a smile. He withdrew a bag from his pocket and placed it on the table. "Like so many other things, I can offer my *kin* a resource that I could offer no other. I offered Verrot repeatedly, but until Katherine accepted my bond, I couldn't offer this to her. Before today, I could not ask you to cause Ajani's heart to cease its function, but"—he smiled at Katherine—"today you are as my own pack, Katherine. That man poses threat to my kin, to the mate of my kin, and one I call friend. I give to you this resource to do as you will."

Katherine took the bag.

Once she did, Garuda spoke again. "I already miss being connected to your mind, Katherine." He watched her with the same sort of fond attention Jack had seen him bestow on only his most favored pack-mates. "Do not die. I would mourn you."

She put her hand on his. "I will not die, but I will dispose of the man who has plagued us."

"Can your pack fight with us?" Jack asked.

"To do so would breach etiquette," Garuda said regretfully. "If we could have done so, we'd have removed him years ago."

Katherine nodded. "We can handle him."

"Be safe and well," Garuda ordered and then was gone.

# CHAPTER 36

For the remainder of the day, Chloe felt like she was fighting an endless panic attack. Ajani shared the evening meal with her, during which he asked her a lot of questions about magic and about the world she knew at home. He alternately studied her and ignored her.

After dinner, Ajani excused himself, and she was sent to her room to rest. A short while later, Daniel came to escort her back to Ajani's library. On the way to the room, he said quietly, "If you fail the test, remind him that you are skilled with guns, *and* that Jack is fond of you. Perhaps, if nothing else, he will think he can barter for you."

Chloe went still at the latter part of the statement. "I never said—"

"Even if Ajani hadn't seen how possessively Jack watched you when you met the boss, Jack's reaction when he heard you'd gone to Ajani's house would've made his feelings clear enough. Several of the doxies and a few bystanders sent messages that he was devastated." Daniel squeezed her shoulder gently. "Use that to your advantage. It gives you a value none of us have. I'm trying to help you, but there are only so many rules I can break." He lifted the edge of his shirt to reveal an ugly burn. "I'm no good to Kitty or anyone else if I'm dead."

Chloe was speechless as Daniel opened the door to the library and motioned for her to enter. He bowed to Ajani and left. She heard the turn of the key as he locked her in the room with Ajani. *What sorts of tests require being trapped?* The warnings Jack and Kitty had shared rushed back to her.

"You appear to be refreshed, Chloe. I trust that you've settled in?"

"I am refreshed, and everyone has been very kind," she demurred.

"Sit." He motioned.

She came to sit across from her host, who was already in a matching chair. The furniture looked like it could've been in any number of old-fashioned libraries at home. It was oversize and a bit ostentatious—and fit the overdressed man in front of her. He had a gold-handled cane she'd not seen previously resting against the table beside him, but other than that, he appeared as he had earlier.

He held out a piece of paper. "Read it."

As he stared at her, Chloe held the paper in her hand and read:

I am lord of eternity in the crossing of the sky.
I am not afraid in my limbs,
I shall open the light-land, I shall enter and dwell in it . . .
Make way for me . . . I am he who passes by the guards . . .
I am equipped and effective in opening his portal!
With the speaking of this spell, I am like Re in the eastern sky,
like Osiris in the netherworld. I will go through the circle of
darkness, without the breath stilling within me ever!

When she finished, he asked, "Do you feel *anything*?"

"Such as?" She wasn't sure what he was seeking. She glanced at the paper as if there might be a clue there. "Did you write it?"

The expression on Ajani's face was veiled. "No. Read it again, and pay attention to any sensations you have as you read."

Chloe read the paper again, trying to do as he asked.

"What do you feel?" Ajani prompted, leaning forward in his chair.

"Honestly? Afraid. Confused."

Ajani had her set the paper aside. "You're not a connoisseur of history or the arts, are you?" When she shook her head, he continued: "No matter. You don't need to *know* the finer arts to feel. It's a singular feeling, Chloe, when it works. The universe unfolds, reveals itself to you, and the man who can wield such power is a god."

He reached out and went so far as to stroke her wrist, as if to calm her, but his touch and his words did little to ease her discomfort.

"I can try again," she offered.

Then he smiled at her. "Good, Chloe. All you need to do is read the poem like you *believe* the words, and then let me know how you feel upon doing so."

She tried once more, but again, she had nothing to tell him. They went on this way for the next hour: she read, inflecting different words, trying different speeds, while Ajani alternated between his discomfitting attempts at being supportive and chastising her. Chloe had begun to think that this strange reading and questioning would continue all night when they were interrupted by one of Ajani's obsequious servants opening the door.

"Sir?"

Ajani turned his gaze on the young man with a predatory look. "You are fortunate that she wasn't successful."

"I am, sir."

The words were barely out of the man's mouth before Ajani was across the room with his cane. He slammed it into the man's throat, and when the servant fell, Ajani spun the cane around and pressed the head of it to his chest as if holding him in place. "You are happy with her failure?"

"Of course not!" the servant swore.

Ajani stayed still, the cane pushed against the servant, and Ajani himself breathing heavily as if he had been exerting himself. Chloe wasn't particularly comforted by his flash of rage, and she wondered what would happen when she didn't eventually give him the answer he apparently sought. She stayed perfectly still, like she had so long ago when she'd been in a relationship that had turned ugly. *Don't draw his attention.* Jason had been quick with his fists when she spoke too loudly—or too softly. He'd thrown things when she wasn't dressed nicely enough or sometimes when she was dressed too nicely. If she had been interested in sex, he accused her of being a slut; if she wasn't interested, he thought she was unfaithful. She'd tried to be what he wanted, but years later, she realized that what he wanted was simply someone to hurt. All of those feeling came back to her as Ajani kept his servant pinned with his cane.

*That could be me.*

Chloe wished that she had her gun back. Killing wasn't easy, but knowing that you could pull the trigger made it easier to escape.

Apparently, Ajani had been speaking to her while she sat frozen in fear. "Chloe?" he asked.

She swallowed and looked up at him. "Yes?"

He smiled, aiming for the considerate facade he'd had at dinner. "There was a cave-in at one of my mines earlier this week. I need to speak with someone about it."

Ajani released the servant, who stayed motionless even as Ajani stepped away from him. "Fetch Daniel."

The man hastened away, and Ajani smoothed out his sleeves as if the burst of activity had left him rumpled.

In only a moment, the servant returned with Daniel behind him.

"Take her with you. Perhaps she'll find it inspiring. Her performance so far has been lackluster, despite my encouragement," Ajani said, and then turned his back and left them.

"Come with me," Daniel said.

In the courtyard outside the house were two uniformed men. Between them was a man who looked as terrified as Chloe felt.

The two watched her expectantly as Daniel said, "If you can do this, he'll trust you more."

For a moment, Chloe stared at him. "Do what?"

He held out a gun.

"You want me to *kill* him?" she prompted.

"Ajani has decided that an example must be made. The foreman's death will motivate others to work harder." Daniel's expression wasn't judging, but he wasn't flinching away like Chloe wanted to. He motioned to one of the uniformed men, who promptly forced the prisoner to his knees, and then he told Chloe, "Ajani himself doesn't kill. He doesn't watch a killing either if at all possible."

She couldn't speak.

"Take the gun, Chloe," he said quietly. The look he gave her was pleading, as if he needed her to understand that what was about to happen here wasn't awful. The problem was that murder over a failed mining tunnel *was* awful.

Chloe tried to think of circumstances where this murder wouldn't be heinous. Maybe if Ajani was punishing a man for shoddy work that had cost lives or polluted a water supply. Maybe if the foreman was callously responsible for collapsing the tunnel on purpose. Neither of those was the case, however. Ajani had ordered the foreman's death because the man had cost Ajani time and money. It was simply business to him—and a lesson to "inspire" her.

"I can't." Chloe turned her back on the prisoner for a moment. "Daniel, you don't have to do this either. Just let him go. We can both walk out and—"

Daniel stepped around her, aimed, and fired. The prisoner slumped to the ground, a bullet hole in his forehead.

"Tell the boss it's done," Daniel said.

Once the two men went inside, Daniel turned to face her. "Wait here." He glanced toward the door where the men had gone and lowered his voice. "You need to toughen up, Chloe."

Then Daniel turned away and left her alone in the courtyard.

Waiting with a corpse wasn't high on her list of acceptable plans, so a moment later she followed Daniel into the house, but Ajani was coming out as she went in. He held the paper she'd read several times already, and then he took her arm in his and led her back to the courtyard and the still-bleeding body.

"Read it again," Ajani ordered as he handed her the paper.

As he stared at her with an oddly excited look, Chloe took the paper and read it aloud again.

> I am lord of eternity in the crossing of the sky.
> I am not afraid in my limbs,
> I shall open the light-land, I shall enter and dwell in it . . .
> Make way for me . . . I am he who passes by the guards . . .
> I am equipped and effective in opening his portal!
> With the speaking of this spell, I am like Re in the eastern sky,
> like Osiris in the netherworld. I will go through the circle of
> darkness, without the breath stilling within me ever!

When she was finished, Ajani shook his head. His excitement had vanished.

"You're just like the others," he said. "Another failure."

# CHAPTER 37

When they reached Ajani's house, Kitty felt a mix of excitement and fear. They were going to end this ongoing conflict with Ajani. It wasn't the same as finding a way home, but after her bonding in the desert with the bloedzuigers, she wasn't as sure that she wanted to leave. The Wasteland was her home as much as the land she'd left behind; truth be told, she'd lived here longer than she'd lived in California, so the Wasteland might be more her home.

"Ready?" Edgar asked.

She nodded, and Jack pushed open the front door. It wasn't locked, but they expected a servant to be standing on the other side. She was poised to grab him and yank him out of the house. She wasn't prepared to see Daniel on the other side of the door. She saw the look of hope in his expression—and the resignation that followed when he saw that she wasn't alone.

"Just go," she whispered, stepping in front of Edgar and Jack.

Daniel didn't raise his weapon, but he already had it in his hand. "You know better than that."

"Please don't make me shoot you," she said.

Behind Daniel, a servant vanished into the depths of the house.

Kitty knew they had only moments before Ajani—or his other

killers—arrived. Daniel glanced past her for a sliver of a moment, but he didn't address Jack or Edgar. Instead, he begged, "Go away, Kitty. Let them handle this."

"Shoot him, or move away so I can," Melody called from behind Edgar.

"Please," Kitty half begged. Shooting him seemed less acceptable after she'd seen what Ajani had done to him.

Daniel lifted his gun. "You know I can't let you walk past me unless I'm down." He smiled at her before inviting, "Go ahead and shoot me, Kit. It's okay."

Edgar pulled Kitty to the side, and Melody fired. It wasn't a killing wound, but it was more than Kitty would've liked.

Daniel fell backward, smiling up at her. "Once more so I can't come after you." He paused, took a visibly pained breath, and told her, "He has four fighters in the house. Two upstairs."

Kitty had shot Daniel herself not too long ago, but the memories of his torture were too fresh in her mind. "Danny . . ."

Jack stepped into the foyer, and Daniel looked at him. "Chloe was with him in the library."

"Let's go." Jack didn't glance at Daniel as he strode into the house with Melody and Hector behind him.

As shots started to ring out from deeper in the house, Kitty knew they needed to move, but she couldn't shoot Daniel again—yet if she didn't, it would be worse for him if Ajani saw that he'd let the Arrivals into the house. "I can't shoot you," she whispered.

Daniel met Edgar's eyes. "Let me take her out of here."

"Can't," Edgar muttered.

Daniel sighed. "I'm sure *you* don't mind: shoot me so I can't follow."

Edgar shot him in the head; then he bent down and grabbed the pistol that Daniel could no longer hold. He handed the gun to Kitty. "Stay behind me."

The chaos in the house grew louder as they walked farther from the door. Thuds and yells mingled with the sounds of breaking glass. Interspersed with it were gunshots.

They found Hector hunkered down at the doorway of a dining room. "Melly's upstairs," he said. "I've got these. Go on."

Daniel was one of the best of Ajani's group of trained killers, and he'd eliminated himself. The staff at Ajani's house was trained to fight, but they also weren't apt to step into the middle of a fracas between groups of people who didn't stay dead. Melody was hunting the two shooters upstairs, and Hector was exchanging fire with another. That left one unaccounted for—as well as Ajani. Kitty was feeling optimistic until she heard Jack's voice inside a nearby room.

"This is not what we agreed on," Jack said.

Gun at the ready, Kitty pushed open the door and slid inside. Edgar was close behind her. Standing just inside the room was her brother, and walking toward them was Chloe.

She walked in front of Ajani. There was blood spatter on her arms, but she appeared uninjured.

"I think I can still hit him," Edgar murmured from beside her.

"No." Jack darted a look at him and answered quietly, "The poison would kill her if you missed. We wait till we have a shot."

Edgar looked at her briefly. His loyalty to her surpassed his loyalty to Jack. She put a hand on Edgar's wrist and shook her head. They would wait.

"Hiding behind a woman?" Jack scoffed.

"Oh, but she's not just any woman, is she, Jack?" Ajani was midway across the room, standing near a pair of exceedingly ugly chairs. Chloe was in front of him like a shield. He slid one hand possessively around her waist. "She's one you're willing to break our accord for."

Jack said nothing, but his expression darkened. Kitty likewise didn't point out that the accord had already been broken. She might be impulsive, but she wasn't foolhardy enough to poke a rattlesnake.

"Sadly, she's not as special as I'd hoped she would be." Ajani tsked.

Suddenly, Chloe tried to jerk away, but Ajani's arm tightened.

"I'll kill him," Ajani said casually. "He won't shoot *you* to get to me, but I will kill him if you force my hand." When she stopped moving, Ajani made an approving sound, and then, with his other hand, reached up and stroked his fingertips down her cheek and around the curve of her shoulder, stopping his hand just above her breast. "She has her uses, and I'm happy to enjoy her, but she's still not what I need. We could trade."

"Get behind me, Kit," Edgar said.

"You know better, Cordova. Miss Reed won't hide." The look Ajani gave them was that of a patronizing father. "You also know that my people don't stay dead. We can exterminate every one of you, or"—he glanced at Kitty with a creepily hungry look—"you all walk out of here, and Katherine stays. I'll treat her like the queen she is."

"No." Kitty's temper flared, and she drew her gun reflexively. The rounds in the third and fourth chambers were poison filled, but she had bullets in the first two that she could shoot first. Those bullets wouldn't kill him, but they'd make her feel better.

Ajani's gaze dropped to the gun in her hand. "My dear, I am willing to let Cordova live, and if you are obedient, we can even negotiate visits with him. Plus, while you're here, you can have Daniel as your lackey too."

"My sister isn't going to stay here." Jack had his pistol trained on Ajani. "The bullets are filled with poison. I *can* kill you permanently this time."

"Is that why you've broken our agreement? To kill me?" Ajani asked. "I think we can come to a better accord. The position of governor has recently opened up, and I'd be happy to install you in his position."

"We worked for him to stand *against* you. Why would we work for you?" Kitty kept watching for a chance. She could see that Chloe was poised, waiting for an opportunity to escape. They just needed a moment.

"The governor has worked for me since before you arrived," Ajani told them. "It didn't seem particularly prudent to tell you that, but then you frightened him, and he became more irritating, so I had him retire early."

"He was torn apart by a demon," Jack said.

"I know. You always clean up the demons after I have them do their jobs. You're quite good at it; that's part of why I use them so often." Ajani paused and smiled, clearly drawing out the tension for his own amusement.

Kitty looked at Jack. The expression of incredulity on his face matched what she felt. Everything they'd fought for was a lie.

"If you won't trade for Chloe, and you don't want to be governor . . ." Ajani turned his gaze to Kitty. "Perhaps, you should do your own negotiating."

Kitty stepped away from Edgar. "Let's talk."

Edgar started, "Kit—"

"Katherine," Jack said at the same time.

She ignored them both. "Let them all go, and you and I will talk. You had an agreement with Jack for years." She watched Ajani as she spoke. The hint of instability that Daniel had mentioned was there, but so was the keen alertness she'd always known. "This isn't the way we have to be."

Ajani smiled and shoved Chloe away suddenly. Kitty heard the hammer of a gun, and the whine of a bullet. She thought it was Edgar who had fired, but then he fell forward, pushing Kitty to the ground, keeping her safe from return fire. Vaguely, she realized that Jack had lunged for Chloe too.

When Kitty felt dampness on her back, she realized that Edgar hadn't simply been pushing her out of the way. She scrambled out from under him and was frantically searching for a pulse. "No. No. No." She rolled him over and leaned down to feel for breath. "You can't do this to me, Edgar."

She realized that Hector stood in the doorway only when he started to speak. "I took care of Melody. She's dead . . . and"—he glanced at Kitty unapologetically—"so is Edgar, I believe."

"*Hector?*" Jack said.

Kitty felt like her world had just ended. She couldn't look, but she couldn't *not* look at Hector either. Her hands were still on Edgar's motionless body. She was vaguely aware that Jack had lifted his gun, but Hector had already turned and walked away.

"I do apologize, Katherine," Ajani said, "but you didn't seriously think that I would lack a plan for this day?"

She stared at him as she knelt beside Edgar. "He's dead."

Ajani took a step forward, and Chloe ran over and grabbed the gun that had fallen from Edgar's hand when he fell. She stood in front of Kitty and Edgar, her gun aimed at Ajani. "You leave her alone. Just . . . just *stop.*"

Without speaking, Jack lifted his weapon as well, but before either Jack or Chloe fired, Ajani said, "If you do that, Cordova will stay dead."

Kitty hated what she was about to do, but there was no alternative. "Jack, don't. Chloe, please don't shoot him."

Her brother glanced her way, and she saw the understanding in his eyes. He would let Ajani live for her, let things continue to fall apart all around them, all because she couldn't bear life without Edgar. *This* was what she'd resisted for so long, the desperation to keep Edgar in her life.

"Just hear him out," she asked in a voice that was far too close to begging for her liking.

Jack walked over to Chloe and gently pushed the muzzle of her gun toward the floor. "Wait."

With a confidence that Kitty hated, Ajani turned his back to them and walked to one of two high-backed, gaudy chairs that were on either side of an ornately carved table. On the table were a crystal decanter and two glasses. He glanced over his shoulder at her before reaching for the decanter. The clink of it being unstoppered sounded strangely loud in the room. "I'd offer you all a drink, but I have only the two glasses here." He poured some amber liquid into both glasses, looked back again, and added, "However, I suspect you would probably *all* drink out of the bottle, wouldn't you?"

All the while Chloe and Jack still stood, pistols in hand but not upraised. They didn't react to the disdain in Ajani's words or actions. Kitty didn't feel nearly as calm or focused as the other two appeared.

"Unless you cooperate, Edgar will not wake," Ajani announced.

# CHAPTER 38

For a moment Jack wasn't sure he could resist shooting. Edgar was dead on the floor; Katherine's hands were wet with her lover's blood. Chloe was staring at Ajani with horror plain in her expression. Somewhere in the house, Melody was dead—by Hector's hand—and in the darkened library, Ajani had the temerity to sip his brandy in silence.

The bullets in Jack's pistol would stop Ajani from rising again, and Jack wanted almost nothing more than to use the toxin that Garuda had provided. The one thing that mattered more to him was his sister, and she would be devastated if Edgar's death were permanent. If his death could be undone, Jack would still his hand.

Still, he felt it only right to point out to Ajani that they weren't powerless. He had his pistol trained on Ajani as he said, "The bullets are filled with poison. I *can* kill you permanently this time."

Ignoring Jack, Ajani held out a glass to Kitty. "Since your brother seems otherwise occupied . . ."

She shook her head. "He's not joking about the poison, Ajani."

"I realize that." Ajani watched them with a bemused expression. "I wonder, though, are you willing to gamble? What if I told you that I could send one of you back?"

"You can't be serious—"

"To open the portal, I require a sacrifice," Ajani said in an obviously falsely saddened voice. "That's the cost of the opening. I've tried deaths from here, shed the blood of every species of beast and being in the Wasteland, but it appears that only someone from our world will do."

"*Our* world?" Chloe echoed.

"Yes," Ajani answered her, but his attention remained fixedly on Katherine. The extent of his obsession with her became frighteningly clear. There was no way Jack was walking out of this house without Ajani dead on the ground.

Quietly, Jack told Chloe, "The bullets in Edgar's gun are filled with the same poison."

She smiled in a way that was eerily reminiscent of Melody in a good mood, but she said nothing.

Ajani didn't even glance at them.

"I'd hoped it wouldn't ever come to this," he said. He paused and smiled, clearly drawing out the tension for his own amusement. "I'll give you a choice. Would you like to go home, Katherine? I can send you or Jackson back."

Katherine stayed silent, but Jack saw her hesitate, an expression of incredulity on her face that matched what he felt. Of all the things he had expected Ajani to offer, that was nowhere on the list. After far too many years in the Wasteland, they were being offered a chance to return to the lives they should've led.

"Go home?" Kitty echoed. "Like you could—"

"I was the first," Ajani interrupted. "I have the spell that opens what people at home have come to call a *wormhole*—peculiar name, isn't it? The spell simply calls it a portal." He lifted his hands in a wide what-can-you-do gesture. "I can't guarantee the *year*, but I have experimented a bit, so I'm fairly certain that it would be near the time you originated."

At Katherine's silence, Ajani lifted one shoulder in a delicate shrug. "Fine. I am willing to even send *two* of you back, alive."

"To the same time?" she asked.

"You can't go to a time earlier than your own." Ajani gave her a small smile. "Cordova would arrive dead if I tried to send him back to a time before he was born. I can send him and Jack to their rightful years, or I can send you and Cordova to your rightful years, or I can send you and Jack."

"So no matter what, I give up Edgar? *Why?*" Katherine's temper flared and her hand went to her own gun.

Ajani smiled, his gaze on the gun in her hand. "Call it a lesson. It takes a death to move between worlds. That's the cost I've had to pay each time."

Jack had watched his sister, knowing her decision before she even made it. "Right. If you can really open the *wormhole*"—Jack drew the word out, finding it even more ridiculous as he said it—"does that mean all the people here are here because of you?"

"Not the natives," Ajani replied drolly.

"Us, though? The ones from home. Did we all end up here because of you?" Jack prompted in what he considered a reasonable tone.

Ajani sipped his brandy in silence for a moment before answering. "Yes, I brought you here. All of you."

Chloe pulled the hammer back, the sound loud in the room. Jack glanced at her, but only Katherine moved, stepping in front of her, placing her back to Ajani in the process.

"Send Chloe home," Jack said quietly.

Katherine looked at him in shock.

"I'm not leaving you here, and Edgar would rather die than be apart from you." Jack shook his head. "But there's no way you're going to let him stay dead. Send Chloe back."

"Bravo, Jackson," Ajani said. "If you want to stay here—and I'm assuming Katherine wants Edgar to live—let's send Chloe back. She's of no use to me." He walked to the desk and lifted a piece of paper. "If you're able to do this, Katherine, in time I'll also send Cordova and Jackson back."

Kitty swallowed audibly. "What do you want me to do?"

He held out the paper. "Read it, Katherine. Show me that you're every bit as rare as I believe. I kept hoping another would come, but they all fail. No one else is like me. They can't do spellwork. Only you."

Jack watched his sister try not to shudder at the zealotry in Ajani's voice. Silently, she took the paper Ajani held out. Her voice was shaking, but she began to read clearly: "I am lord of eternity in the crossing of the sky. I am not afraid in my limbs . . ."

The air in the room felt wrong, as if it were growing too thin.

She paused, and Ajani aimed his gun at Jack. "Don't disregard our accord, Katherine."

Jack gave his sister a comforting smile, and she resumed: "I shall open the light-land, I shall enter and dwell in it . . . Make way for me . . . I am he who passes by the guards . . . I am equipped and effective in opening his portal!"

The air in the room was visibly swirling, as if a vortex was being created.

Shakily, Katherine read the rest. "With the speaking of this spell, I am like Re in the eastern sky, like Osiris in the netherworld. I will go through the circle of darkness, without the breath stilling within me ever!"

The portal opened, looking like a fire opal grown large, and Ajani beamed at Kitty. "I knew you could do it."

He walked toward the strange swirl of darkness and color, and as soon as he was directly in front of it, he glanced over his shoulder at Chloe. "Go ahead."

Chloe took several steps toward him and stopped. "It takes the death of someone from there. How do you know which death will stick? Could it be Melody *or* Edgar who lives?"

Ajani hesitated, and Jack saw the truth on his face before he opened his mouth to answer. Ajani had said that a death of one of them was necessary to open the portal. Logically, that meant it could be Edgar, Melody, or even Daniel who stayed dead. Ajani didn't say *how* or even if there was any way to determine which Arrival stayed dead. All Ajani managed to get out was, "Chloe . . ."

"Someone from home has to stay dead," Chloe said, and then she shot him. She fired bullet after bullet into his body, and he jerked and jumped like a puppet in a storm.

Neither Jack nor Katherine moved.

Chloe glanced at Katherine. "He was from our world, too. If it's last killed that doesn't wake, that's him now. If it's just random, Edgar's odds just improved. Twenty-five percent is better than thirty-three."

"Thank you," Katherine choked out around the sobs that were coming over her.

The darkness swirled, and Katherine stared at it and then at Jack. She looked like the weight of Edgar's death was too much to process, like she needed to be protected or, at the very least, given space to mourn. She dropped to her knees. Her hand covered her mouth, but it didn't muffle her loud sob.

Chloe lowered the gun. "Will Ajani stay dead with that poison?"

"Garuda thinks so," Jack said. "If not, you'll be safer once you go back to your time. If you're not here, he can't reach you if he does wake."

Chloe looked at Katherine, and then at Edgar, and finally back at

Jack. "If he doesn't stay dead, he's going to come after her . . . and you. All of you." Carefully, she placed her pistol on the floor and grabbed Ajani's feet. She stood and looked at Jack. "I'll stay here," Chloe whispered. "Ajani should go . . . just in case."

Jack wasn't sure he was any less overwhelmed than his sister. Ajani was defeated, but at what cost? Edgar, Melody, and Daniel were all dead; Hector had betrayed them. Katherine was crying louder by the moment.

Chloe stared at Jack. "Help me get rid of him so he can't hurt either of you again."

He nodded, and together, they hauled Ajani's lifeless body to the wormhole and tossed it in.

As the darkness closed in on itself, Chloe leaned against Jack, and they watched the darkness vanish.

# CHAPTER 39

Over the next week, Kitty was a fury of cleaning and removing anything that made her think of Ajani. Chloe and Jack let her lead them through the house—which by Wasteland law was now Chloe's possession, as were all of Ajani's holdings.

Garuda had nominated Jack for governor the very same day the Arrivals went after Ajani. They'd learned that the morning after Ajani's death, and what with the persuasive powers of Kitty and Garuda, Jack's every objection to the position was quickly dispelled.

"We could burn it all," Kitty suggested again. "I hate seeing it."

Jack sighed. "Katherine, why don't you rest? Chloe and I can sort through this pile."

They went on that way for hours, gathering Ajani's possessions and then sending them away to be claimed by anyone who wanted them. The idea of doing the same thing at his other houses was daunting, but for now, all they really needed was one place free of his presence.

Edgar, Melody, and Daniel were dead in three of the house's rooms. Francis was recovering in another room, and five of Ajani's other people were staying on in Chloe's employ. A few others were debating what to do, and some had simply left. It was an odd state of affairs, and the tension in the house was wearing out everyone.

No one knew for sure if all of the Arrivals were now immortal, but as much as they could figure based on what they'd learned from Ajani, they'd only died permanently, up until now, because he'd needed their deaths in order to open the "wormholes." Of course, Kitty had pointed out that she could do the "same damn thing as Ajani, so they'd better not fuck up."

Garuda's frequent visits helped her to feel calm, but even his influence couldn't keep the panic at bay, and Jack and Chloe spoke daily about what they'd do if Edgar stayed dead. Oddly, Chloe and Francis took turns waiting with Melody, but the only people Kitty would let near Edgar were Jack, Chloe, and Garuda.

So when Edgar, Daniel, and Melody all awoke, Chloe actually wept with joy.

"Fucking Hector" were the first words Melody said when she opened his eyes. "Where is he?"

In the other room, Edgar and Kitty locked the door and didn't come out for hours.

Things in the house were far from what Chloe had once considered normal, but she wasn't sure that she wanted the kind of normal she'd once sought. She glanced at Jack, and together they walked to the sitting room, where they'd been spending hours talking about everything from how to handle Ajani's possessions to movies she'd seen back home.

They closed the door behind them, and for a moment they stood staring at each other. Chloe wasn't sure there were words enough to explain the things she'd figured out the past couple of days, but she owed it to Jack and to herself to try.

"I'm not ready for this," she started.

Jack nodded, but he still frowned.

Chloe took the nod as encouragement to keep talking. "A few days ago I lived in a world with televisions, smartphones, and about a million other things that don't exist in the Wasteland. That world also lacks the kinds of monsters that are here, and"—she caught his gaze and held it—"also the kind of men here."

The way she felt in his arms wasn't the sort of thing she wanted to ignore—neither was the fact that he was a good man. He'd stood by his sister, put her well-being before his own, and that kind of devotion was rare. He'd protected his team, tried to make the Wasteland a better place, and didn't put his own needs before anyone's. Even now, he was looking at her with concern.

"I'm sorry, Chloe. Katherine can't endure the idea of killing someone in order to send you back. She thought about doing it to Hector after what he did, but . . . she's sick of killing," he said.

"I chose to stay," she reminded him.

The frown he wore vanished, replaced with a look of hope. "I'm sorry I called you Mary. Before, I mean." He swallowed nervously. "She was a good friend, but I meant what I said. We weren't what you and I . . . what I mean is . . . I'm hoping that you and me . . ." His words faded, and he pulled her to him and kissed her.

Chloe didn't resist. Of all the things in this world that didn't make sense, she was pretty sure that *this* did. Her lips parted under his, and her arms wrapped around him.

When he pulled away from the kiss, she kept her arms around him and murmured, "Me too. I want to get to know you, Jack."

He smiled. "I'm awfully glad you're not hurt. Ajani and I had an accord of sorts, that we didn't force anyone to side with either of us, but I wanted to . . . I would've broken all the rules for you if I could have." Jack leaned his forehead against hers. "I don't remember the last time I let my own wants get in the way of the good of the group. You're different. This is . . . not just lust."

"Good." Chloe laughed a little at both of them. He'd stayed pressed up against her so tightly that she was having a difficult time not telling him to shut up so they could get back to kissing. In a not so subtle move, she rocked her hips forward. Jack slid his hand up her spine, holding her to him.

Chloe stilled as she heard Kitty's voice. "You need to go slowly, Edgar. What if—" Her words ended abruptly on a squeal and a thump.

Chloe and Jack exchanged a look. "You two need your own house," Chloe yelled. "I'll even give you this one. Early wedding present."

Jack laughed, and she led him outside to the courtyard. Once they were away from the blissful couple, Chloe continued, "I'm staying, and since I am, maybe we can go on some sort of dates or whatever, too." She smiled at him, the new governor, as they stood in the courtyard of one of her houses and teased, "If you wanted, you could court me."

Jack's bemused expression was endearing as he loosened his hold on her. He cleared his throat and said, "I don't know the rules for your time, but I can try."

Chloe tilted her head so her lips were closer to his ear and whispered, "In *my* time, courting doesn't mean no lust, Jack. It just means we do other things too."

The wicked smile he gave her was enough to make Chloe glad he already had his arms around her.

# AUTHOR'S NOTE

The Coffin Text used by Ajani to open wormholes and assign himself deathlessness is modified from Coffin Text 1031. To the best of my knowledge, Egyptian spells have absolutely no connection to wormholes, nor would travel through a wormhole allow a person deathlessness.

Saloon girls didn't use modern idiomatic phrases. If Kitty were back in her rightful time (late 1800s), she would not have said, "Seriously!" The characters use language from eras other than their birth eras to reflect their years spent in the Wasteland with people from later eras. If you do happen to fall into a wormhole and end up in an 1800s Wild West town, do avoid giving yourself away by using modern phrases.

Each character's name is selected for meaning as well as a vague sense of "fitting" that I can't explain in any remotely rational way. Here are a few of my etymology notes that started the book.

- **Jack (Jackson Reed)**—diminutive form of John (God is gracious) or Jackson (son of Jack)
- **Katherine (Reed)**—pure
- **Chloe (Mattison)**—verdant and blooming
- **Edgar (Cordova)**—rich spear
- **Francis (Miller)**—free

- **Melody (Blankenbecker)**—song tune
- **Hector (Soto)**—anchor, steadfast
- **Ajani**—he who wins the struggle
- **Garuda**—king of birds
- **bloedzuiger**—literally "bloodsucker"
- **Verrot**—rot/rotten
- **lindwurm**—a wingless dragon of Nordic folklore
- **cynanthropy**—a mania in which the patient thinks he is a dog

# ACKNOWLEDGMENTS

My sincere gratitude goes to the following people without whom this book would be nothing more than incoherent scrawls scattered throughout various notebooks and on the backs of receipts:

Liate Stehlik, Kate Nintzel, Seale Ballenger, Jean Marie Kelly, Brianne Halverson, and Shawn Nicholls astounded me with stellar support for *Graveminder* as I was writing *this* book. You've all been quite kickass.

Ashley (via her mother, Stephanie) lent me her name through winning a charity auction. Meeting you at FaerieCon made me smile, so I hope your namesake in the story makes you smile.

Dr. Scott Paulson answered my physics questions, so I could *try* to grasp the possibilities of timespace (although the physics in the text was quite corrupted by the liberties I took). You're still very patient.

My research assistant, Christopher Scheirer, procured articles on various oddities (all while working on his PhD). My personal assistant, Laura Kalnajs, read and proofread this book repeatedly—all while keeping my daily chaos in check. Thank you both.

Merrilee Heifetz has had the unenviable task of handling my bouts of crazy, and I'm ever indebted to you for the unwavering faith in this (and every other thing). You are an amazing guardian/warrior angel.

Kelley Armstrong and Jeaniene Frost repeatedly assured me that I could write this book. You were ultimately right, *but* I'm not sure if I could've done it without your cheering.

Dylan shared cryptid expertise, as well as his stacks of books and DVDs to help me build monsters. Asia read drafts and reminded me that I have, in fact, written books before so could do this again. Clearly, I'm the luckiest mother in all of the possible universes because you are my children.

Loch provided emotional support, food, and caffeine; he read drafts and listened without impatience as I ranted, rearranged furniture, and planned last-minute family vacations. Your steadiness is enough to merit awards.